Love, Checks
and Balances

Lou Black

Respect The Pen LLC

Love, Checks and Balances is a work of fiction.

Names, characters, places, and incidents are either products of the author's imagination or are used fictitiously, and any resemblance to actual persons, living or dead, business establishments, events, or locales is purely coincidental.

To Thomas B. Black Jr.

July 12, 1967-March 28, 2019

As I write this, the tears just won't stop falling. I've cried everyday since you've been gone. Antaeus told me that he always looked at you like a superhero. I have to confess that he wasn't the only one. I saw you exactly the same way. I don't think anyone asked me about the progress of this book more than you did. Every time I saw or spoke to you, it was always, "What's up with the book?" Or, "When do you think you're going to be finished?" I tried so desparately to get it done before you left us, but you just couldn't hold on any longer. I apologize for taking so long, but it's finally here. I hope I make you proud.

Love you, "Br'Unc".

Sleep Forever In Peace.

Acknowledgements

First and foremost, I would like to thank God for putting some kind of sense in my head to be able to write *anything* worth reading. I have to thank my mom, Ms. G. Black, for always being supportive. Never, ever have I encountered a more beautiful and selfless individual. The world would be a better place if there were more like you. I'm blessed and grateful to have you as my mother. I love you, "My Sunshine."

Thank you to my children, Lashawn, Joel, Von, Dartanyon, Larry, and Maya. Maybe you'll actually take the time to read this one. Who am I fooling? A man can still dream, can't he? Love you, kids.

I want to thank Mr. Black's other girls. My lovely aunts: L. Black, F. Black, and J. Black, for all of your love and support. Love you, ladies.

To my "Br'ousin," Thomas "TC" Riley @tcrdesigns, @iam_artist_jai, and @brooklyndave88 who are the geniuses behind the artwork on this project. Thank you TC, for all of your support and creative input. Your vision is what makes people want to pick the book up in the first place. I can't thank you enough for that. It's just you and me, now. We all we got. Love you, "Br'ous-O."

To my cousins: Ajene, Antaeus, Dorian, Lawrence, Amber, Sydney, Uriah, Cameron, Isaiah, Dakota, and Mylez. I'm grateful to have you in my life, and to call you my family. I thank you for your support. I love you all.

I would like to extend a very special thank you to Ms. Tia Ross @WordWiserInk, the best editor in the literary world. If you like the way this story flows, you should thank her, too. She took my li'l ol' manuscript and turned it into what you see before you. You're the best! (My editor for life)

To my brothers, all from other mothers: Alfredo "Bugsy" Lopez, Kevin "Tef" Smith, and Charlie "Buck" Hvasta. I thank you for always being there. Love you all!

These next four brothers are more than special to me. Blood is the only thing that could make us closer. A person doesn't have to be blood-related to be considered "family". They are the true definition of that word.

Harold "Took" Smith. You're probably my oldest and closest friend. You've been a part of my life since the first time I stepped out of building 106, and you came out of 104. These past few weeks in particular have been extremely trying for me. You and your wife (love you Vette,) have been there holding me down every step of the way. Words can't express how much that means to me. I thank you for considering me as your brother. You're my family for life. Love you, bro.

P.S. Stop telling that story about how I almost killed you when we were kids.

Jamie-O Wright. Your sense of humor is what I love about you the most. You're always ready to crack a joke or say something crazy to make me laugh. I need that, so don't ever change. I'm so proud of the transformation you've made from what we used to be, to the respectable man you are now. I aspire to do the same. Keep rising to the top! Love you, bro.

Anthony Cary. What can I say about the the most lovable pain in the ass I've ever known? Through all of the ups and downs you've been right there by my side. And although you were more than likely the cause of some of those "downs", God couldn't have given me a better brother. Believe me, I asked Him. In the past few years I've watched you mature in ways I never thought possible. I'm so proud of you, and even more proud to call you my brother. I love you, bro.

Nairobi G. Washington. Don't worry. I'll never tell what the "G" stands for. As far as I'm concerned, it means "Greatest". Of all my brothers, you and I share the closest bond. You're my confidant. I can talk to you about anything, and I probably already have. You're my voice of reason. You've always been there to talk me off the ledge when life became unbearable. Who knows where I'd be if it wasn't for your words of wisdom? You're my biggest supporter. Whenever I come to you with my ideas, you always say, "Well, let's do it!" We will, bro. One day we will. You're my mentor. Although I'm older, it never ceases to amaze me how much I still learn from you. I can

5

go on and on, but ain't nobody got time for 'dat. My world is a better place with you in it. I love you, bro.

Sidebar: I can't wait until you give me the "green light" to write your story, 'cuz the shit that comes out yo' mouf is UN- BEE- LIEVE- ABLE!!!

You four are the true definition of "Love and Loyalty." It's the motto we live by. The one I will die upholding.

Last, but by no means least. For the people who took a chance and supported an unknown author, who had never written anything longer than a book report or a prison letter, I offer a humble and sincere thank you from the bottom of my heart. I hope the li'l black boy from 139th Sreet doesn't disappoint.

If my brain neglected to acknowledge anyone it was purely an oversight. Please know that my heart didn't forget you.

Leave me alone! I'm old!

Lavian Taylor and Sean Prescott

On a chilly night in November, of 1996, Lavian Taylor and Sean Prescott stood on 139th Street near 7th Avenue waiting for customers to come buy the crack they were selling. It was kind of slow that night, but the customer traffic usually had its ebbs and flows. Partners in the drug game, the two men alternated between the packs they sold.

On one pack Lavian, (Lay for short) took the money while Sean made the sale, and vice versa. On this particular pack, Lay had the work and Sean was taking the cash when two customers approached and asked for three. Before making the transaction, Lay noticed one of them was wearing a pair of thick-rimmed Steve Urkel-looking glasses that had white tape around the left arm, close to the lens.

For some reason something about those two didn't sit right with Lavian. These customers looked *off*. Their clothes appeared ragged, almost looking staged, as if they had worn costumes. Sean took the cash from Urkel, and Lavian handed the other one the three vials.

After about five minutes of them waiting for the next customer to show up, a slim light-skinned man walked up from Lenox Ave and approached them wearing all black with a skully on his head. When he was approximately five feet away from Lavian and Sean, the man pulled a gun out of his pocket and, pointed it at them.

"Get your hands in the air!"

When Lavian saw the gun his first thought was that they were being robbed. But when he heard, "Get your hands in the air", he knew the guy was a cop. It was only then that he bothered to pull out his badge. A black unmarked car was pulling up from Lenox at the same time, and two more officers jumped out.

A van rounded the corner from Seventh and another four cops hopped out of it. They were coming from everywhere!

Lay had five bottles in his left hand and thought about making a run for it as he was instructed by the first cop to,

"Open your fuckin' hands and get down on the ground!"

There were too many of them. Lay had no choice but to drop the vials on the ground, get down on his knees, put his hands behind his head, and try not to get shot that night.

The police surrounded Lavian and Sean, slapped cuffs on, and led them to the van. The last time Lay had NYPD jewelry on his wrists was in '89, and that feeling of helplessness and despair came over him once again. He hated that shit. That night, he and Sean were caught up in a buy and bust operation conducted by T.N.T., as part of the aggressive efforts to meet quotas for the November elections.

This was a classic case of shit rolling downhill. Politicians put pressure on NYPD chiefs. The chiefs in turn, cracked down on captains. Captains came down on lieutenants, sergeants, and officers. Then the officers came down hard on the street hustlers. That's the reason Lay and Sean were dealing hand to hand on the street in the first place.

Previously, T.N.T. had raided their building every single day and locked up all of their workers, putting the fear of God in them. No one wanted to work. With no employees, Lavian and Sean had to step up to the mound and pitch themselves, thereby becoming more susceptible to inevitable arrest. All year long, shit on the block flowed smoothly, but around election time, the police went crazy trying to fill those quotas.

That's why the rich people who sat at the top usually took the entire month of November off. But Lavian and Sean didn't have that luxury. They *had* to be on the block, or their money would've stopped altogether, which meant they'd starve. And that was a no-no! With fresh new drug cases, off to the 32nd Precinct they went-, or so they thought.

T.N.T. had more busts to make, so they left Lay and Sean cuffed in the van for over an hour as they rode around snatching more hustlers off the street. When the van was full they stopped on Broadway and got something to eat. Dudes were starving like crazy, and had to sit there and smell the officers' food as they ate.

When their bellies were full, the officers processed all the perps in the van before taking the long trip downtown to Central Booking. Sean and Lay thought they would never get those cuffs off! Once inside, they found spots on the benches and relaxed until it was time to see the judge because there was nothing else to do. Waiting was their only option.

Sean was extremely tired, so he wrapped himself in his jacket like a cocoon and quickly drifted off to sleep. Lavian, on the other hand, reclined on the bench staring up at the ceiling thinking about how stupid he felt. He knew there was something up with those two bummy motherfuckers! Now he and his brother had open cases for some bullshit because he failed to open his mouth.

The lesson was learned that night to always trust your first instinct. If shit feels funny, there's a reason for it. But that wasn't the only thing on Lay's mind. He was trying to figure out how he was going to explain this shit to his girls. Not girls as in his daughters, but the two women he was engulfed in a love triangle with, Celina and Jocelyn- (pronounced Joe-se-lin, Josie for short).

They were going to kill him, because neither wanted him hustling anymore, and for that reason Lay knew he would never hear the end of this shit. He was probably worried more about what Celina and Josie were going to say, than the judge.

Celina was Lavian's main girl, whom he'd been with since '93. He was head over heels in love with her. She was six years younger than him with light-brown skin and had a body like she just got off a plastic surgeon's table. But Celina's was all natural! Her 34C breasts were perfect-, not too big not too small. But Celina's ass was on 1,000! Her flat stomach and small waist made that thing sit up just right!

When the two met she had a son who was only eight months old, but her body snapped right back into the perfect hourglass figure she previously carried. Lavian looked after shorty like he was his own, and Celina loved him for that. He was kind of a good dude. However, being the sucka ass cheater he was, Lay got heavily involved with Josie in '94 when she moved to 139th Street with her two sons. They started a romance very quickly. Josie was two years older than him and had her shit together a little more than Celina. That played a big part in the attraction he had for her.

Josie had a career in law that was going quite well. Although she was a single mother, she was able to take very good care of her sons. Josie was caramel complexioned with long black hair, thick in all the right places and stood about five feet, six inches tall. The passion they shared was incredible. Not saying it wasn't the same with Celina, because they had a great sex life as well.

But there was just something about Josie that Lay couldn't get enough of. She knew he was in a relationship from the beginning and didn't care, but Celina didn't find out about Josie until a few weeks prior to this arrest. Guys are dumb and always end up moving sloppy. They're always getting caught.

Sean's main girl at the time was Desi, but he was a whore and dealt with many more on the side. Desi was a feisty little light-skinned chick with a fat ass, who loved drama. Sean definitely had his hands full with that one, but it would be wrong to place all of the blame on Desi. Sean had a way of driving women crazy with his shenanigans.

After spending an ample amount of time thinking about his chicks and the new dilemma he found himself in for what seemed like hours, Lay finally fell into a light slumber. Not much later, he was awaked by the sound of the CO calling names to see the judge. It was time to get up and pay attention. When their names were called, Sean and Lay walked into the courtroom, stood before the judge and were arraigned.

Josie and Desi had been in the gallery all evening waiting for the two men to be brought out. Lay was disappointed when he didn't see Celina in the gallery. He hoped she had heard about his arrest and showed up to court for the arraignment, but she had had enough of Lay's bullshit. Her attitude was, "if you want him, you can have him. *All of him.*"

Although Celina was still very much in love with Lay, she was not going to compete with another woman for someone she felt was rightfully hers. So, she was content to let Josie handle things from then on, and kept her distance.

They were charged with 'criminal sale of a controlled substance'. Bail was set for Lay at $2,500 and $7,500 for Sean.

Sean's was slightly higher because of a recent bullshit charge he was previously arrested for. They were given a new court date and remanded until that time. Before walking in the back, Lay and Sean turned to give Desi and Josie the look like, 'You know what to do'.

Back in the bullpen, Sean made small talk with some of the other detainees, and this went on for the next few hours before the CO started calling names of people to move into another holding cell.

When he called their names, Sean asked, "What are we going over there for?"

"You're going upstairs to the Tombs," the CO replied.

Sean said, "No we not! We gettin' bailed out!"

The CO looked at Sean's paperwork and said, "Your bail is $7,500. Unless you have seven large in your pocket, you're not going anywhere right now. Until then, move your ass to the next cell."

Sean said, "Man I don't give a fuck how much it is, we ain't going over there! We gettin' up out this motherfucka! Bet that!"

Lay looked at Sean and shook his head as he grabbed his jacket and began walking to the other cell. Another CO approached carrying two large manila envelopes. "Sean Prescott. Lavian Taylor," he yelled.

Lay stopped in his tracks. "Right here!" he and Sean answered the same.

The officer said, "Grab your shit. You made bail."

As he walked out of the cell, Sean looked the first CO up and down and said, "Told you I wasn't going to no motherfuckin' Tombs! I'm outta this muhfucka!"

Lay simply looked at this big-mouth nigga and laughed.

11

After being processed out, they walked to the train station in the cool November night air. "You always talkin' shit," Lay said. "Somebody is gonna knock your motherfuckin' ass out one day."

Sean said, "Man, fuck them motherfuckas, Lay. They wasn't keepin us in that nasty joint. We out!"

Lay and Sean fought their case for eight months before finally accepting a plea in July of '97. Lay knew he was going to prison because of his prior convictions so he paid his lawyer to keep getting postponements to stay free as long as possible. When it was all said and done, Lay pleaded guilty to a term of two and a half to five. Sean received three to six years in New York State prison, and was scheduled to be sentenced in September. With only two months of freedom left, Sean and Lay got their affairs in order as best they could, but it wasn't easy because their building wasn't the same after the arrest.

It seemed like the flow would never reach levels of $5,000 to $10,000 a day like it had once upon a time, thereby making it a struggle to maintain the lifestyle to which they'd become accustomed. The last two months were kind of rough, and what made things more difficult for Lay was the breakdown of his relationship with Celina.

The back and forth game he played with the two women had taken its toll on her and she left him. Deep down, he was heartbroken but he knew the best thing to do was let Celina go because he knew he was never going to end things with Josie. Lay saw the pain and damage his infidelities caused Celina, but it still wasn't enough for him to straighten up and fly right. Although his heart was with Celina, Lay made it his business to hold on to Josie with everything he could. He loved her too, but Lavian was *in love* with Celina.

Sean, on the other hand was focused on stacking his bread and putting things in place before leaving to do his bid. Their sentencing date was right around the corner, so there wasn't much time. But little time or not, Sean would find a way to get himself in some shit.

On the morning of September 10th, Lay and Sean met up at the train station on 135th Street and Lenox and prepared to take the ride downtown to 100 Centre Street and surrender themselves to the court.

They had talked previously about going on the run, but neither one had taken the other seriously. That day was different. Lay brought up the idea again and asked Sean what he was going to do.

"Release the hounds!" Sean said. "Fuck that shit, Lay! They gonna have to get the dogs out for me!"

Lay bursted out laughing and said, "You a fuckin' fool."

Sean said, "Man, I'm dead serious. They gotta catch me when they can!"

"Fuck it bro. I'm with you," Lay said.

And that was that. The two men became fugitives of the law. It was time to be extra careful and smart about every move they made. But somehow, Sean, smart and careful didn't mix well. It was like oil and water to be exact.

He and Desi had their share of issues and parted ways a couple of months after the arrest. In true Sean fashion, he started a relationship with a chick that lived in Desi's building. To make it worse is his new lady and Desi didn't care for one another. Her name was Holly. She was slim and brown-skinned with natural hair and possessed an air of sophistication. She liked the finer things in life.

But Holly also had some thug in her, and was not to be played with.

In a situation as delicate as being a fugitive, a rational person would do everything possible to keep a low profile. That was next to impossible for Sean. Although he and Desi were broken up, he doubled back once more and slept with her a few months prior to going on the run.

Since then, she had been trying to get back into a relationship with him, but he wasn't having that. His focus was on Holly, staying free, and figuring out how to put some money in his pocket since he couldn't be on the block anymore. But Desi really wasn't trying to hear that. And when she found out he was fucking with Holly, it made her go extra hard.

After they'd been on the lam for only a couple of weeks, the shit reached its boiling point.

Holly woke up one morning and was getting herself ready for work. Sean was still in bed watching TV as she moved about the apartment through her morning ritual. When Holly was ready, she leaned over the bed to give Sean a kiss before leaving.

Thinking about the sex they'd had the night before, he tried to go for round three. As Holly leaned over the bed and kissed Sean, he slid his hand up her skirt and rubbed her inner thigh, slowly moving it up toward her panties. Her legs were silky smooth to the touch, and the body oil spray she used made her skin feel even softer beneath his fingertips. When Sean's hand reached her panties, he pulled them to the side and slid his middle finger into her already moistening vagina. Holly softly bit his bottom lip and tried to pull away, even though she was enjoying every second of it.

"C'mon, you got time for a quick one," Sean coaxed.

She moaned. "No I don't." But her soaking wet pussy was saying, 'yes I do!'

Sean pulled her closer and she couldn't resist anymore. Holly dropped her Louis bag on the floor, pulled up her skirt and started to slide her panties down when the phone rang.

'Damn!'

Sean glanced down at his rock-hard dick, then back at Holly with a look that asked, 'Are you really gonna leave me like this?'

She looked back at him. 'Saved by the bell,' she thought.

Holly pulled her panties up and adjusted her skirt. "Get that. I'm going to be late messin' with your nasty ass." She walked out of the bedroom.

14

Sean fell backward onto the bed and shook his head with disappointment at how close he had been to getting some that morning. By this time, the phone had rung about eight or nine times.

'Who the fuck would let the damn phone ring that many times this early in the motherfuckin' morning?!?' he thought.

The phone was on Holly's side, so he rolled over the bed and answered it with a serious attitude.

"HELLO!" he barked.

The female voice said, "Hello."

It was Desi.

Sean said, "Yo, how the fuck did you get this number?!?"

She said, "Don't worry about it."

"Listen, don't play no games with me. Don't call here no more. You fuckin' buggin."

"Come downstairs," Desi said. "I want to see you."

"Man, I'm not comin down there." He hung up the phone. Sean picked up the receiver immediately to call the phone company.

"I need to change this number, now!"

The associate told him it was going to be a $45 charge added to the bill and would appear on the next cycle.

Sean said, "I don't care how much it costs. I need it done now!" "How long will it take to go into effect?"

"About an hour."

He said, "Good. Do it." Sean wrote the new number down and let out a sigh of relief.

Holly would still be on the train while the number was being switched, so he could just call her job to give her the new one when she got to work. He was in the clear.

Sean had drifted into a light sleep. Two hours later, the phone rang again. Sean picked up and said,

"Hello."

The female voice said, "I don't care how many times you change that number, motherfucker. I'm going to get it! So you can stop wasting your $45."

Sean's eyes shot open. "Yo, you buggin! You need to stop playin' yourself!"

"Oh, I'm playing myself?" Desi yelled. Ok, I'ma call your *bitch* now!"

Before he could protest, Desi hung up the phone.

'Damn. This chick is really crazy!' Sean thought. 'And how the fuck did she get Holly's job and cell number, too?!'

He was scared to death when his cell phone rang a few minutes later. Sean hesitated for several rings before he finally answered. It was Holly.

"What the fuck is going on, Sean?!? I just called the house and it said the number has been changed. And did you give that psycho, Desi my number?!?"

Sean replied, "Hell no! Why the hell would I do some dumb shit like that?!"

Holly said, "That bitch just called my job, talking about how you keep calling her. She's fucking with my livelihood, Sean! I'm gonna fuck her dumb ass up!"

The house phone rang again. "Hold on Holly," Sean said, reluctantly picking up the other phone.

"Yeah, I just called that bitch's job," Desi said. "Don't fuckin' play with me, Sean. Don't fuckin' play!"

Sean went back to Holly. "That was that crazy mufucka' on the house line. She's lying. How could I be calling her when I'm on the phone with you?"

Holly said, "I know she's lying! *And* she's calling my house, too?!? How the hell does she have that number and I don't even have it?! I'ma fuck that bitch up! And if you're behind any of this I'm going to kill you, Sean! I'm on my way uptown!"

Sean wanted to talk her out of it, but before he could say two words, Holly hung up the phone, grabbed her bag and walked out of her office door.

In the forty minutes or so it takes to get from 17th Street on the train, Desi continued her phone harassment campaign. Sean had had enough of that shit, so he got dressed and went downstairs to try to meet Holly arriving from work. As he walked outside, Sean saw a Suburban double-parked in front. He recognized whose truck it was and shook his head.

Holly had called for reinforcements. Roz, who's about five foot nine, and six-foot Katrina got out of the truck and started yelling at Sean. "Tell your bitch to come downstairs! We got something for that ass!"

Sean looked at Roz, who was wearing a football jersey, spandex and track sneakers, and Katrina had on a hoodie, spandex, and Tims.

'Damn,' he thought. 'These chicks gon' kill Desi!'

When Sean looked up the block, he noticed Holly coming down the street toward him with Sheri, another one of her girlfriends. Sheri was a petite super slim, high-yellow dainty little thing with huge breasts and natural hair that came down to her ass. Lay always had a thing for her, but felt she would never give him the time of day, even if he tried, so he never did. Sheri looked like she couldn't hurt a fly, and was too prissy to be fighting. But she was right there with Holly, holding her down.

Sean tried to get her to chill out and rethink things, but Holly was hearing none of that. He looked at Holly's hands and noticed she had several

17

rings on all of her fingers, almost like brass knuckles. 'Lord, please help this girl,' Sean thought.

Holly and Sheri were now standing by the truck with Roz and Katrina, who were gassing Holly up as if it was hardly necessary, since she had left work solely to administer this ass whooping, personally!

She called Desi to come downstairs so they can get to shaking, but Desi wouldn't answer the phone. Holly tried the intercom. Still no Desi.

At this time, Desi's friend Tonia pulled up, but she couldn't have helped much, because she was pregnant. Tonia got out and asked Sean what was going on. Sean said,

"I don't know, but if you love your friend, tell her don't bring her ass outside."

Tonia said, "C'mon. We're not doing this today."

Sean admonished her to stay out of it.

Thirty minutes later, Desi came out of the building looking as beautiful as she wanted to be. Dressed in beige linen, wearing shades, and her hair done up, with heels on looking like she was ready for New York Fashion Week, Desi walked up to Holly and asked her if she was looking for her.

Holly said, "Yup", and punched snot out of Desi's nose!

The force from the punch sent her stumbling backward into the scaffold. Her pocketbook fell as well, scattering some of its contents onto the ground. Desi had a meat tenderizer, a steak knife, and a small dumbbell in her bag. When Holly saw all of this, she said, "Oh, you brought weapons, bitch?!?"

She grabbed Desi by her shirt, dragging her away from the bag and repeatedly punched her in the face. When Holly got Desi close enough to the next beam of the scaffold, she started banging her head against it until Desi's face was battered and bloodied.

Sean grabbed Holly from behind and pulled her away from Desi. "That's enough, Holly!"

As fucked up as she was, Desi still kept talking shit and laying threats.

Holly gave her a look that clearly said, *'Sean is not gonna be here to break it up next time; keep talkin shit.'* But she didn't say a word.

Desi got herself together and left.

Suddenly it had just dawned on Sean that he was a fugitive and the police would probably be there any minute. He turned to Holly and said, "I gotta get outta here."

Sean flagged down a cab and rode uptown to the home of yet, another chick he was messing with-, named Cynthia, who was tall thick, and brown-skinned.

He wasn't there for five minutes when he got a call from Holly. Sean told Cynthia to be quiet in her own house while he took the phone call and stuck his head out of the window so it would seem like he was outside. In a calm even tone, Holly said, "You need to get back home. Right now."

Sean didn't know what the fuck was going on, but his baby needed him. So he left Cynthia's crib, caught another cab and headed home. When he got there, Holly was lying on the bed under the covers, sore and stiff as a board. Beating Desi's ass had evidently taken a lot out of her.

"What's wrong?" Sean asked.

"You need to go down to the eleventh floor and tell me what you see."

Sean asked "What for?"

"Just go down there."

So Sean took the elevator to the eleventh floor. As soon as he stepped out he saw blood on the walls and tenants' doors stretching from the elevator down the hall. Sean ran back up the three flights to their fourteenth floor apartment, and into the bedroom to check Holly's body.

He ripped the covers off the bed and examined her for any damage. Startled, she asked, "What's wrong with you?!?"

Sean was scared to death. He said, "Are you okay?!?"

Holly pushed his hands away. "Boy, get off me. That's not my blood."

"Well, what the hell happened down there? That shit looks like a crime scene!" Apparently, Holly and Desi had a rematch in the building that didn't go to well for Desi again.

Holly then told Sean about the second fight and that she'd pressed charges and had her arrested.

He said, "So you beat her up twice, *and* had her locked up?!"

"Yup. Sure did."

Sean knew Desi was going to be out for blood after all of this, so his best bet was to stay clear of her.

A few days later, he ran into Desi. He tried to ease the tension by at least saying hello and apologizing for everything Holly did.

"Oh no motherfucker! Don't talk to me now! You're gonna talk to them people!" was Desi's response.

"Man, whatever," Sean said.

They each walked away and went about their business. Desi knew Sean was on the run, and that was a dangerous secret for someone as vindictive as her to have.

About a month after the original confrontation on an early October morning, Holly was getting dressed for work as she typically would when there was a loud banging at the door.

Sean jumped up out of bed and ran to the door to look through the peephole. It was the fugitive squad! He ran to the refrigerator, and started removing food and the shelves so he could fit inside.

He told Holly to close the refrigerator door, but his foot was still hanging out. She said no, but he pleaded with her to keep trying. She refused and left him in the kitchen, opening the door for the police so they wouldn't break it down to search for him.

Sean was safe for a few minutes because none of them expected his crazy ass to be in the refrigerator. He heard one of the officers say, "He's gone! We missed him."

Another one said, "I know he's in here somewhere."

Sean couldn't stay in that refrigerator for much longer in his boxers and wife beater. Before waliking out, one of the officers noticed the refrigerator door ajar and opened it all the way to find Sean crammed inside.

He said, "Good morning Mr. Prescott. I have a warrant for your arrest."

There was no need to pull out his gun. Sean was far from being a threat, having almost frozen to death in the refrigerator. The officer grabbed Sean by the arm and led him to the bedroom so he could get dressed. Holly sat on the sofa with tears streaming down her cheeks. A female officer questioned her as they took Sean out of the apartment.

Just like that, his fugitive days were over. On the elevator Sean asked how they found him.

"A little birdie told us."

Sean knew exactly who that birdie was, automatically.

They said, "You must've done *something* to piss her off."

All Sean could do was shake his head. On the trip downtown he thought of Holly and how fucked up she looked sitting on the sofa. He knew he really messed up this time.

Lay's situation was the complete opposite of Sean's. He kept an extremely low profile, rarely leaving the house for much of anything. When Lay became a fugitive, Josie being the ride or die that she was, moved out of her apartment in 139th Street so he would have a safe place to live since the warrant was issued for his address on the block.

They, along with her two sons moved to her mother's apartment on 129th Street and Convent. Lay spent his days and nights watching TV and playing video games. That wasn't a life for him though. Shit, that wasn't a life for any respectable man. He couldn't just sit in the house every day and let Josie take care of him, the bills, and the kids.

But everything he tried, failed to work in his favor. He tried to partner up with one of his friends to run the block while he stayed in the house. That plan fell apart because this particular friend had a serious gambling habit. As soon as he made a significant amount of money, he would go down the block to the park to start a dice game. Lay had to nip that operation in the bud before it got out of hand. At the end of every flip he would only have enough money to re-up. He was basically hustling to pay his connect and support his partner's gambling addiction.

Lay had enough, so he just gave the block to his friend and walked away from it altogether.

This left him disheartened because he and Sean had worked hard for years to make the building what it was.

Then, an opportunity fell in his lap for him to make some bread in Durham, North Carolina. Lay still had connections, and it wasn't a problem getting his hands on some work. He got a brick of coke, made arrangements for it to be transported and hopped on Amtrak to meet it there.

When Lay arrived, his man Dave was there to meet him at the station. He chilled that night while Dave made the necessary phone calls so they could get rid of the coke the next day.

The next afternoon, Dave told Lay he had a buyer for the whole bird. Lay said, "Good. Let's do it."

Dave called a chick to drive the key to the buyer's crib while he and Lay rode in a separate car. When they arrived, they were greeted by a tall slim Jamaican guy with dreads draped down his back. Dread was very hospitable, and the three men made small talk as Dread and Lay got to know each other.

Dread checked the work to make sure it was legit. Once he was satisfied, he walked over to the oven, opened it and began pulling out stacks of money, and placed them on the kitchen table where Dave and Lay were sitting. When he finished, Dread rewrapped the brick and told Lay to count his money, before leaving the kitchen to go stash the coke he had just purchased.

Lay counted out the $28,500 and stuffed it in a plastic bag that Dave pulled out of his pocket. The deal was done, so they left Dread and went back to the crib. Lay grabbed a stack out of the bag and handed it to Dave. That was his cut, for making everything happen. Lay had to pay $24,000 for the brick, $500 to transport it, and the $3,000 was his profit.

That wasn't bad for a day's work. Lay made his reservation on Amtrak for the next morning and chilled the rest of the night at Dave's crib. On the ride back to New York he thought about how smoothly that trip had gone, and how he could get used to this. All he had to do was make three or four trips a month, or as needed and shit would be okay.

It didn't measure up to what he and Sean used to get on the block, but it definitely beat sitting in the house doing nothing while Josie took care of the family.

Lay had a hook-up in the DMV to get a license that would be registered in the New Jersey State system. It only cost $800 and he had that covered easily from the trip he'd just taken.

Lay met the guy, gave him $400, and told him he wanted the name on the license to be Chris Jackson. The guy met Lay a couple of days later and showed him the permit with the name Chris Jackson on it to prove everything was legit. Satisfied, Lay gave him the other $400. The guy said he would call Lay to let him know what day they should meet to take the photo for the license.

23

A week went by, no call. Two weeks passed by. No call, no answer. By then, Lay knew he'd gotten played. He should've never paid in full until the actual license was in his possession. You live and you learn. But he promised, when he caught that motherfucker it was going to be a problem. Lay was no gangster, but he was far from being a sucker too. One thing he didn't play about was money. This fuck-up meant he had to move around without ID for a while longer.

About a week later, Lay's people informed him that they had another brick for him. He called Dave and let him know he would be on his way down in a day or so. Everything went smoothly, just like last time. However, this trip took longer because Dave didn't have any buyers who were ready to re-up.

So, Lay had to sit for a few days. That wasn't a problem, but he just wanted to get back to Josie. On the fourth day, they finally got a buyer for half of the brick. Dave pulled out a scale, weighed the 500 grams and wrapped it up while Lay put the other 500 back in the stash. This time, instead of calling the chick, the buyer, named Bird came to Dave's crib, which was even better.

There was only one problem. Bird came without the money. Something told Lay to make him go get the bread and come back for the work, but Bird coaxed Dave into hanging out on his side of town after the deal was done; and was too lazy to drive back and forth. 'Fuck it,' Lay thought. 'We'll do everything in one trip.'

So Bird got in his truck with the half a brick and drove to his crib while Dave and Lay followed. Bird drove a little faster than Dave, and they got caught at a light as he sped through it. While sitting at the light, Lay noticed a police car approaching the cross street when Bird flew through the intersection. The lights and sirens went on, and the police car made the right to catch up with Bird. 'This can't be happening,' Lay thought. The two men sat in silence until the light turned green and Dave stepped on the gas.

They were less than a mile away from Bird's crib when Dave and Lay saw flashing lights from the police car up ahead. 'This can't be'. Sure enough, the police had Bird pulled over. As they got closer, they could see him cuffed on the ground while one officer stood over him and another searched through the car. They, of course found the work.

Lay's heart sank. 'Damn. I can't catch a fuckin' break. What the fuck am I going to do now?!?'

It was a good thing Lay's connect was a friend; otherwise he would've really been in a jam. He told Lay to bring the other half back and they would figure out the rest later. But he wasn't in the clear yet.

How was he going to get a half a joint back to New York? He damn sure couldn't get on Amtrak with it. Lay didn't have a license, so he couldn't drive. What was he going to do? He called Josie and in code, explained the situation to her. Like the rider she was, Josie said,

"I'll be down there to get you Friday after work."

She worked the rest of the week, drove nine hours to N.C, picked Lay up and drove all the way back to New York. He thought, 'I cannot live without this woman in my life. I'm gonna marry her one day.'

When Lay and Josie got back to the city, he called his man so he could return the half a brick. That was cool for the time being, but now Lay was back to square one. He only had a little bit of money left over from his first trip, and that wasn't going to last very long. He needed to figure out a way to generate some income.

Everything he tried went to shit, and Lay was getting frustrated with not having steady income. He definitely couldn't let Josie keep taking care of him. After being on the lam for eight months, Lay couldn't take it anymore, so one night while they were watching TV he told Josie he was going to turn himself in, do his time, come home and start all over.

Josie loved her man very much and didn't want him to leave, but she respected his decision. She knew she would support him no matter what, and that's what made Lavian love her even more.

On Friday May 8th, Josie drove Lay downtown to 100 Centre Street so he could surrender to the court, but it was after five o' clock when they arrived.

Lay hugged Josie, kissed her and told her how much he loved and appreciated everything she did as the tears rolled down her cheeks. He then turned and walked toward the front of the courtroom, got a bailiff's attention and said,

"Excuse me. My name is Lavian Taylor. I'm surrendering myself on a warrant."

The court officer looked at his watch and said, "Not today you're not. Come back Monday morning."

Lay looked at him like he was crazy, but didn't stay there long enough for him to change his mind. He was out!

Josie looked at Lay in confusion as he walked past her to the back of the courtroom and out the door. She quickly grabbed her Gucci bag and followed.

She asked, "What happened back there? What did he say?"

Lay said, "That lazy muhfucka' probably didn't feel like doin no paperwork, so he told me to come back Monday."

Josie practically jumped on his back in sheer joy!

She was hugging and kissing Lay like they had just won the lottery! They drove back uptown and chilled together all weekend. Sunday night came entirely too fast for both of them. After eating dinner, they watched TV for a while until Lay got up to take a shower. Josie joined him and they each washed the other's bodies in the steamy bathroom.

Lay grabbed the back of her neck and kissed her passionately as their tongues danced around in the other's mouth. With his other hand Lay caressed Josie's soapy back, sliding it down to the crack of her ass. He then cupped her cheek and lifted her thigh so she could put her foot on the side of the tub. Josie knew where he was going and followed his every move.

Lay slid his hand along Josie's thigh to the opening of her moistened vagina and spread her caramel lips apart. He slid his middle finger inside as Josie stopped kissing to look him in his eyes. Lay pulled his finger out and

26

stuck it in his mouth, then hers. He then knelt down and gently licked her clitoris as Josie gasped and grabbed Lay's head with one hand and used the other to grab the soap dish hanging on the shower wall to keep her balance.

This went on for a couple of minutes when Josie said breathlessly,

"We gotta take this to the bed."

Lay stood up and kissed her again, and they both exited the shower. The two dried each other off and went into the bedroom. Lay sat on the edge of the bed with the towel around his waist. Josie grabbed a bottle of her Victoria's Secret body oil from the dresser, dropped her towel and climbed onto the bed.

Sitting closely behind Lay, she hugged him, pressing her breasts against his back. He felt the heat from her body as Josie kissed the back of his neck and rubbed his wavy hair with her left hand. This aroused Lavian immediately. He reached to open his towel to reveal his growing dick, but she beat him to it. Josie was opening the towel and began rubbing some of the oil on his shit, making it even harder.

She knew when her man was fully erect, and when she got him to that point, Josie nudged Lay and told him to stand up and turn around. She was in control now, so he did as she wished. Josie took the towel, wiped the oil off of his dick and started sucking it. Lay grabbed the back of her head and gently played in her long black hair as she enjoyed every inch of him.

Lay was in ecstasy, but he didn't want to get too excited because he wanted this session to last for a while. Feeling a climax coming he slowly backed out of her mouth, bent down to kiss her soft full lips, and pushed her back onto the bed. Lay took the oil and massaged every inch of Josie's caramel-toned body. When he was done, he put Josie's left leg over his right shoulder, lowered his face between her legs, pushed her right leg to the side, spread her lips with the two fingers on his left hand and stuck his tongue inside of her already dripping wet pussy.

Josie moaned with pleasure as he licked her with strong deliberate stokes of his tongue. After being in there for a few minutes Lay moved up and concentrated on her clitoris, sucking the small round piece of flesh gently at first, but then more fervently as Josie began to swivel her hips and moan ecstatically.

He knew that this was her weak spot. 'It won't be long now,' he thought. Sure enough, Josie grabbed the back of his head and pulled it closer as she began to climax.

The strangest thing happened next. As she reached the peak of her orgasm, a warm fluid that smelled like urine shot out of her pussy into Lay's face and onto the bed! That shit was everywhere! He jumped up.

"What the fuck is that?!? Did you just pee in my face?!?"

Josie was a little embarrassed, but she said, "No! That's not pee! I must've squirted! That shit never happened before!"

Lay had never experienced that before either, but he's a nasty motherfucker, so that shit turned him on. He was ready to eat her again just to see if he could make her squirt once more, but since Josie's clit was too sensitive for that, they just had some good old-fashioned sex and fell into a deep sleep. In the morning they did it all over again before making their way down to 100 Centre Street. Lay kissed Josie, said goodbye, and began his three-to six-year sentence.

Robert 'Bobby' Charles

Although Sean and Lay were close like brothers, and partners on the block, Sean also had a clique he hung out with aside from Lay. They consisted of Evan, Justin, Daryl, Tony, and Bobby. The six of them were regulars at Skate Key and would meet up every Saturday to attend the weekend's festivities.

Lay was a few years older than they were and had been going to The Rink out in Bergenfield, New Jersey since the 80's, whenever he did decide to get out. Skate Key was an every now and then thing for him. It was around '93 when Sean and Bobby both returned to the street from doing their first bids that they met. They had Evan, Justin, Tony, and Daryl as mutual friends, but the two of them bonded together so well because of their recent incarcerations they had both experienced.

Evan, Justin, and Daryl were all working dudes, who never really indulged in street activity but were still cool to hang out with. Chilling together every weekend turned into almost every day for Sean and Bobby. When Sean wasn't on the block with Lay, he was with Bobby, and the bond they shared had grown just as close.

Bobby and Lay were always cool, but didn't really hang out with each other. Lay was the type to always stay close to the block while Sean ran around and had fun with the Skate Key crew. His motto was, 'no one is going to take care of my business better than I will,' so he played the block closely.

In '97, when Sean got snatched up by the warrant squad and went away, Bobby was devastated. His closest friend was gone and he didn't know what to do with himself. At this time, he was working at Harlem Hospital in communications. With a newborn son to care and provide for, the hospital salary just wasn't cutting it. He had to do something, and fast, so the hustler's spirit inside of him came to life, once again.

Bobby had hooked Evan up with a job at the hospital so he knew what his salary looked like. 'This dude can't be satisfied with that little bit of change, so I'ma see if he wants to get some real bread,' he thought.

Bobby went to Evan with a proposition. He told him that he wanted to put their paychecks together and buy some coke so they would be partners.

"Nah, I gotta buy me some sneakers for this party," Evan said.

Bobby was disappointed but replied, "Okay," and moved on.

He wanted to start with an ounce, but without Evan's half the grind just had to be a little harder. So, Bobby took his check, added about 85 lbs. of pennies that he rolled up and took to the bank, bought a half of an ounce of coke and began to make sales to the people he knew in the neighborhood.

Doing everything alone, he grinded until fourteen grams turned into twenty-eight grams. Twenty-eight turned into fifty-six, and so on. Bobby was now in the coke business. Along with his paycheck from the hospital, he was doing well for himself. After work, he would sit in Jewel's bar on 138th Street and 5th Avenue where he became a regular, and his sales damn near quadrupled. Bobby was off and running, buying up to two hundred to three hundred grams in no time. Business was great, so taking care of Bobby Jr. wasn't going to be a problem for him at all.

Bobby's coke run went on for a few months before things started to get shaky. That game has its ups and downs, and is very unpredictable. He found himself hanging out with Evan and Justin almost every day, since Sean wasn't around. Even though he was doing okay with the coke, he kept hearing about this check game that a few dudes were playing with.

There was a guy from the hood named Mustafa, who put certain people on to it, but Bobby didn't really know him, so he couldn't get the inside scoop. Mustafa was a super smart guy who always had his hand in some kind of white-collar criminal situation. He never had a job but always managed to keep a lot of bread in his pockets. If he didn't tell you personally, there was no way of figuring out how he earned his money.

Bobby always wondered how Mustafa did what he did, but had no way of getting close enough to find out. Evan and Justin knew this dude named Nick that had learned the game from E.J., who was schooled by Mustafa, the originator. Nick was a short big-headed guy who always acted kind of nervous and talked really fast. This cat was killing 'em with the checks! He rode around Harlem in brand new cars, fully paid for in cash.

Nick had a Mercedes Benz CLK430, and a BMW M3, both paid for. He even rode around with the titles to his vehicles in the glove compartment so he could stunt on anyone who thought he wasn't the real deal. Dudes hadn't done it like that since the 80's. But Nick was getting to it with those checks, and a blind person could see it.

Bobby didn't know what Nick was doing, but his interest was piqued. Tired of being on the outside looking in, Bobby got up the nerve one day and asked Ev and Jus, "What the fuck is that nigga Nick into? I know he's gettin' some bread, but how?"

Because they trusted Bobby, they gave the goods up without thinking twice.

"He fucks with the checks," Justin said.

But Bobby was still stuck.

That little bit of info left him in the same place as he was when he first asked the question.

"How? What you mean he fucks with the checks? Fucks with them how?"

"I don't know," Evan said, "but he has everything in his crib. A computer, printer, scanner, and some shit called Versacheck."

That's all Bobby needed to know.

He immediately went to Staples and bought all the supplies Evan and Justin said Nick had in his crib. Every day after leaving the bar, he would go home and practice trying to duplicate one of his old paychecks. Bobby had moved from Harlem by this time and was living with his girl Danise, in Glenwood Gardens, an apartment complex in Yonkers. He had rent and two car notes to pay, so the coke money was only maintaining his monthly bills. There was nothing extra coming in to put in the stash.

31

Besides that, his flow with the coke gradually slowed because of all the time he spent trying to master the check process. Finally Bobby felt he was ready to test the waters. He got a copy of a check from someone and duplicated it to the best of his ability.

One Friday, Bobby grabbed a chick he knew from the hood named, Stacey who had an account at Fleet Bank and had her deposit a check for $8,000.

Danise, whom (everyone called her Niecy,) had just left to go to Miami with her girlfriends. Bobby still had some coke, but only had $3,000 cash left to his name. He had given Niecy $1,000 of that for her trip, so this drop he did with Stacey had better work or he was fucked!

The first thing Bobby did the next morning was call the automated system to check Stacey's balance, which stated, "Your available balance is $8,462.12"

Bobby's eyes got as big as two BBS rims! He said out loud, "That shit worked!"

He called Stacey immediately and told her to get dressed because he was on his way to pick her up. She heard the excitement in his voice but didn't know any specifics because he didn't discuss it over the phone. That was a no-no!

Bobby flew down the Saw Mill Parkway and jumped on the Major Deegan Expressway, making it to Harlem in about fifteen minutes. He never drove fast. That's normally a twenty to twenty-five-minute drive. Not that day, because Bobby was flying! He picked Stacey up from her house and shot down to the Fleet Bank on & 79th and Lexington Avenue. He sat in the car while Stacey went in the bank, reappearing a few minutes later holding a white envelope filled with $100 bills.

She passed the envelope to him and said, "That shit was easy. The teller knew me, so I didn't have *any* problems. I gave her my ID and she just gave me the money. I counted it and walked out."

Bobby opened the envelope, saw all that crisp new money and almost got an erection. He counted out $4,000, gave it to Stacey, and her face lit up like Times Square. They never discussed what her cut was going to be, so when she got half, she was elated to say the least.

That was Bobby's introduction into the check game. His first experience was a hit! Stacey was so hyped up, she told Bobby she was going to get all of her girlfriends and put them on to her new come-up.

Trying to conceal his excitement, Bobby's response was, "Say no more."

Stacey got six of her friends together, schooled them to how everything went down, and they got on board. These chicks were thirsty to go! If they didn't already have one, Bobby would have the girls open accounts, let them sit for a week, and make the drops after seven days. With the coke money still having a decent flow, along with his newfound hustle, Bobby was back on his feet in no time.

He kept a safe at a sub-leased one-bedroom apartment in Harlem that had about $60,000 in it, and one at his crib in Yonkers that held around $45,000- all, which was cash Bobby had accumulated in a matter of two months. It was his first time ever touching $100,000 cash at one time in his life. You couldn't tell him shit!

Bobby was the type who had to master whatever he was into. So, while everyone was still using the Versacheck software that limited creativity, he abandoned it and learned how to duplicate his checks from scratch. He even went the extra mile and started using fraud deterrent paper before anyone else had even tried. Whenever new technology was introduced, Bobby was the first to jump on it. He developed his technique to suit his needs and built a small white-collar crime operation. But that was nothing compared to what the future held.

Malcolm Jones

Bobby had built a decent life for Niecy and himself. They lived in a nice apartment in Yonkers, not too far from Harlem where she worked, and he handled most of his business. The commute wasn't bad most of the time, so unless there was traffic, it wasn't a headache going back and forth. They lived a stone's throw away from the Cross County Mall on Central Ave, a popular shopping area that had stores like Macy's, Victoria's Secret, and other brands.

Further up in White Plains however, was The Westchester Mall Niecy loved, where the high-end stores like Neiman Marcus, Louis Vuitton, and Gucci were located. Bobby kept his baby laced with the finest things money could buy. You name the brand, and she owned it. Things were going well for Bobby, and life was good.

Danise had an identical twin sister named Latise, (called Tiecy for short,) who moved up to Yonkers and got an apartment a couple of buildings away, in Glenwood. The twins were half Puerto Rican and half Black with long hair, caramel-brown skin, and banging bodies. They were both fine as fuck!

Tiecy's boyfriend, Malcolm lived in Douglass Projects and would use the Metro-North to visit her on the regular.

Neither one had a car at this point, but they made do. It was cool for a little while, but the commute was tiring and expensive, so Malcolm moved in with Tiecy after a while. She worked at a dentist's office on Park Avenue and Eighty-Eighth Street, and Malcolm was a supervisor at Sprint on Seventy-Seventh and Broadway.

Most of the time on Fridays, Malcolm and Tiecy would take the Metro-North home or catch a ride with Niecy. Bobby used to see Malcolm in passing, but never really made much conversation, simply speaking cordially and keeping it moving. One late evening, Niecy called Bobby and asked if he would pick Malcolm up and bring him to Yonkers because he had to work late, and she and Tiecy were already home.

Bobby said, "Ok baby. Where is he?"

"His office is on Seventy-Seventh and Broadway."

Bobby said, "Tell him I'll be there in twenty minutes. I'm finishing things up right now."

"Thank you, handsome."

That put a smile on his face, and he said, "Don't worry about it, baby. See you in a minute."

When they hung up, Bobby counted the rest of the money he already had in his hand when Niecy called, put it in the safe, and went to get Malcolm from his job.

Arriving at Seventy-Seventh Street twenty-five minutes later, Malcolm was just walking out of the door when Bobby pulled up.

He hopped in and said, "What's happenin', Home Team? I appreciate this ride, man. You don't know how much I hate riding that muhfukin' Metro-North."

"Don't worry about it. It's cool."

Malcolm always noticed how laid back and quiet Bobby was.

He never heard about him crossing cats or being on some grimy shit. He always saw Bobby as a super-smooth dude. On the way up to Yonkers, Malcolm noticed the Presidential Rolex with diamonds in the bezel on Bobby's left wrist. It was nighttime, but the diamonds still danced every time they drove under a street light in Bobby's silver Denali.

Malcolm looked at how Bobby was dressed. 'This dude always looks fresh to death, every time I see him,' he thought. He was curious about Bobby, but they barely knew each other and he didn't feel comfortable asking. Instead, he remained silent while the music was playing. They didn't know one another well, so there wasn't much to say. The two men bobbed their heads to the music and Bobby's silver Denali cruised through the night traffic.

Despite himself, Malcolm glanced over at Bobby once more. He looked down at the Sprint button-up shirt he's wearing, and back at Bobby. He couldn't take it anymore.

At the next light he asked Bobby to turn the music down for a second.

Bobby obliged and said, "What's up?"

Malcolm said, "Yo B, what you into?!?"

Bobby let out a little chuckle and said, "I'm into a couple of things. What you into?"

"Man, you see what I'm into. I work."

"That's cool. Ain't nothin wrong with a steady paycheck."

He thought for a second and asked Malcolm if he knew a chick with a bank account.

He said, "Yeah, Tiecy got one."

"Not your wife. Another chick."

"Oh, definitely." Malcolm smirked. He was a big whore, and was sleeping with all the chicks that he worked with, so that didn't present a problem for him at all.

Bobby said, "Cool, get the chick's debit card and we'll take it from there."

Malcolm said, "Bet."

They exchanged numbers and Bobby dropped Malcolm off at his building. He thanked Bobby again and stood outside for a minute to make some calls before going upstairs. He couldn't make them upstairs while Tiecy was home. Malcolm had been given a homework assignment, and got right on it.

The next day, Malcolm called Bobby and said he wanted to link up. Bobby got himself together and met Malcolm in front of his building. As soon as he jumped in the truck, Malcolm showed Bobby the debit card. Bobby thought, 'this muhfucka didn't waste no time.' He looked at the name, and then went upstairs to print out a check. Shortly after, they drove to a bank on Broadway in Yonkers and dropped a check for $1,500.

"Now what?" Malcolm asked.

"We wait."

The next morning it cleared. Bobby went to the ATM with the card and withdrew $500. He immediately called Malcolm and told him to get shorty to take the rest of the money out. Malcolm got on his bike once again and got busy. He called the chick and had her withdraw the remaining $1,000.

Malcolm gave her $500 and kept $500 for himself, splitting everything evenly, and making everyone happy.

"Now you see what I do," Bobby said. "So if you get you a girl, I can get you some money."

Malcolm was the perfect candidate for that job. That night he called Bobby and told him to meet him in front of his building.

When Bobby got downstairs, Malcolm had ten more debit cards! Bobby thought, 'this nigga ain't playin!' With all of those cards now in his hands, Bobby had his work cut out for him. He had to put all that work together that night in order for it to be ready in the morning. He went upstairs and got busy.

In the morning, the two met and Bobby gave Malcolm the checks, all made out in amounts of $1,500. Malcolm rounded up all of the girls and collected their debit cards so they could make the deposits.

The first phase was done. Since it was the weekend, they had to wait until Monday for everything to clear. But Bobby checked each account, and $500 was available for all ten checks, which was a good sign. He went to their banks and withdrew the $500 each for all ten. His $5,000 was secure, but he didn't dip into it until the rest of the bread cleared. Meanwhile, Malcolm anxiously waited all weekend to see what the results were.

Monday morning Bobby got up bright and early and started making the calls to check all ten balances. They'd all cleared. He called Malcolm and said,

"Get those chicks together, bro. You're about to get some money today!"

Malcolm jumped up, showered, got dressed and was out the door. While on his way to work, he called all of the girls and told them the good news.

They were instructed to make the withdrawals and meet him at the job. Malcolm had to be strategic with the times he told them to come because he didn't want one bumping into the other. He was sleeping with 90% of them, and that would've been disastrous if they did! As the day went on Malcolm met each chick, got his $500 and gave them their $500 until the last one came through.

When it was all said and done he cleared $5,000 for one day's work. This motherfucker was open! He couldn't wait to do some more drops! He told all of his girls to be on standby because he would be calling again. They all were eager to participate in such an easy payday, so that wasn't going to be a problem. Malcolm met with Bobby later that night and explained how the day went. Bobby was extremely happy to put some money in his newfound friend's pocket. From there, the two formed an unbreakable bond that lasts to this day.

Malcolm and Bobby did a few more runs over the next couple of weeks. Things were going well for them both. Malcolm was touching a few extra bands aside from his paycheck, and that shit felt good. Damn good!

One day Bobby was chilling in his truck waiting for Stacey to come out of the bank when his cell phone rang.

It was Niecy. He answered, "Hey baby, what's-..."

She cut him off before he could finish and yelled, "Bobby, why would you do that?!? What's wrong with you?!? Why would you do that?!?"

Bobby was dumbfounded. He moved the phone away from his ear, looked at it for a second, then put it next to his ear again and calmly asked, "Do what? What did I do?"

He was trying to play cool while his heart was beating a mile a minute. The first thing that came to his mind was some chick he was humping called Niecy and said she was pregnant, or some dumb shit like that.

She said, "Why would you tell Malcolm to quit his job?!?"

"Huh? Quit his job? Baby, I didn't tell Malcolm to quit his job. I don't know what you're talking about. I didn't even speak to him today."

Niecy yelled, "Well, he quit his job, and Tiecy is all stressed out! You know they have a baby on the way! How are they supposed to make ends meet with one income, Bobby?!?"

Bobby looked at the phone again, then put it back to his ear and said, "Baby, I don't know how they're gonna make it on one income, but all I wanna know is, why are you yelling at me?"

Niecy said, "Bobby, I swear you better not have anything to do with this!"

"Baby, I don't."

But Niecy didn't hear him because she had already hung up the phone. By this time, Stacey had come back to the truck in time to over hear one end of the conversation. She was looking at Bobby like he was crazy.

He put his hands to his face and thought, 'what the hell just happened?'

After Bobby dropped Stacey off, he immediately called Malcolm and asked, "My nigga, what did you do today?"

Before he could answer, Bobby said, "Where you at? I'ma come scoop you."

Malcolm gave him his location, and Bobby headed over there. When he arrived, Malcolm got in the truck and explained what happened that morning.

He said, "I went in that muhfuckin' spot, threw my shirt and tie on the floor and said man, check this shit out. Fuck this job! I'm outta here!"

Bobby looked at Malcolm and said, "Listen bro, I appreciate your dedication, but if you don't have a job, you *have* to hustle! You do realize that, right?"

"Well, that's what I'm gonna do!"

"So what are you gonna tell Tiecy?"

"I'm gonna show her this muhfuckin' bread I've been making with you, and that will keep her ass quiet."

"Okay cool, bro. I'm glad to have you aboard, officially. But there's one thing I need you to do before I take my ass home tonight."

"What's that?" Malcolm asked.

Bobby said, "Could you please tell my baby *I did not tell you to quit your damn job?!?*"

Malcolm bursted out laughing!

A few months had passed, and Malcolm and Bobby were still doing their thing. When Malcolm said he was going to hustle, he wasn't kidding. He turned all the way up! When he started, neither he nor Tiecy had vehicles. But all that changed because Malcolm was getting money now. He bought Tiecy a brand-new black Toyota Camry and a Champagne colored Denali for himself.

They got all new furniture for the house and laced the baby's room with a crib, toys, and all kinds of stuffed animals. Bobby's silver Denali was the previous model, so he upgraded and bought a white one just like

Malcolm's. For Niecy, he got a blue Lexus ES 350. Things were going beautifully. Every now and then, Bobby would think, 'damn, I wish my brother, Sean was here to be a part of this'.

He wouldn't have to wait long.

Welcome Back

In November of '99 Lavian was transferred from Hale Creek Correctional Facility in upstate New York to a federal/state halfway house on Thirty-First Street between Fifth and Madison Avenues. There he stayed for another year and a half until being released on parole in May of 2001. While there, he got a job at American Express Travel processing airline tickets for the executives at Coty, a huge perfume and cosmetic conglomerate.

The job didn't pay much, but it kept the P.O. off his back, and it allowed him to help Josie with some of the bills. Things were kind of tight, so Lay would just give her his entire paycheck, minus what he needed for lunch and transportation for the week, which didn't leave much of anything to spare. Josie had held Lay down his entire bid like the ride-or-die chick she was, so he felt it was only right for him to put her and the boys first.

In the beginning, she went to see him weekly; then once Lay was settled, she went monthly. It didn't matter how far, she made those trips faithfully, and Lay loved her for that. He felt like he owed her for the sacrifices she made to secure his well-being. Lay wanted to give Josie the world, and he intended to make that happen.

On Lavian's last day of reporting to the P.O. at Lincoln Correctional Facility, Bobby spotted him coming out of the train station on 110th Street and Lenox Avenue. He made a u-turn and pulled up on Lay as he was about to turn the corner.

Bobby jumped out of the truck and said, "Ayo Lay! What's up, my nigga?!?"

Lavian stopped when he heard his name and turned to see Bobby walking toward him looking like a million dollars.

He was wearing a navy velour Enyce t-shirt with gold lettering, and the matching sweatpants. On his head Bobby wore a blue Yankee fitted, of course. But on his feet were the official hustlers' slippers, white on white Air Force One's. Harlem cats wore those kicks so much that in the prison system, people from other boroughs called them 'Uptowns'. Back in the 80's, it was

Reebok Classics, or maybe Adidas Shell-Toes. But the new millennium definitely belonged to Nike AF1's! Technically, that's what Nike called them. Not Bobby and his crew. To them they were and would forever be known as 'Icey-Whites'. That's because of the way they seem to sparkle like ice when they come fresh out of the box.

On Bobby's wrist was that pretty Rolex all iced out, now accompanied by a diamond pinky ring. In Lay's mind he was thinking, 'damn, Bobby really came the fuck up!' When he left, Bobby was still working in Harlem Hospital. He just couldn't believe the transformation Bobby had made. Lay was genuinely happy for him.

The two men embraced and expressed how good it was to see the other. Lay asked if he had kept in touch with Sean.

Bobby replied, "Of course. That fool should be home in a couple of months."

"I know," Lay said. "What the hell are we gonna do with him? That motherfucka' is a handful."

"I have something in mind for him. You too-, that's if you're both interested. You know, y'all had a pretty good thing going on in your block. He might just want to pick up where he left off. We'll see."

Thoughts of hustling were far from Lay's mind. All he wanted to do was enjoy his freedom. But the allure of his prior lifestyle ate at his very core. It wouldn't be long before he found himself back in the street. The two men exchanged numbers and parted ways for the moment.

Memorial Day Weekend was approaching and Bobby intended to treat himself to a trip for all of his successes over the past couple of years. After Sean went away, his status on the streets of Harlem escalated considerably, and he wanted to celebrate. Sean wasn't home yet, but Bobby still had Malcolm by his side every step of the way.

He hit Malcolm and the rest of the Skate Key Crew and they all flew to Miami for the weekend. Booking a room at The Loews Hotel, they were set for four days of sun, fun and "freaknastiness." Niecy and Tiecy would've killed those two if they knew what was about to go down on that trip. It didn't matter; Bobby, Malcolm and the rest of the crew were ready to take Miami down.

After check-in Bobby shed his clothes, threw on some Sean John trunks and went down to the Jacuzzi to see what was popping. Relaxing in the hot tub, he recognized Latiya, a short, light-skinned, thick cutie with natural black hair cut in a 'bob', chilling by the pool with her all-girl crew.

There were about eight of them stretched out in two cabanas, looking sexy as fuck. Bobby had been trying to get with Latiya for months, but Niecy busted him and put an end to that whole situation before it could even get started. Being the gentleman he was, Bobby sent four bottles of Cristal with some strawberries and other fruits to her and her girlfriends. He knew this would be the perfect opportunity for them to reconnect. Upon receiving the Cris and platter of fruit, Latiya raised her flute and acknowledged Bobby by licking her top lip.

'Aww shit! I got this motherfucka' back. This trip is gonna be crazy,' thought Bobby. His focus on Latiya was interrupted by a half-dozen ladies from D.C, who joined him in the Jacuzzi. Small talk was made, numbers were exchanged, and they promised to meet up in his room later that night. After a while, the D.C. ladies left Bobby in the hot tub and got ready for the night's activities.

He sipped on his drink while thinking about all of the ass he was about run through that weekend. When exiting the Jacuzzi, Bobby accidentally knocked his cell phone into the water which turned out to be a gift and a curse. On one hand, he lost all his contacts, including the baddies he just met from D.C. On the other, Niecy wouldn't be able to reach him unless he was in his room, giving him freedom to play as much as he liked. Because he had been drinking since he landed, Bobby was 'wet' by the time he got to the club that night; and the fun hadn't even begun. While in the club, he hooked up with a babe from back home named Sheema.

She was a slim light-skinned chick with huge breasts and long, sexy legs. The two found themselves in a dark corner where their kissing and fondling wouldn't be noticed much. With no one paying attention, Bobby and

Sheema started fucking right in the club. He had Sheema damn near naked as he lifted her in the air and sat her on his dick. Half drunk, it was a wonder how he was even able to hold her up. Bobby bounced Sheema up and down as he sucked on her huge nipples.

She was trying to look around to see if anyone noticed them, but couldn't concentrate because the sex was just too good. Before long she said 'fuck it', and just enjoyed her session. When they were done, he stumbled to the bathroom to clean up, as Sheema did the same, then on to the dance floor to enjoy the rest of his night.

There were many people from New York in that particular party and Bobby ran into another chick he used to knock down named, Tee Tee and her girlfriend, Danni. Dancing with both of them, Bobby's drunken ass turned and kissed Danni in the mouth. Tee Tee punched him in the chest and said,

"Bobby, you just kissed my girlfriend! What's wrong with you?"

He grabbed the back of Tee Tee's head and kissed her too. Bobby then grabbed Danni's head as well and, pushed their faces together so that the two ladies could kiss. After a few seconds, he joined in and made it a three-way tongue-fest. Normally this would've turned him on, but he was too 'saucy' to realize it. Next thing you know, Bobby took off his shirt, climbed into the dancer's cage and started dancing as the DJ played Tupac's "California Love."

When the bouncers urged him to get his ass down from there, he headed back to the dance floor. Digging both hands into his pockets, he pulled all of his money out and threw it up in the air; making it rain with about $2,500 in five-dollar bills.

Somehow Bobby made his way to the bar and ordered a bottle of Cris and some cocktails for a group of ladies who were dancing there. One of them asked, "Baby, how are you going to pay for this? You know you just threw all your money in the air, right?"

Bobby was so drunk, he didn't give a fuck. He just slid away from the bar as soon as the bartender left to fill the order. Eventually, Tee Tee found him in the crowd. She did her best to settle Bobby down because he was going crazy in the club. She grabbed his hand and led him to the exit and out the door.

Walking back to his hotel in the rain, shirtless, moneyless, and drunk out of his mind, Bobby suddenly became extremely horny. 'I'ma fuck the shit outta this chick,' he thought. Stumbling to the elevator and finally to the room, Bobby and Tee Tee got straight to business. He was humping so hard and fast, his dick kept slipping out.

Frustrated, Tee Tee said, "Stand up baby. Let me suck it."

Bobby stood up with his back to the bed while Tee Tee went to work. Ten seconds into the oral session, Bobby fell back onto the bed and passed out from intoxication. Tee Tee couldn't believe this motherfucker. She took his jewelry off, placed it in his pants pocket, got dressed and left him alone to sleep it off.

The next morning, Bobby woke up buck naked with the hangover of life. He didn't know *what* the hell happened the night before, but that wouldn't stop him from doing it all over again. He hooked up with three more chicks that weekend before taking his ass back to New York. Needless to say, that was a trip he would remember for all time!

A couple of weeks after Bobby's Miami trip, he and Lay took the drive upstate to pick Sean up from Hudson Correctional Facility. They were both happy to have Sean out, but not as happy as he was. On the ride home, the three men laughed and did all the necessary catching up. Lay and Sean hadn't seen one another in four years, so there was a lot of shit-talking going on.

Upon reaching the city, they stopped at Floridita on Broadway and 125th Street to grab a bite to eat. It was there that Bobby filled them in on the success he had found in the check game. Although both men were intrigued, they were apprehensive about stepping into a new realm of criminal activity and decided to try their hands back on the block instead.

Promising Josie he would do the right thing when he got out, Lay hadn't even attempted to hustle without his partner. It had been almost two years he spent just barely getting by. But now that Sean was back, it was a different story. He was ready to hit the ground running a hundred miles an hour, and Lay was ready to run right alongside him. Bobby offered to join him and Malcolm in the paper game but they respectfully declined.

He told them he would loan them some seed money to put them back in the crack game-; enough to buy one hundred grams. That was more than enough to put the Dynamic Duo back on their feet. After receiving the cash from Bobby, Lay and Sean went to the block to set up shop again, only to find that things had changed considerably. There weren't an abundance of available workers at their disposal, and this presented a problem because selling hand to hand is what got them a free ticket to the New York State countryside in the first place.

Being on parole didn't make things easier for Sean, either. Coming in direct contact with the work put him at risk of getting a positive reading on a drug test, and his curfew limited the time he was able to be on the block as well. They needed to find a way to work around Sean's parole situation. Those restrictions didn't apply to Lay because although he was still on parole, his status was inactive.

He didn't have to report or submit to urinalysis tests. The only stipulation for Lay, was not to be re-arrested. When they finally found employees, Lay gloved up, bottled all of the work and took the evening shifts while Sean came out in the mornings. Things were starting to look up for them financially, and Lay began to feel some relief in his household.

There had been some tension between him and Josie, mainly because of bills and also due to readjusting to one another after his incarceration. Because money was flowing a lot better than before, Lay made good on one of his promises. Josie had been driving a 1997 Nissan Altima for the past few years so he surprised her with a top-of-the-line black 2001 BMW X5, just because he felt she deserved it; in appreciation for all of the sacrifices she made for him and the boys.

Lay parked the SUV down on 83rd Street and Columbus in front of Flor De Mayo and took a cab uptown to wait for Josie to get home from work. When she arrived Lay grabbed her by the hand and led her into the

47

bedroom. Josie looked confused as he explained that he was taking her and the boys out for dinner, and happy she didn't have to cook after that long day at the firm.

Josie showered, changed into more comfortable clothes and the four of them headed to the restaurant. On the drive down, Josie's cell phone vibrated, but she didn't answer. Lay noticed it went off a couple of times while she was in the shower, but paid it no mind. However, declining to answer while it sat in her lap raised an eyebrow.

Lay made a mental note of it but kept driving, because nothing was going to steal his joy tonight. Walking into Flor De Mayo, Josie noticed the shiny BMW with a big red bow on top of the hood and said, "That's nice! Whoever bought that for his lady is getting some tonight!" Lay just smiled to himself as they entered the restaurant.

While eating dinner, Josie's phone went off again. This time she answered. Lay could clearly hear a man's voice talking loudly on the line as Josie tried to remain as cavalier as possible and responded to every question asked of her in an even tone. When she hung up, Lay asked if everything was okay because she was clearly shaken by the call.

Josie replied, "It's nothing. Just my boss tripping about work stuff."

Lay said okay, but it didn't sound like her boss on the phone. Lay had been to her job plenty of times and knew that wasn't Mr. Lieberman's voice on that call. Another red flag went up in Lay's mind, giving him a real uneasy feeling, but he didn't want to ruin the evening, so he let those thoughts subside. For now.

After dinner, Lay, Josie and the boys stepped outside the restaurant as Josie's eyes again focused directly on the new vehicle sitting before her.

Lay smiled and said, "You like that, huh?"

"Yes! It's so shiny and pretty. I love it! Some lucky girl is gonna be smiling in the morning when she sees this! I hope nobody messes with her bow."

As he walked over to the car Lay said, "You can untie it if you want to."

Josie said, "I'm not touching that car! Are you crazy?!?"

"You can untie the bow, lean on the car, do whatever you want. Here, lemme show you," Lay said, as he pulled the ribbon that was hanging by the passenger side windshield.

Josie yelled, "Lay, get off of that car! What is wrong with you?!?"

"Stop worrying. You worry too much." Lay had his left hand in his pocket on the key remote as he pulled the ribbon with his right, pressing the button to disarm the alarm on the X5 with a "Beep Beep," as the door unlocked and the lights flashed.

Josie's mouth and eyes opened wide.

"See, you play too much. Somebody is coming to get you for messing with their car, Lay!"

She grabbed the boys' hands and started walking away like they were all in trouble.

"Ain't nobody gon' do nothing to Ms. Taylor's son," Lay said.

He walked around to the driver side of the car and opened the door.

Josie yelled, "Lay! What the hell are you doing?!?"

"I'm getting in your car," he replied casually.

"*My car?* Lay, no you didn't! How-..?"

Lay left the door open as he walked over to Josie to grab her hand. He led her to the driver seat and handed her the key. The boys jumped up and down excitedly while Josie sat in the car, looking at Lay through the tears puddling in her eyes. She was speechless because she now realized why Lavian had been keeping all those late hours.

She stepped out of the vehicle, threw her arms around Lavian and hugged him for what seemed to be an eternity.

Wiping her tears, Josie finally said, "Lay, you did this for me? I can't thank you enough. I don't deserve this, or you. I love you so much."

"Baby, you deserve this and so much more. I'll never forget how you held me down from day one. I owe you the world, and nothing is gonna stop me from giving it to you. Now wipe those tears and let's get these boys home."

Josie did just that. She drove uptown thinking about her man and the wonderful gift he just gave her. Lay and the boys followed in the Altima as he smiled to himself, feeling great about how happy he made his baby.

Sean was doing his best to reintegrate into society, get some money, and stay out of his P.O.'s way in the process. It's a good thing he had a cool one, who didn't put any real pressure on him. With the money he made from the block, Sean was able to set himself up in a bachelor pad on Fifth Avenue between 112th and 111th Streets, lacing it with Italian furniture, a pool table and a couple of video games for when the fellas stopped by.

Although he will probably be a whore until they threw dirt on his coffin, Sean was the type who always wanted to be in a relationship because there was just something about coming home to a beautiful woman every night that he loved. Sean and Holly had fallen out of touch while he was away, but that didn't stop him from loving and wanting her.

He was determined to get her back, and nothing was going to stand in his way. She had moved from her old apartment, but Sean still remembered where she worked. He anonymously sent a dozen red roses to her job with his cell number attached. If she still worked there, maybe he had a shot; if not he had no choice but to move on.

As time ticked away without receiving a call from Holly, he thought all was lost. At 5:15 however, a 212 area code popped up on his cell, from a number he wasn't familiar with. He answered and immediately recognized the sweet voice on the line as Holly's. The two talked while she walked to the train station and made plans to catch up over dinner on the weekend.

50

Holly was glad Sean was home, but a relationship with him wasn't what she had in mind at the time. She loved Sean, but Holly also remembered the drama that came with dealing with a man like him.

That didn't matter because Sean was on a mission to get his baby back. After a couple of dinner dates, Holly informed Sean how much she enjoyed spending time with him, but getting back together wasn't an option for her.

Sean was crushed, but that didn't slow him down from being a player. He just moved on from one chick to the next while he waited for the next one who would eventually capture his heart.

Back on the block, things were going smoothly for Lay and Sean. As weeks passed, their clientele and flow increased tremendously.

One evening, McBride and Knight, two detectives cruised through 139th Street and stopped in front of Lay who was sitting across the street from the spot.

"How you doin', Mr. Taylor?" Det. Knight asked from the passenger seat of the unmarked car.

Lay looked at the two cops and ignored the question, wondering how they even knew his name. This prompted Det. Knight to exit the vehicle and approach Lay.

"What's up? Cat got your tongue?" he asked.

"Nah, I can talk. I just don't have nothin to say to *you*."

"Well, you don't have to talk. Just listen. We have a pretty good idea you and your boy are up to your old tricks again."

"I don't know what you're talkin about."

"I figured as much. Okay, put it like this. I *know* what the fuck you're out here doing, and it's only a matter of time before I catch your black ass red- handed. When I do, you and that fuckin' friend of yours won't slip through the cracks with a skid bid like last time. I'll make sure your shit gets kicked up to the federal level!" Det. Knight barked.

"That's crazy. I didn't know sitting in front of a building was a federal offense," Lay retorted.

"Oh, you're a smart-ass," the detective barked annoyingly. "As a matter of fact, get the fuck off this block! And if I see you or your fuckin' buddy, Sean out here again I'm locking both of you the fuck up! Do I make myself clear?"

"Crystal," Lay replied. He stood up, looked Det. Knight square in the eye and walked away from them, wondering where this heat was coming from.

Lay went into the McD's on the corner and immediately called Sean to inform him of his encounter with New York's Filthiest. These weren't ordinary detectives, and Lay didn't know where they came from, but he wasn't sticking around to find out, either. He and Sean were making decent money again, but it wasn't enough for another trip to the can. If they couldn't hustle on the block anymore, what the hell were they going to do for income?

Lay didn't want to go back to working a nine to five again, and Sean never had a job in his life, so that was definitely out of the question for him. It's a good thing they were almost at the end of their package, and there was only a couple of G's left before re-up. So they paid a couple of friends $100 a day to run the block for them until the work was finished.

The question still remained: what were they going to do after that? With their backs against the wall, Lay and Sean looked to their good friend Bobby Charles for answers.

A New Hustle

Lay and Sean gave Bobby a brief rundown about the block situation, so he arranged to meet them at Mekka's to discuss what their next move would be. He brought Malcolm along as reinforcement to assist in convincing the two men to make the transition from the coke game to earning money with the checks. Bobby gave them his spiel, and the two men were sold without Malcolm having to utter a single word.

At the dinner, Lay and Sean agreed without hesitation that the check game was the next best wave. Bobby told each of them to get as many girls as they could find to work. By this time, he had made the transition from making deposits to cashing the checks directly over the counter through the teller because the previous method had become too risky.

Being the ladies' man he was, it was no problem for Sean to round a few ladies up to get his show started. Lay on the other hand was more laid back, and introverted. He didn't associate with too many chicks so it was a little difficult for him in the beginning. Before long, he linked up with Sammi (short for Samantha).

She was a super cool, brown-skinned cutie he knew from the hood with an enormous ass. After explaining what the deal was, Lay got Sammi to join the team. Lay informed Bobby that he found a willing participant, who was ready to go. With Sammi's info, Bobby printed ten checks and MapQuest directions for Lay to go on his first mission.

When he got home that evening, Lay must've looked at the small rectangular pieces of paper a half a dozen times trying to figure out how this was going to work. He still had his doubts even after all Bobby and Malcolm had explained, but felt following their lead was definitely worth a chance. After all, what did he really have to lose? Besides, 'Bobby was pretty successful at it, so what the hell,' he thought.

Lay put the checks away when his youngest son called him into the dining room for help with his homework. About fifteen minutes later, Josie walked through the door, kissed all three of her guys and hopped in the shower so she could start dinner. Lay heard his cell phone ringing from the bedroom and sent his son to retrieve it.

Of course, being a kid, he grabbed the first phone he saw, upon entering the room. When he got the phone, Lay opened the flip, and before he could say hello, heard a man's voice he vaguely recognized.

"Hey Babe, did you make it in yet? I was trying to catch you before you did."

That's when Lay realized it wasn't his phone that had rung; it was Josie's.

They both had the same model, so his son didn't bother trying to distinguish one from the other. He just grabbed the phone that was ringing and brought it to Lay, like he was instructed to do.

Without saying a word, Lay calmly got up from the dining room table, walked into the bathroom, handed Josie the phone while she was still in the shower and said, "It's your babe. He tried to catch you before you got in, but he was about ten minutes late."

Dumbfounded, Josie looked at Lay like she had been blindsided. She knew deep down inside she was busted. Lay left the bathroom and went into the bedroom. There he sat on the chaise lounge and, waitied for Josie to explain what the hell was going on.

Stepping into the room, with the towel around her soaking wet caramel body, Josie quietly broke down how she met Dante while at work. He was an ex-NBA player, now playing overseas in Italy who used her firm to review his contracts when he'd made the transition three years ago.

"So you've been fuckin' this motherfucka for three years? That means you started fuckin' with him as soon as I left. Damn, Josie. Our relationship didn't mean shit to you. It's like you couldn't *wait* for me to leave."

"It didn't start out like that, Lay. We were just friends at first. Then one thing led to another."

"Just like that, huh?" Lay asked.

"I mean, I don't know what to say."

"Not much you *can* say, is there?" "Do you love him?"

Josie hung her head in shame. She said, "Don't do this, Lay. Please?"

"Do what? I'm merely asking you a question. Do you love him?"

"Please don't make me answer that."

Lay sat in silence while he waited for a response. After a long pause, Josie finally responded, "Yes, I think I do."

"Too much to leave him alone?"

"Lay," Josie said with a feeling of helplessness.

"Answer me!" Lay shouted.

He had remained composed until then, but Josie's continual stalling frustrated him.

"I don't know," she replied.

"Enough to lose me?"

"Never. Don't say that. Lay, I'm so sorry. I was so lonely, and you were away. And I just kept thinking about all we had been through with Celina-..."

Lay cut her off abruptly.

"Celina?!? Don't try to use her as the reason for your shit, Josie! You always had a choice, and you chose to stay. I never forced myself on you. I didn't have anymore secrets. And I left Celina alone completely for you. For us! And it's been about you ever since, so don't give me that bullshit!"

By this time, Josie was sitting on their bed, still in the towel, with her hands folded and tears welling in her eyes.

After a silence that seemed to last for an eternity, Josie spoke again.

"He was just a shoulder to lean on-..."

Lay cut her off mid-sentence. "Well, he's clearly more than that, now, right Babe?"

"That's not my Babe."

"You certainly are *his*. That muhfucka didn't have a problem letting *that* be known."

"Lay, please!" Josie implored.

"Did you use protection?"

"Yes, every time."

"You expect me to believe you were sleeping with this man for three years and you never fucked him raw? You must really think I'm stupid."

"Lay, I wasn't fucking him for three years, and I wouldn't do that to you."

"Nah, you did enough," Lay said as he began to pack his Hugo Boss duffle bag.

"Where are you going?"

"I'm going out of town tomorrow."

"When will you be back?"

"Tomorrow night."

"So, where are you going now?"

"I'm getting a room for the night. I need a clear head for my business. I don't even know if that's possible after all this. I just know I can't be here."

"Lay, I wish you wouldn't do this."

"What do you expect me to do?"

Josie had no response, and sat wordlessly as he eyed her with disgust.

"Just like I thought."

After his bag was packed, Lay grabbed the checks out of his nightstand drawer and went to say goodbye to the boys. He jumped into the Altima and drove across the bridge to New Jersey and booked a room at the Marriott at Glenpointe. Once he was checked in and inside the room, Lay stretched out on the bed and contemplated what he was going to do about Josie. He wondered if all that happened was karma coming back to bite him in the ass for all the pain he had dished out to Celina.

Trying to put it out of his mind, he made arrangements for his man, Kev to pick Sammi up and meet him at the hotel at four a.m. sharp. It was a five-hour ride to Virginia and Lay wanted to be there by the time the banks opened.

Kev and Sammi were right on time, and the three of them hit the road. On the way down I-95, Lay had plenty of time to think about his plight with Josie. He loved her very much, but didn't know if he would be able to move past this betrayal. The situation weighed so heavily on his mind, Lay hadn't noticed the "Welcome To Virginia" sign just ahead.

They had arrived.

'Okay, Lay. Time to shake this shit off,' he thought. He pulled out the directions and guided Kev to the first bank. Sammi was asleep in the back seat so he woke her up so she could get herself together. She fixed her hair and slipped on some flats. She was instructed to wear corporate attire with comfortable shoes just in case things got 'funky.'

Lay reached into the envelope and handed her a check in the amount of $1,500. Sammi got out and walked toward the door of United Bank. Lay and Kev watched as her huge ass bounced almost as if it was moving to a beat. They looked at one another and said, "Damn!" almost at the same time. A few minutes later Sammi returned to the truck holding a white envelope filled with money and handed it to Lay.

He took the money out, counted it and asked if she had any problems. She said they asked about her I.D., since it was from New York, but that was it. Thinking on her feet, Sammi told the teller she had just moved there and hadn't had the chance to switch her credentials over yet. It was a good thing the teller didn't ask where she lived, because that would've stumped her.

From that first encounter they knew what to expect when they reached the next spot. Lay stayed calm but he was excited about what had just transpired. 'I just made $1,500 in a matter of minutes. This beats the block by a long shot!' They had the same success at the next spot, and the day continued until Sammi said she was tired and wanted to quit.

When Lay checked the envelope there was only one check left. "You did good, baby," Lay said as he began to count the day's take. Altogether the total was $13,500. Sammi made $2,700-, $300 for each check. Kev got $100 a check which added up to $900. Bobby's cut was $1,350-, for $150 a check, and the rest was Lay's to keep.

He told Kev to point the truck north and burn the highway up, as he turned on the radio. Coincidentally, "Get This Money" from "The Best of Both World's" by R. Kelly and Jay-Z was playing. It was a good trip; and an equally good day. Lay could now relax on the ride home. He adjusted his seat all the way back to where he was almost in Sammi's lap.

She reached over and rubbed Lay's chest and massaged his temples. He had no idea where this attention was coming from, but he didn't resist, either. Thoughts of Josie and the bullshit back home ran through his mind as he drifted off to sleep.

When he awakened, they were just reaching the New Jersey Turnpike. 'Only an hour and a half to go,' Lay thought. He also noticed he had a few missed calls from Josie, in which he didn't bother to return.

Arriving at the hotel, Lay checked to see if the Altima was ok, which it should've been, since he booked the room for two days.

Lay counted Kev's money and gave it to him with a handshake. He then counted Sammi's and passed it back to her in one of the bank envelopes. Lay told Kev to get his lucky lady home safe.

"I don't want nothin' happenin' to her. She's gonna make me rich."

Sammi asked, "Is it okay if I stay with you tonight, Lay?"

He was shocked, but kept his composure. "Of course, if you like."

The two of them got out and went up to Lay's room, where they each showered, ordered room service, and chilled. Sammi thanked Lay for the opportunity to make some money with him because she had never made that much change in one day.

There's something about the paper game that sometimes makes a chick fall for the dude that's putting money in their pockets. It's almost like the pimp game, with the exception that the ladies get to keep their own money. After chatting for a while, Lay's eyes got heavy, and he was getting drowsy. He wanted sleep, but Sammi had other plans.

She got up to turn the bathroom light off and slipped her bra and thongs off before getting back in bed. She reached under the covers and rubbed on Lay's dick until it became semi-erect. Then she stuck her head under and began to suck it until it was rock hard. At this point Lay was trying to play like he was asleep, but he was quite awake.

The oral session went on for a few until Sammi was ready to ride. She straddled Lay and rode his dick until she came all over it. Lay told her to turn around so he could see her ass while she rode him. She obliged, and it was a beautiful sight, indeed. He told her when he was about to cum so Sammie jumped off and caught it all in her mouth. She then went to spit Lay's babies in the toilet, gargled with the hotel mouthwash and returned to bed. Sammi lay her head on Lay's chest and they both drifted off to sleep.

In the morning Sammi ordered breakfast and went another round with Lay before checking out. He felt a little fucked up about sleeping with her and also giving her a ride in Josie's car, but she had no other way of getting home so that guilt subsided quickly. Lay dropped Sammi off and told her to keep her schedule clear because they would be going to work again, soon.

She said she had planned to recruit some of her girls before Lay even asked her to.

'This is going to be a beautiful situation,' he thought. He hit Bobby and let him know he was ready to meet up. They agreed on Aahirah's Palace on 116th Street, since Bobby hadn't eaten. There, Lay explained the day he had with Sammie, as well as the night. He passed Bobby his cut under the table as Sean walked in the dining area with two ladies at his sides.

Sean dropped Bobby's cut on the table in front of onlookers, and said, "I ain't never goin' back to that block again! They can have that shit!"

Apparently, Sean had twice the success Lay had on his first day out. Two girls, twenty checks equaled a lot of motherfucking bread, and he was happy as shit! Sean reached into Bobby's plate, snatched a piece of turkey bacon and ate it.

Bobby looked at Lay, then back at Sean and told him to sit his crazy ass down and stop making a spectacle out of everything. He sat down like Bobby requested, but left the two ladies standing. Bobby looked at Sean again. Catching on, he told them to grab a table and he would be with them in a minute. The three men chopped it up as Malcolm arrived a few minutes later.

He topped Lay and Sean's total with twenty-five checks cashed. This proved to be a very lucrative day for Bobby and his team. He made $150 for every check cashed that day. Lay had done nine, Sean did twenty, and twenty-five for Malcolm. That's added up to fifty-four checks at $150 a pop, totaling out at $8,100 just for printing.

That didn't include what he and Stacey may have done as well. About forty minutes pass as the four men trade stories of the previous day's events until Sean stood up, dropped two C-Notes on the table and said, "This one's on me, gentlemen. I'm out." He reached into his pocket, peeled off another one and paid the bill at his ladies' table.

They had finished eating a while ago but he made them wait anyway. The remaining three parted ways as Lay mentally prepared himself for his home situation. Walking through the door, he was surprised to see Josie was home. It was the middle of the afternoon so she must've called out from work. Lay was really only there to grab more clothes and pay the bills for the next month.

He didn't want to face her again, at least not this soon. Lay sat down on the couch next to Josie who was wearing one of his wife-beaters and some boy-shorts. Her voluptuous thighs were looking extra good to Lay. He loved that look on her, and she knew it. Although his heart and his groin wanted to make love to her, his brain knew it wasn't the best thing to do at that moment. Lay went on to explain how he felt that a break was necessary.

It didn't mean forever, just not right now. She didn't like it, but Josie conceded. He said he would continue to pay the bills and give the Altima back. "It's your car and I don't want to keep it. I'll get something soon."

"It's fine, Lavian. You can use it as long as you need to."

After the discussion, Lay gathered some more gear and left the bill money and car keys on Josie's nightstand.

Little did he or she know, it would be the last time he stepped foot in that bedroom. Lay took a cab down to 79th Steet and Broadway to pick up a rental car. He then called Sammi and asked if she wanted to spend the weekend with him. She said yes, so he picked her up and they drove to Atlantic City and booked a room at Caesar's Palace.

The two spent the entire weekend enjoying one another, and making plans for next week's work schedule. Sammi had two of her girlfriends that were ready to go, so she gave Lay their info to pass on to Bobby. Lay couldn't wait. Because they were cashing payroll checks, the team really only worked on Wednesday, Thursday, and Friday, when people usually got paid.

Sometimes, one might try a Saturday, but that was rare. On Tuesday night, Lay met up with Bobby to pick up the paperwork for the next day. He called Kev so he could scoop the girls up and meet him at four a.m., same as before. Everything was in place, so Lay and his crew headed down to

Virginia like clockwork. This time Lay and his crew cashed eighteen checks, clearing $19,170 for himself, after paying everyone.

Friday, he and his crew went back and had repeat success. That's damn near $40,000 in two days. Lay was feeling great about this newfound hustle. Things definitely fell into place financially while his home life was in shambles. The hotels were becoming expensive, so he decided to get a place not far from the city.

Bobby, Niecy, and Little Bobby had recently moved to the Avalon, in Edgewater, so he hooked Lay up with the agency that got him his new place. Lay called them and scheduled an appointment to meet with an agent at the Atrium, in Ft. Lee. It's a hotel style building designed in the shape of the letter "A."

Lay wore a crisp white button-up with navy slacks. On his feet was a pair of navy Mauri gators with a matching belt. Arriving early, Lay informed the concierge that he was waiting for a realtor from The Harris Agency. He was directed to have a seat in the lobby until the agent arrived. Not even five minutes after he sat down an agent approached the concierge desk.

When Lay heard the agent ask for him by name, he sat forward on the comfortable chair. He heard the clicking of heels coming toward him on the polished marble floors. When she turned the corner, Lay looked down at the black Gucci pumps that were making such an enchanting sound. (He loved a woman in heels).

His eyes moved up to the perfectly shaped smoothly shaven legs to the tight-fitting black skirt, hugging the most curvaceous hips. That walk. It was all too familiar. It was almost like she moved in slow motion. As his eyes rose, he skimmed over the neatly tucked-in royal blue, black and white blouse and locked eyes with none other than Celina, his long-lost love.

She looked absolutely stunning in her work attire. Classy, but oh, so sexy at the same time. Lay stood up and greeted her with a tight embrace. Celina smelled delectable, as the Issey Miyake fragrance she wore gently caressed his nostrils.

In the back of Celina's mind she thought the exact same thing about him.

"Celina Barnett. How have you been, Ms. Lady?"

"I've been okay. And yourself?"

"I've been holding on," Lay replied.

"I should've known you were the Lavian Taylor I was meeting today."

"You should've. How many niggas do you know named Lavian?"

"No, I didn't. And you're the only one."

"Are you saying if you knew it was me you would've cancelled?"

"Oh no! Never that! I don't turn down commission for no one. A sister needs *all* her coins."

"I hear that."

"You look well, Mr. Taylor."

"Thank you. And you look way more than well. You look fantastic."

"Why thank you, sir."

Lay wished Celina would stop being so formal, but he respected the fact that she was working.

"I see you listed a one bedroom as your first choice. Is there something you care to share?"

Lay let a little smile form as he replied, "Correct. Josie and I are separated."

"Oh, I hadn't heard you were ever married."

"We're not. Never was," Lay clarified. Clearing his throat, he continued, "We're not together at all anymore."

"Is that right?"

"Yes. That's absolutely right."

"Well, I'd be lying if I said I was sorry to hear that."

Lay looked down at his shoes and felt a little ashamed. He deserved that last remark. After an awkward pause, he switched the focus off of him and asked, "So, what about you? I don't see a ring on your finger."

"Nope, I'm as single as a dollar bill, Mr. Taylor. And I intend to stay that way."

"That's a shame, because I had every intention of changing your marital status if I ever saw you again."

Shaking her head and smirking cynically, Celina looked away and beamed inside. Secretly, she was enjoying the flirtatious banter between them.

Lay stood extremely close to Celina, even though they were alone in the elevator. She couldn't help but feel the irresistible attraction she still had for him. Celina had dated a few guys after Lay, but none ever measured up because although he was a jerk for cheating, he had set the bar very high.

Celina was angry with herself for still being in love with Lay. She had no idea when or if she would ever see him again, and those were the feelings she wanted to avoid until he was totally out of her system. They came rushing back, nonetheless. He'd done a number on her when he allowed her to leave. The fact that Lay didn't fight for their relationship made her feel like he chose Josie over her.

When they reached the fifth floor, Celina stepped off first and led Lay to a two-bedroom apartment with updated appliances and wall-to-wall carpet. As soon as they entered Lay said, "I'll take it."

"But I haven't shown you anything yet."

"It doesn't matter. I respect your opinion. You wouldn't have shown me this unit if you didn't think I would like it. A sister needs her coins, right?"

"I sure do."

"So, I know you're not wasting my time or yours. Draw up the paperwork and I'll sign."

"You don't even know how much it is."

"Once again, it doesn't matter."

Celina was trying to remain professional but in the back of her mind she thought, 'This negro is doing too much.'

Celina said, "Okay, I'll have my broker get in touch with you once everything is finalized."

"*Why don't you get-in-touch with me?*" Lay enunciated as he seductively stepped so closely behind Celina that she felt every syllable on the back of her hair as he spoke.

"Because, that's not how it works."

"Let me take you to dinner."

Before Celina could respond, Lay asked, "What's your commission? I'll double it if you call me personally. Triple it if you let me take you out."

Celina paused for a minute and responded, "You have a deal, Mr. Taylor. This unit is $2,700 a month, so that will be $5,400 for a month's rent and security, plus $8,100 for my li'l old Gucci," as she pat her bag three times.

"No problem," Lay said as she locked the apartment door and they walked to the elevator.

"So when can I pick you up?"

"You can't. But we can meet Friday, at seven o' clock."

"Meet, where?"

"Here. We'll meet here."

"Bet. It's a date."

"No, it's not. It's just dinner," Celina clarified.

"Okay, Ms. Barnett, it's just dinner," Lay said as he walked her to her Honda Civic.

"Can I let you in on a little secret?" Celina asked.

Lay opened her car door to let her get in. "What's that?"

"You had me with the invitation. Oh, and changing my marital status didn't hurt either. You never talked about marriage when we were together. I think I like this new Lavian."

All he could do was smile while thinking about all the money he could've saved if he was just a little more patient. She was worth every cent. He shut her car door and Celina backed out of the spot to pull off. They both were on cloud nine in anticipation of Friday's dinner. Celina thought Lay and Sean must be up to their old habits to be able to throw cash around like that.

Bobby and his team had continued success over the next couple of weeks as the commas in their safes grew and grew. For the first time in his life Lay touched over $100,000 at one time and it was a great feeling. The whole team was winning. Lay and his faction brought their missions up north after having a couple of unsuccessful trips to the nation's capital region. Malcolm and Sean didn't miss a beat, however. Money was coming in by the pile.

Tired of the city life, Sean copped a one-bedroom condo on Park Street in Hackensack, and furnished it. He also snatched a 2001 Mercedes CLK 430 that was plum-like in color. Sean was showing his ass, as usual. Malcolm kept his Denali but also grabbed a champagne Cadillac STS. For some reason, he had a thing for American cars.

Not to be out done, Lay picked up a black BMW 530 and threw some chrome and black Asanti's on it. Bobby topped them all, picking up a 2001 white Mercedes Benz S430 and threw some Brabus rims on it. That motherfucker was so pretty! There was something about white cars that Lay loved so when he saw Bobby's Benz, he vowed his next car would be white. It was a very prosperous time for the team, and the best was yet to come.

Tony Brown

Around this time, Tony had just returned to Harlem from doing a two-year state bid and bumped into Bobby at Jimbo's on 145th and Lenox. They had been friends going back to Skate Key days, and when Tony saw how Bobby was shining, he didn't care what was going on, he wanted in. After eating breakfast, Bobby took Tony out on a mission to show him exactly what it was he did for a living.

They spent the entire day together. Tony saw Bobby receive envelope after envelope from Stacey filled with $100 bills until it reached well over $10,000. Tony didn't need any convincing after that.

He was already sold when he first put his ass on the plush leather seats of Bobby's new Benz. Tony was ready to go.

Bobby told him to get some girls together and he would set him up. The only problem was, Tony was fresh home and didn't have a whip yet. Even though it was against his better judgement, Bobby told Tony he could go into the banks like the girls until he built his bread up to buy a car, and he agreed. Tony was fine starting off like that because it meant he got a bigger percentage that didn't have to be shared with anyone.

That night, Bobby printed ten checks in the amounts of $1,500 for Tony. The next day, every one popped. The split was 50/50, so Tony made a cool $7,500 in a couple of hours; that was a decent piece of change for someone just coming home. With his earnings, Tony bought a used blue Ford minivan to use for his new hustle. He was definitely about his business. Tony didn't even have his license yet, but he was raring to go.

A couple of more outings with Bobby, and Tony found himself sitting on about $25,000. His license was in place, so he snatched up three chicks and put them to work.

By this time there were five teams going out on a weekly basis at least three days a week. The bank most frequently used was HSBC, due to the amount of branches located in and around the city. In fact, there were locations worldwide, so the sky was the limit, as long as they continued to be fruitful. The city was becoming saturated, so the team decided to venture outward. Tony was just getting his feet wet so he stayed close to home. On his first outing with his own crew, he did seventeen checks.

After paying everyone, he cleared $17,850 for himself. Not bad for a day's work. And that was the case for the rest of the team as well. Using the walkie-talkie function on their Nextel phones, the team would communicate their progress to Bobby throughout the day. "Popping bottles" was the code used to indicate how many checks were cashed.

Malcolm hit: "I popped twenty-six bottles already!"

Sean: "I'm sitting on dubs, Bobby! I'm saucy like a muhfucka'!"

Lay: "I'm at fifteen so far!"

They would always fuck with him because he never popped more than twenty-five bottles in one outing. He still made his bread, but they were always more successful. It didn't matter to Lay, because he was eating, *well*.

A few more weeks went by, and Tony had done really well for himself. He concentrated on his finances so much, he hadn't made any time for a social life.

'Shit, I only slept with one chick since I've been home,' Tony thought.

One day, he and Lay were standing outside of the Famous Fish & Chips spot on 145th Street and St. Nicholas Avenue when some chocolate brown thickness got out of a Land Rover LR3 and walked inside.

Tony said, "Damn, she thick as hell! I think I know her from somewhere, too."

"Say something to her when she comes out," Lay urged.

When she emerged, Tony approached and a conversation ensued. He had found out that he did know her. She was sisters of one of his homie's girl. They exchanged numbers and it was on from there. Her name was Yvette. She stood about 5'5" with dark brown skin and was built like a brick house.

The two of them started a whirlwind romance that included trips with her family and sometimes just as a couple. She was very close with her family and they had dinner at her mother's almost every Sunday. Tony fell in love quickly, and so did Yvette. He deserved love after doing this last bid, and the whole team was happy he found it.

One Saturday after having a sensational week, Tony told Bobby he was ready to put a ring on Yvette's finger. Bobby laughed at first, but quickly changed his tune when he saw that Tony was serious. Bobby shook his hand and hugged him simultaneously.

"Can you take me to see Burt?" Tony asked.

"Shit, let's go get some 'ice', my nigga!" Bobby exclaimed. "In fact, let's *all* go get 'icy.'"

He called everyone on the team and told them to meet him and Tony at The Jewelry Center on Route Four in Paramus, N.J.

"And bring some change with you," Bobby said.

Malcolm brought $60,000. Lay brought $50,000, even though he had no intention of spending that much. Sean, being on 1,000 at all times, brought $75,000. Who knows what he planned to do?

Burt looked happy as hell to see all those vehicles arriving at almost the same time. But when he saw Bobby walk through the door, he knew it was going to be a good day. This time, he brought some friends along, so actually it was going to be great!

When the whole team was inside, Bobby said, "Tony has an announcement to make." Pointing both index fingers in Tony's direction, he said, "Go ahead."

When he had everyone's attention, Tony said, "I'm getting married."

They all burst out laughing at first, just like Bobby, but then realized Tony wasn't kidding.

Bobby waited until they collected themselves and said, "Our brother is tying the knot. It's a celebration!"

He sent Lay to the trunk of his car to get two bottles of Cris and some cups. Burt put the bottles in his fridge while the team got ready to spend some change. Tony went first because he was the reason they were there in the first place.

He selected a two-carat round diamond in a white gold setting for Yvette that set him back $25,000. For himself he grabbed a white gold Presidential Rolex with a blue dial and diamonds in the bezel, and an iced out cross on a Cuban link chain. Those two items were $27,500, bringing his total to $52,500 that day.

Malcolm dropped $4,500 on a pinky ring and white gold Presi with ice in the bezel, totaling $24,500. Sean did the same, minus the ring. Lay was simple with it, buying a plain white gold Rolie with a black dial. But he also grabbed a pair of studs in a platinum setting for Celina-; three quarter carat each for $6,700. Bobby told Burt he wanted to do something special, so he ordered five platinum dog tags and had "Love & Loyalty" engraved on each one for himself and his team.

After Burt counted all the bread and put it away, he brought the bottles out and they toasted for Tony's engagement. He now had a wedding to plan, and the team had a bachelor party to throw.

Things had been going well since Lay and Celina reconnected. They had gone on several dates since then, and things started to heat up between the two. It was good that the passion they once shared still remained strong after all that time. That night, while having dinner, Lay shared the news about Tony and Yvette's engagement.

Celina was happy for them. 'They just met, and she got a ring already? It must be nice.'

The words weren't spoken but they might as well have been, because they showed on Celina's face. Lay sensed it too, so he decided against giving her the studs that night. That could wait.

After their meal, Lay dropped her off at her apartment in the Bronx. When he walked Celina to her door, she barely gave him a half of a kiss as she said goodnight and went inside, leaving Lay on her doorstep confused and equally frustrated.

On the drive home, he tried to figure out what was wrong with her.

'She was the one who said she was going to stay single,' he thought.

Lay didn't understand, but that's women for you. When he got home, he placed the studs in his safe, showered, and went to bed. Tomorrow was a new day. Maybe she would feel better then.

The Bachelor Party

Lay and Bobby's favorite TV shows were *'MTV Cribs'*, and BET'S *'How I'm Livin'*. Both programs gave the viewer an inside look at the houses, cars, jewelry, and all-around lifestyles of celebrities, athletes, rappers, rock stars, and the like. The two of them would talk for hours about previous and upcoming episodes, as well.

With all the success magazines like, *'F.E.D.S.'*, *'Don Diva'*, and *'F.E.L.O.N.'*, were having, Bobby came up with the brilliant idea to create a magazine that catered to the *'MTV Cribs'* audience.

He said, "We'll call it, *'Celebrity Lifestyles Magazine'*."

Lay was definitely on board with the idea. The first order of business was to form an LLC.

Bobby and Niecy came up with the name, 'UN-STOP-ABLE ENTERTAINMENT'. The next thing was to compile a list of celebrities who had already guest-starred on these programs that were willing to open their lives and homes to the public. Next, they needed to figure out a way to get in contact with such celebs.

It just so happens, a friend of Malcolm's was cool with Luther "Luke" Campbell, so he made arrangements for Bobby and Lay to fly down to Miami for an interview and photo shoot. Lay thought it would be a good opportunity to make a guy's trip out of it and celebrate Tony's bachelor party with the "King of Nasty", himself.

Bobby hired a photographer, booked flights and rooms for all seven of them, and they made their way to Miami. Recalling how much fun he had on his Memorial Day trip, Bobby of course wanted to stay at The Loews again. This time he booked a suite for himself, and an adjoining one for Lay. That evening, the seven men went to Club Rolexx where the introduction to Luke was made. The crew met him out front and made small talk before going inside, where he had the VIP section reserved and waiting for them.

They entered the VIP with Luke wearing iced-out Rolie's and 'bling' everywhere else. They were sporting every urban designer under the sun, from Rocawear, to Sean John. The dancers knew money had entered the building. Luke whispered into a bouncer's ear, after which he signaled about twenty dancers who lined up at the entrance to the VIP.

Lay looked at Bobby, and without words they exchanged a glance that said what they were both thinking, 'Some disgusting shit is about to go down in here tonight.'

When Sean and Malcolm saw all the dancers lined up, they took their shirts off. The dancers entered to find them standing in the middle of the room in their wife-beaters, boxers, and Icey-Whites, each with about $1,000 worth of singles in their hands.

The photographer looked on in amazement when the baddest women he had ever seen entered the VIP butt-ass naked. This was nothing like the strip clubs in New York, where the dancers were semi-nude. These chicks showed everything, pussy and all! Bobby told Luke that Tony was getting married, and this was part of his bachelor party.

Luke grabbed one of the dancers and whispered in her ear. She got the attention of three other girls and they led him to a private room where God only knows what went on. After a few lap dances, and money being thrown everywhere, Sean and Malcolm were almost as naked as the girls. This was a typical night for Luke, so he wasn't fazed by any of it. He just sat back, smoked a cigar and watched the festivities take place.

Bobby and Lay set up a meeting to visit Luke's home the next day to do the photo shoot. The day after that would be an interview at his office. After finalizing the arrangements, Luke told the bouncer to take care of the team and called it a night. Just then, a short brown-skinned cutie named Destiny with a short hair cut and a bubble butt sat on Lay's lap and gave him a dance.

He didn't have any singles so he gave her a $100 bill. After that, she stuck to Lay like glue for the rest of the night. When he got up to pee, she waited outside the bathroom door for him to come out. The dance already made him horny so he asked, "How much for you to leave with me?"

She said, "I have to give the club $400 to tip-out."

"And, how much for you?"

"We'll discuss that later," she replied.

Lay reached in his pocket, peeled off $400 and slipped it in her hand. She wasn't wearing any clothes, so she left the VIP room to get dressed. Bobby and the rest of the team followed suit and almost everyone there ended up at the Loews in the suites for the night. Bobby ordered some Cris up to the room and it was a party all over again.

Lay and Destiny went to his suite, and the session began. She danced a little for him before they got down to business. Afterward, she said, "I knew y'all had money the minute y'all walked in the club."

"Why? Because we were with Luke?"

"No, because y'all niggas just look like money!" she exclaimed.

Destiny's comment definitely stroked Lay's ego.

Secretly, he liked shit like that, even though he wasn't as flashy as the others, which he saw as a hood mentality that he hoped would fade one day with age and maturity.

In the next suite, the team had big fun and the ladies were paid well, that night. Tony's bachelor weekend was kicked off with a bang in a major way.

The next day, however was strictly business. Bobby, Lay and the photographer drove to Luke's house to do the photo shoot for C.L. Magazine. His home was beautiful, with five bedrooms, four and a half bathrooms, swimming pool, studio, and a golf course in back. The shoot took most of the day, and both Lay and Bobby were satisfied with the outcome.

That evening, the plan was to take Tony out for dinner to celebrate his last few weeks as a single man. But first, they headed to the mall at Bal Harbour to get fresh. They bought gators, linen, and Versace, it seemed like by the pound. Everyone had their slacks tailored on the spot, and was readied for the night's festivities.

Bobby and Malcolm were the only ones who had been to Miami before, so they selected the restaurant. That night the team dined at a posh eatery where celebrities and Miami's elite gathered to get their grub on. Bobby sat at the head of the table, and Tony was at the other since the dinner was in his honor.

Once again, their style of dress and the manner in which they conducted themselves caught the attention of others in their midst. One in particular, was a thirty-something-year-old Hispanic man who dined with his wife and two young daughters. Two bodyguards stood at each end of the arch shaped booth. As he ate with his family he observed the gentlemen who sat not far from his table.

Well into the meal, Bobby sent for bottles of Cris, and when they were uncorked and poured, he proposed a toast in Tony's honor.

Lay, not much of a drinker, raised his glass, took a couple of sips, then excused him self from the table. When the Hispanic gentleman saw Lay walk toward the restroom, he excused himself and did the same. He had been waiting for this opportunity all evening. Upon entering, Lay nodded to the bathroom attendant and proceeded to the latrines.

A few seconds later the Hispanic man came in and whispered into the valet's ear.

"Yes sir, Mr. Lopez," he said, and quickly exited.

Mr. Lopez locked the door and waited for Lay to finish and wash his hands. When he was done, Lay turned around expecting to see the attendant, but instead saw Mr. Lopez with his hands folded in front of him. Behind him was one of the bodyguards from the table.

"You don't work here," Lay said.

"No, I don't. I gave him a break."

"Well, are you gonna give me a hand towel, or do I have to air dry?"

"But, of course. Here you are," a smiling Mr. Lopez said while passing him a hand towel.

"Allow me to introduce myself. My name is Alfredo Lopez."

"How you doin'? Nice to meet you, Mr. Lopez," Lay said as he extended his hand to be shaken.

"And you are?"

"Confused, more than anything, but I'm Lay... umm, Lavian Taylor."

"No need to be confused Mr. Taylor. It's nice to meet you as well. I noticed your friends are having a celebration."

"Yeah, he's getting married."

"Nice. Family is important. And you?"

"Me? No, not yet. Maybe, one day."

"You're probably wondering why I followed you into the baño."

"That's an understatement."

"I noticed you and your friends when you entered. I admire the way that you are dressed and the manner in which you carry yourselves. Like gentlemen. I like that. Me gusta."

"Thank you Mr. Lopez. We try."

"Call me Fredo."

"Okay, Fredo."

"You're not like most black guys."

The statement left Lay confused and slightly offended. "What's that supposed to mean?"

"Forgive me, but I meant no disrespect. You're different from most guys our age. You don't wear big clothes. You're not loud. You don't wear your pants sagging off your behind. Like I said, you carry yourselves like gentlemen."

Having a little more clarity, Lay thanked Fredo again.

He still wished a point would be made. This was beyond weird.

"I have a very lucrative business opportunity for you and your associates-..."

"My brothers," Lay corrected Fredo while cutting him off mid-sentence.

"Even better. Let me ask, do you know anything about cocaine?"

Lay was taken aback for a second. He paused for a moment, and answered hesitantly, "I do."

"Good. Well, I am in the cocaine business. In fact, *I am* the cocaine business. Name a place in this country and my cocaine is there. I guarantee that. I'm always looking to expand my business, and you gentlemen are the pedigree I need in my organization."

"I appreciate the offer Mr. Lopez. I mean, Fredo. But we don't indulge in that life anymore."

"What is your line of business, might I ask?"

Reluctantly, Lay answered, "Banks."

"Oh, white collar. That's interesting. How's that working for you?"

"Very well, as you can see," Lay replied as he took a step back and raised his hands to the side so Fredo could get a better look at his outfit.

Alfredo smiled and pulled a business card out of his pocket and handed it to Lay.

"This says you're in real estate."

"Well, it certainly can't say that I sell cocaine, can it?"

"You're right about that."

"If you change your mind, give me a call. If not, the next time you're in town, call anyway. I'll bring you to my home to meet my family."

"How do you know I'm not from here?"

"I know everything that goes on in my city. Enjoy the rest of your evening, Lavian. Oh, and tell your brother I said congratulations."

The bodyguard unlocked the door. Alfredo Lopez walked out of the restroom with his bodyguard in tow. Lay threw some water on his face then dried it with a small white towel, needing to collect himself before returning to the table. When he returned and sat down, Bobby asked him if he enjoyed his cigarette.

"Whatever. You got jokes, Foolio."

"You see that dude with his family sitting at the next table?"

Bobby said, "Yeah, why? What's up?"

Lay said, "Raise your glass to him."

Bobby and Lay raised their glasses simultaneously, and Fredo and his wife returned the salud.

"You wanna tell me who the hell that is?"

"Well, he might as well be Pablo and his wife, Griselda Blanco. That's what took me so long. That motherfucka had me trapped in the bathroom!"

"What you mean, trapped?"

"He offered to put us back in the coke business. Heavy too, bro. I mean, like we've never imagined."

"I wonder why us?" Bobby asked.

"He said he liked our style, and how we moved."

"What did you say?"

"I told him we don't fuck around with that anymore. But he gave me his info just in case. The motherfucka even invited us to his crib the next time we came to Miami."

"Oh okay," Bobby said nonchalantly.

"Okay?!? Nigga, you didn't think that shit was weird?"

Bobby chuckled at Lay's naivetee.

"What the hell is so funny?! I'm trying to find the humor in this whole shit and you keep laughing." He stared at Bobby in disbelief.

"Nigga, that might be the feds fuckin' with us and you giggling like you're at a Bernie Mack show!"

Every statement made Bobby laugh harder. The more he cackled, the more irritated Lay became.

Bobby finally collected himself and said, "Get used to it, my brother. When you touch the amount of paper we're touching, shit like that will happen more often than you think." "Your paranoia is getting the best of you, bro. Feds don't bring their wife and kids to an investigation. Lighten up, champ."

Bobby held his table napkin over his mouth and laughed at Lay once more.

Lay cut his eyes at Bobby and sat back in his chair for a minute to take all of what was happening in. 'This motherfucka' thinks everything is a joke,' he thought. It really began to sink into his brain that they were on another level when it came to making paper.

The team enjoyed the rest of Tony's bachelor dinner and the rest of the evening. The next day Bobby and Lay did the interview at Luke's office, and they all prepared to take the trip back home.

The Wedding

In August, Yvette and Tony held a bridal dinner at Carmine's on Broadway where the entire party met so everyone could get acquainted. There they dined on some of the finest Italian cuisine the city had to offer. After the meal Yvettte and Tony stood at the head of the table and thanked their friends and family for attending, then, Yvette took over. She pulled a piece of paper from her Gucci bag and read from a long list she'd written.

She announced all rehearsal locations and schedules, firmly stressing punctuality. The groomsmen were instructed where to get fitted for their tuxedos, and the bridesmaids for their dresses. The ladies would wear royal blue gowns and the groomsmen would wear all white tuxes with royal blue accessories to match.

When Lay heard white was the color, he got a sick feeling deep in his gut. 'I hope she doesn't make us wear those ugly ass white patent leather shoes that come with the tux,' he thought. He despised white shoes! He hated to be the one rocking the boat, but he reluctantly raised his hand to interrupt Yvette while she was spewing off more instructions.

"Yes, Lavian. May I help you?"

"Uhh, I'm not trying to be difficult, but do we absolutely *have* to wear white shoes?"

Almost everyone found humor in the question except for Yvette, of course. She put one hand on her hip and asked, "And what's so wrong with white shoes, Lavian?"

"They're ugly as fuck! That's whats wrong with them. The only time a grown man should wear white shoes is if he's dancing on stage with his four brothers."

Yvette took her hand off of her hip, threw the list in air, looked directly at Tony and said, "Get your friend. Get him before I kill him."

Now, everyone was definitely laughing at Lay, mostly because they couldn't believe he was the one who spoke up in protest about the shoes. He was always the quiet one. Deep down inside all the men agreed, including Tony, but he wasn't trying to turn Yvette into more of a Bridezilla than she already had become.

"He does have a point, babe," Tony said while rubbing both of Yvette's arms, trying to soothe her nerves.

Yvette turned back to the table and asked, "I'm probably going to regret this, but what do you suggest, Lay?"

"Why can't we wear Icey-Whites?"

"What the hell are those?!?"

Tony leaned in to whisper in Yvette's ear.

"Oh, okay! Shit, if that's what y'all want to do, be my guest. Just make sure they're all white!"

At that moment, all the men stood up and gave a round of applause for Lay speaking up, and for Yvette being so understanding.

The weeks flew by and it was the wedding day before they knew it. The night before, most of the groomsmen stayed at a hotel near the venue. Lay opted to stay in the Bronx with Celina that night so they could leave together the next morning. He woke up early, showered and waited for Celina to get herself together.

He thought she was beautiful everyday, without even trying, but there was something about the process Celina went through whenever she prepared for an event, that Lay loved. He would sit and stare as she moved about the bedroom taking her time to dedicate attention to every little detail. The way she lotioned every curve of her body, the way she slid her undergarments on, and how she sprayed the perfume in just the right places nearly drove Lay wild.

Celina carefully slid into a periwinkle dress with floral print, lifted the back of her hair and motioned for Lay to zip her up in the back. This was the part he loved the most, and she knew it. Lay stood up from the bed, moved closely behind Celina, zipped up the dress and nestled his nose in her neck. He took one long sniff and closed his eyes with an expression of extreme pleasure on his face. The gesture made Celina close her eyes and gently lean back into him.

"You're always smelling me," she said.

"It's so good," Lay responded.

Lay spun her around and kissed Celina ever so passionately on the lips.

"Mmm, I had to get that in before you put on your gloss."

"You're so fresh."

Celina pushed him away, turned back to the mirror, adjusted her dress and began to apply some light makeup. She noticed Lay staring at her in the mirror. She smiled inside and thought, 'this man really loves me.'

When Celina was finally dressed, she and Lay made the drive to Antun's of Westchester where the ceremony was to be held. He walked inside with Celina, made sure she was situated, and then left to join the rest of the groomsmen. Most of the guys were already there so they sat around relaxing and telling jokes until it was time to get dressed. About an hour later they all got themselves together and gave Tony the business about his last couple of hours as free man.

He took it all in stride and laughed it off. Tony knew he was getting the better part of the deal. Yvette was a firecracker, but she was also the best thing that ever happened to him. Tony was marrying the woman of his dreams and he wouldn't have it any other way. A couple of hours passed and Yvette finally arrived in a white Rolls Royce Phantom, looking absolutely stunning.

She wore a form-fitting all white Vera Wang gown with Swarovski crystals and a cascading six-foot cathedral train. With everyone in place, Yvette was escorted down the aisle by her dad as the audience looked on in awe. Tony stood at the altar in great anticipation for his beautiful bride to be given away. The pastor asked everyone to be seated as he began his opening remarks.

When he stated the traditonal, "if there's anyone who feels this marriage should not take place, speak now or forever hold your peace," Yvette turned to the audience with a look on her face that clearly said, 'I wish one of you motherfuckers would!'

That look brought the entire audience to laughter. When it quieted, she turned back to the pastor and said, "You may continue," which made everyone chuckle again.

Yvette had to smile herself as she noticed even the pastor was laughing a little. The ceremony flowed smoothly without a hitch. Vows and rings were exchanged, and the couple was pronounced husband and wife. When the pastor instructed Tony to kiss his bride he lifted the veil from Yvette's face and rubbed his hands together as if they were standing outside in twenty-degree weather. He proceeded to drag each foot back one by one as if he was a bull about to charge at a matador, which brought delight to the crowd, once again.

Trying to keep a straight face herself, Yvette placed both hands on her hips and said, "Man, if you don't stop playing and kiss me."

Tony got the memo and gently placed his hands on both sides of Yvette's face to kiss his beautiful bride as the entire audience rose to their feet and cheered for the newlyweds. The flashes went off like paparazzi as Mr. and Mrs. Anthony Brown turned to face their guests. Tony and Yvette walked hand in hand down the aisle and out to the Phantom where they would meet up with the rest of the wedding party for photos.

After the photoshoot, the wedding party went back to Antun's where the family and guests were waiting. One by one, the emcee announced each couple's name as they walked in and faced one another. When it was time for the bride and groom to enter, each bridesmaid held their bouquet in the air and each groomsman held up a hand forming an arch for the newlyweds to walk beneath.

"And for the first time, I present to you, Mr. and Mrs. Brown!" announced the emcee.

When Tony and Yvette emerged on the other end of the human arch, the emcee announced the couple's first dance as husband and wife. The DJ played "For You," by Kenny Lattimore as Tony and Yvette began their dance. Suddenly, the crowd was on their feet clapping and cheering as Kenny Lattimore stepped from behind the curtain to begin his ballad.

Yvette had no idea what was going on until she noticed people were pointing in Kenny's direction. Tony spun her around and when she saw Kenny, Yvette screamed with delight and jumped up and down in Tony's arms so excitedly he almost lost his balance. Kenny Lattimore's performance was a surprise Tony and the team had put together for Yvette as a wedding gift.

When she finally regained her composure, they danced as Kenny serenaded them. Tears rolled down Yvette's cheeks as she thought about how happy her life was going to be with the man she loved so much.

The evening proceeded and the guests enjoyed it tremendously.

Three days later, Tony and Yvette left to honeymoon on the beautiful islands of Turks and Caicos where they enjoyed the sun, the beach, and each other for a week.

After the wedding and honeymoon, it was time for the team to get back to work. Up until this point Bobby had received all of his check copies from people he knew that worked in banks, and that had worked well for him. One day, while in the barber's chair at Danny and Mel's, Stew, a guy Bobby knew from the hood asked if he could have word with him after his cut.

Bobby obliged Stew and after the talk he discovered that he had struck gold. Somehow Stew got wind that Bobby was in the check game and wanted to offer his services. Apparently, he worked in a clearing house where banks from all over the region would send their checks to be processed and cleared for cashing. This information was music to Bobby's ears.

The two men exchanged numbers and Bobby assured him they would be in touch.

"Quick question, before you go. How did you know about my business?"

"Oh, Nick told me you played with the paper."

'That big mouth, big headed muhfucka,' Bobby thought. It was all good, but he still couldn't wait to see Nick about speaking his business.

With an inside man on the payroll, Bobby and his crew had access to any bank they wanted.

All they had to do was get the routing number and it was all she wrote. This put Bobby's team at an advantage over other crews. There definitely were others, but, Bobby and his crew were like the B.M.F. of the paper game. Bobby told Stew he would pay extra if he dealt with him exclusively, and he agreed. The team was already paid, but now it was about to excel to another level.

Bobby called the team and told them to meet him at the office at seven p.m. He shared with them news of the good fortune he'd stumbled upon, and they were excited, to say the least. Bobby instructed them to scour different areas and find new banks to hit. It was time to expand, and they were ready.

The following day, Celina asked Lay if he would mind driving upstate to visit her mother who recently purchased a home in the capital region of Albany, N.Y. This was perfect timing, since Lay could take that opportunity to look for banks in that area and report back to Bobby. On the two-hour drive up, Celina asked Lay what his plans were for the next five years.

"Hopefully I'll be married to you," he replied.

"Is that right? That sounds good. What else?"

Lay went on to explain the idea about 'Celebrity Lifestyles Magazine,' and Celina was thrilled for him.

"I'm glad you and your friends are trying to do something positive with your money for a change. Have you ever thought about purchasing real estate? Like, even as an investment property?"

"I never gave it much thought. It's only me, so I don't need a big ol' house."

Celina mushed the side of his head. "It's only you, huh? Don't play yourself, boy."

"I'm just kidding. You know it's me and you, Boo."

"Awww Lay, you haven't called me that in a long time. Remember my beeper code?"

"Of course I do."

"What was it?"

"Two-six-six. I'll never forget that, Boo."

"Lay, you're so sweet when you want to be. I love you so much."

"Love you too, Boo."

"Okay. Don't wear it out, now," Celina scolded.

They both laughed out loud.

When they reached her mom's exit, Lay turned his attention to spotting any new banks. He saw some HSBC's and quite a few Key Banks. That was all he needed to see. His homework was done.

He and Celina arrived at her mom's just in time for lunch, and they enjoyed the rest of their visit until it was time to return to the city. Lay couldn't wait to get to work. The rest of the team had similar success as well. Tony went to the South Jersey and, Philly areas and Sean ventured out to Connecticut.

Bobby and Malcolm stayed in the city, but found a couple of new spots to hit as well. Next week, it was on!

The following day, Bobby informed the clearing house connect of all the work he needed for Wednesday. On Monday evening, he met Stew and picked up the copies. He spent the entire Tuesday printing up the work all five crews needed to go out on Wednesday.

Everyone was responsible for their own MapQuest directions. After picking up their checks Lay, Sean, Tony, and Malcolm went to Kinko's to print them. The next day was the best they had thus far, each pulling in an average of $50-$55,000, totaling out to $250-$275,000. Stew's eyes damn near popped out of his head when Bobby met him to give him his portion of the day's take. It came to $2,200.

"All this is mine? In one day?"

"Yeah," Bobby said. "So you don't need to fuck with no other crew. We're the best, yet."

"Say no more," Stew said.

Bobby told him to have the same list ready for tomorrow so his team could go out on Friday.

Stew beamed. "Bet."

The two men shook hands and departed. Needless to say, Friday was just as good as Wednesday, if not a little better. The team was definitely on to something.

Malcolm wanted to do something nice for Tiecy's birthday, so he called Bobby that night to see what he was doing for Niecy. This birthday wasn't a milestone so the twins didn't care and left it up to the men to decide. Malcolm looked online and saw that R. Kelly was going to be at Radio City Music Hall. He hit the team to see if they wanted to go with their wives.

Of course, everyone said yes, so Malcolm charged ten third row center aisle seats. Lay knew how much Celina loved R. Kelly, so when he told her she was beyond excited. He asked her what she was going to wear, and she said she would just wear some nice jeans and heels, since it wasn't her birthday. 'Cool,' thought Lay.

A couple of days before the show, Lay picked Celina up from work and they shot down to Cellini Uomo on Orchard Street. He copped some black Mauri gator sneakers and matching booties for Celina. Next, they went to Alexandro's Furs on 28th Street and he bought her a black cropped mink jacket to match his black bomber.

Lay loved when she wore clothes that flattered her figure, especially that booty. After having three great days the previous week, Lay rode out to Burt and picked up the match to his Rolex that he had previously ordered for Celina, so she could wear it to the show. That evening Lay got dressed at her place, and presented her with the watch and earrings he had been dying to give her. All this brought Celina damn near to tears.

"Lavian, you are such an amazing man. You treat me so good. I can't imagine what I would do if I lost you again."

"Well, that ain't never gonna happen, so stop imagining it." She kissed and hugged Lay, and they got dressed for the show. Bobby and his team arrived at Radio City looking like a million dollars. When they walked down the aisle to the front of the theater, all eyes fixated on them.

R. Kelly gave a hell of a performance, as usual. Afterward, the team and their ladies headed to Benihana for a late dinner. During dinner, Bobby gave Niecy her gift. It was a classic Chanel bag. Malcolm gave Tiecy the same, but a different color. The team enjoyed themselves celebrating the twins' birthday and dining on fine Japanese cuisine.

With Christmas a couple of weeks away, the team went extra hard to close out the year. Bobby had planned to slow things down in the new year so they could concentrate on making the transition to legitimate income with the magazine and possibly the music business as well, since Tony was a pretty good rapper. But then, something else fell in his lap.

Stacey had schooled a white girl who worked on her job named Maureen to the game and got her on board with their crew. When Bobby got this news his first thought was, cha-ching! With a white girl, he knew the sky would be the limit. He could up the ante because of her lack of melanin.

And up the ante, he did. Usually checks were drafted in amounts of $2,500-$3,000. With Maureen, he could make checks out in between $7,000-

$10,000 denominations. It didn't get much sweeter than that! Bobby took full advantage of this newfound situation and exploited it.

The team worked until Christmas and enjoyed the holidays with family and friends. Gifts were exchanged, and it was a beautiful time for all. But, as always, nothing good lasts forever.

Stacey Mack

After the holidays, Bobby and his team continued their joint effort in the paper game, while keeping the magazine in focus. This project was something he wanted to make sure he didn't lose sight of, but in the meantime, they still had to eat. And eat, they did. The team took tens of thousands of dollars from several banks on a weekly basis as Bobby began the slowing down process.

Instead of going out three days a week, the team only went one or two days. He also organized a kitty everyone contributed to once a week for emergencies, such as lawyers, bail, etc. But the most important reason for the contribution was to cover expenses for the magazine. Each team member would share equal ownership and responsibility in the company.

The weekly gross would be divided five ways and then each teammate would contribute one-fifth of their share to the kitty. For instance, if $100,000 was the gross for that week, each one would take $20,000 for themselves, and put up $4,000 for the kitty. That's $20,000 set aside for the team and the magazine.

Of course the amounts varied from week to week, but that was the gist of the plan. In the meantime, Bobby scouted for celebrities to interview for the magazine. Stacey, who was with Bobby from the beginning, was the only female team member. She went out just like the other girls, but there was something about Stacey that set her apart.

Bobby recognized her leadership qualities and made her his 'bottom chick,' if you will. In the pimp game, this was the woman closest to the boss, and her duties were to keep the other ladies in line while securing his money in the process. He trusted her enough to let her take his crew out and bring back all of his money, down to the penny.

While Bobby focused on the magazine, Stacey completed his missions with Maureen for him. The two women would rack up tens of thousands of dollars on almost every trip. Stacey had her own checks to cash, and Bobby also gave her a percentage of every check Maureen cashed. So she was paid very well.

Whenever Maureen wasn't able to work, Stacey took other girls out to make sure Bobby had a steady flow of income. She was so efficient and trustworthy he eventually gave Stacey her own crew to run. That's when her commas went all the way up! With the money she made Stacey bought a charcoal grey Dodge Durango, had a booming system installed and threw some twenty-two inch chrome rims on it.

With Stacey running her own crew, Bobby could concentrate more on the magazine and other ventures, and didn't have to worry about slowing her money down in the process. Whenever he needed to make a few grand, he could grab Maureen and go on a quick mission.

Besides, he still got a cut from the whole team whenever they went out, so he was still financially secure. Stacey took full advantage of this new responsibility and proved herself to be as equally effective as the rest of the team. She stayed in and around the city mostly, hitting the local banks generating a considerable amount of income.

Once, Stacey topped all the guys with a $72,000 payday. She went out with four girls, and everything went in her favor. For some reason, the banks would not say no to any of her girls that day. In this game, in order for a day to be productive, everything must line up perfectly. When the girls are dressed properly, their ID's passed inspection, the work looked presentable-, (which was never an issue, because Bobby was a master printer)-, and the accounts had the money to cover the payroll, the day would almost always be profitable. Stacey had one of those days.

After paying her crew and meeting with Bobby to give him his cut, she wanted to celebrate her best day so far. She grabbed one of the girls, and went down to The Shark Bar to grab some dinner. After the hostess seated them in the last booth in the far corner of the establishment, Stacey summoned a sexy waitress to their table. She then ordered two apple martinis and the honey-glazed fried chicken with macaroni and cheese and collard greens. And for her companion, named Missy, she ordered the shrimp etouffee.

Both women had a couple of more drinks during dinner, and the buzz made them feel an attraction toward each other. Stacey had her "lick-her" license for a while and had been with many women before, but this was altogether new to Missy. She wasn't sure exactly what she was feeling.

Stacey, being the aggressor, moved closer to Missy and started rubbing her thigh under the table. Missy opened her legs wider as she felt Stacey's hand glide up towards her vagina.

The loosely fit slacks she wore made it easy for Stacey to rub her pussy through the fabric. While enjoying Stacey's hands Missy looked at the surrounding tables to see if anyone noticed how her expression had changed. She tried to stay straight-faced but the pleasure was taking over. She unbuckled her belt, opened her pants, grabbed Stacey's hand and guided it to her throbbing wet pussy. Stacey's bold ass didn't give a fuck who noticed.

She stared into Missy's eyes while her fingers went to work, admiring the response she got from dispensing Missy so much joy. Slowly grinding her hips to the rhythm of Stacey's fingers, Missy gripped the cloth napkin while trying to keep her composure. Stacey glanced around to see if anyone was paying attention to her and Missy.

When she saw that the coast was clear she untied the curtain to their booth to conceal what was about to occur and quickly slid her five-foot-nine frame under the table as Missy looked on in astonishment. She was embarrassed but slightly turned on at the same time. Stacey aggressively pulled Missy's slacks down just far enough to spread her legs apart.

The excitement of someone noticing what was going on under the table gave Missy goosedbumps. Stacey maneuvered her body in order to get the perfect position for her next act. She spread Missy's lips apart and licked her clitoris fervently, bringing her ultimate pleasure.

No man had ever made Missy feel this way before. The way Stacey used her tongue was like "magic." Missy gripped the edge of the table as her eyes rolled in ecstacy. She would've pushed it to the other side of the booth if it wasn't bolted to the wall. Feeling a climax coming on, Missy grabbed a handful of Stacey's hair and pulled her face deeper into her crotch. She tried to fight it but it was futile.

Missy let out a little moan and whispered, "Oh shit!" as she came in Stacey's face.

She continued to lick and suck until Missy's legs began to shake and she pushed Stacey's head away from her throbbing clit. Satisfied with a job well done, Stacey gave herself a figurative pat on the back and inched her way back onto the seat.

She wiped Missy's juices from her mouth with a napkin and a smile formed slightly as she watched Missy try to collect herself.

Missy was a wreck. Her slacks were still down around her ankles. One shoe had been kicked off somewhere under the table. Her hair was disheveled from sliding down in her seat. Her vagina was soaking wet and her legs would not stop trembling.

There was nothing left to do but get the check, so Stacey pulled the curtain back and re-tied it. As she summoned the waitress, she noticed the embarrassed looks on the faces of the patrons who sat nearby. One guy was sitting at a table with a huge Kool-Aid smile on his face. His companion poked him in the arm with her fork and glared at him as if to say, "Don't even think about it."

When the waitress arrived with the check, she asked if the ladies had enjoyed their dining experience. As Stacey placed two C-notes on top of the bill, she stared at Missy seductively and replied, "Everything was delicious."

Not quite sure what the comment or the look meant, the waitress grabbed the money and the check and walked away.

There was no need to wait for change. When Missy finally got herself together, Stacey extended her hand and helped her out of the booth and to her feet. She led Missy through the dining room, past the bar and out to the street where the informal valet retrieved her Durango.

"That was a hell of a dinner," Missy said. "I will never look at The Shark Bar the same way."

"I'm glad you had a good time, baby. You might wanna stick around. There's plenty more in store. Tonight was just the tip of the iceberg. We're winners over here, baby."

Just then, the valet pulled up with the truck and helped each lady inside. Stacey gave him a twenty-dollar tip and drove away. On the ride home, Missy leaned closer to rest her head on Stacey's arm. Stacey smiled as she moved through the night traffic thinking that, 'today was a good day.'

Always Some Drama

Lay woke up early one Saturday morning to the sound of his phone vibrating on the nightstand. He let it ring until it went to voicemail. 'It's too early for this shit', he thought. When he finally looked at it, he noticed an unhealthy amount of missed calls from Sammi. 'No one calls that many times for anything good,' he thought.

Surprised he'd slept through all that vibrating, Lay dragged himself to the bathroom for his morning ritual of dropping the kids off at the pool (taking a dump). Reluctantly, he returned Sammi's call.

She picked up on the first ring. Immediately, without even saying hello, she started off with, "What the fuck is up with you, Lay?!? What the fuck is up?!?"

"I don't know what the fuck is up with me, Sammi," Lay sighed, as he responded calmly.

"No, a better question is what's up with us, Lay?!? We don't hang out anymore! We don't fuck! We don't do shit since you got back with your ex, and I think that shit is fucked up! Remember, I was there with you when you went through the bullshit with Josie. Me! I'm the chick who stood by you. I rubbed your back and told you everything was going to be okay! I'm the one who made you all this money when you couldn't go back to the block!"

'Damn, I told this chick entirely too much,' Lay thought remorsefully.

But she definitely had a point. He had genuine love for Sammi. That was undeniable. She'd been there to hold him down and made things great for him when he needed it most. The only problem was he was *in* love with Celina. Having love for someone and being in love are two totally different things.

Lay tried to ease the tension by reasoning. "ATA (that was the nickname he gave her for, All That Ass), you know me and Celina have history together. She was my girl for years before you even gave me a second thought-..."

"You don't know what I was thinking about, Lay!" Sammi interrupted.

"Okay, you're right. I don't know what you were thinking about. But we didn't even cross paths yet back then. We wasn't fuckin' with each other like that. Then, when we hooked up, I thought we were just gonna keep it fun. You do what you want and I do the same. I didn't think you wanted to be in a relationship."

"I *don't* want a relationship, Lay. Don't get souped up, you conceited motherfucka!"

Lay was taken aback by that remark. 'So, what the hell is she beefing for? Me, conceited? Hell no,' he thought.

"So, what's wrong, ATA?"

"What's wrong is, I had to play second to Josie. Now I have to play second to your new girl. What's her name, Shanakateema?"

"Her name is Celina. You know what her name is."

"Whatever. When do I get to be number one in your life?!?"

"Wait a minute. Didn't you just say you don't want to be with me?"

"I know what I said."

"I'm confused. So, if you don't want to be with me, and I don't want to be with you, what's the problem?"

"The problem is you don't even consider me *good enough* to be your woman. That's the problem! As much as I do for you, you should *want* me as your number one! I make it possible for you to take care of your bills, your kids, your ex-girl *and* your new bitch! The problem is not me wanting you. The problem is *you* not wanting *me*! What the fuck?!? I'm not good enough for your black ass?!?"

"Whoa, whoa, whoa. You're taking shit way too far, Sammi. No one said you're not a good woman. You're gonna be great woman, for someone. That someone is not me. In another day and time, who knows what we

97

could've been? The time is not right for us, now. My heart is with someone else at this moment. I can't help that. The heart wants what the heart wants. You know how that goes. Haven't you been in love before?"

"I don't know if I've been in love or not. I'm just tired of motherfuckas always putting me second to the next chick. When is somebody gonna love me first? I treated you like a king! When do I become somebody's queen?"

"Baby, I can't answer those questions for you."

"I'm not asking for your advice, Lay. I just want somebody to think about *my* feelings for once."

Lay sighed, recalling that when a woman is venting, she's not always looking for answers. Sometimes she just needs to be heard, so he shut up for a minute. 'But how does one distinguish when to speak or be quiet? There you go, trying to figure out the female mind again. When will you learn?' he asked himself.

Sammi continued with her rant as Lay silently tried to figure out what this woman wanted from him.

"So, you're just gonna sit on the phone and not say shit?!? Really, Lay?!?"

"Sammi, you just said you weren't looking for advice, so I was letting you speak. You're mad if I talk; you're mad if I'm quiet. Come on baby. Tell me what's really going on."

"You know what? Nothing, Lay. Just forget it. I'll talk to you later." Abruptly, Sammi ended the call.

Lay had stayed on the throne for so long listening to Sammi's tirade, his left foot was asleep. He shook it vigorously to try and get the blood flowing again. He wasn't sure why, but Lay had an uneasy feeling about Sammi. He didn't think she was the type to do anything crazy, but when a person's feelings are involved you never know.

The morning had started off rocky, but he was determined to make the rest of the day much better. Celina had a showing in Franklin Lakes that morning, and they had a lunch date at Houston's right after. Lay was excited to see his baby. He felt like doing something nice for Celina since things were going so well between them.

Lay knew she would never do this on her own, but he was tired of her driving that Honda Civic. Not that she needed it, but Lay wanted to upgrade her vehicle; so he planned to take her car shopping after lunch.

During their meal, Celina brought up the idea of Lay investing in some property again, but she could tell he wasn't taking her seriously. He listened as he devoured his Hawaiian ribeye and fries, but his focus was on the right now, and-not the future. He wanted to put a smile on her face *today*, not think about having to mow some lawn on a house he would eventually buy.

After lunch, he told her to follow in her car, as he had to meet someone on Route 17. She obliged, and in about fifteen minutes they pulled into Park Avenue BMW. Celina was curious as to why they were meeting at the dealership but she rarely asked Lay about his business.

He went inside and purposely left her sitting in her car for five minutes before he returned.

"Come wait inside. My guy is running late."

Upon entering, Celina went to sit in the waiting area while Lay walked over to a black four-door 3 Series with black interior. He opened the door and sat behind the wheel, smiling like a kid in a candy store.

Celina shook her head from side to side as Lay motioned for her to come to the car. Reluctantly, she sighed, stood up, adjusted her skirt, and walked to the driver side of the vehicle wondering, what is this man up to now?

"You like this?" he asked, still smiling.

"Yes, Lavian. It's a very nice car."

Lay opened the door, stepped out and told her to get in. "Let me see how you look behind the wheel."

Celina looked at him suspiciously, rolled her eyes and sat in the driver's seat.

"Yeah, I like the way my baby looks in this joint."

Without uttering another word, Lay left Celina in the car as he grabbed the attention of a salesperson. After making the necessary arrangements, Lay returned to Celina and said,

"She's all yours. A new baby for my baby! All you have to do is sign the paperwork and drive her outta here."

Expecting to see a smile on her face, he was disappointed when he heard, "Lavian Taylor, what did you just do?"

"I just bought you this car, Boo. You said you liked it."

Trying to remain calm, Celina said, "First of all, don't Boo me. I said I liked the car. I didn't say I wanted it." "This unnecessary spending of yours has to stop, Lay. You need to find better things to do with your money."

"Come on, Boo. You're supposed to be happy. I work hard to put smiles on that beautiful face." As he said this, Lay wrapped his arms around her thighs under her ample butt and picked Celina up in the air.

Embarrassed, Celina protested, "I have on a skirt! Put me down! You play too much, fool!"

Lay relented and placed a peeved Celina back on the showroom floor.

"My car is paid for, Lay. You just created another unnecessary bill for me."

"Now what makes you think I'm gonna let you pay for this? You know me better than that."

"A bill for you is a bill for me. Think smarter for a change, Lavian."

"Okay, I'll pay for the whole car so we won't have a note."

"That's not the answer either, Lavian."

"So, you're saying you don't want it?"

She shook her head again, rolled her eyes and went to the dealer's desk to fill out the paperwork. While she did that, Lay cleaned out the Civic and transferred all of her things to the new whip. 'She needs to get rid of all this junk,' he thought.

When Celina was done, she walked out to the lot where Lay waited next to her brand new car with his arms folded and a huge smile on his face. She hugged him tightly and said,

"Don't think I'm not appreciative of everything you do for me, Lay. We just need to make better decisions. We're not getting younger. The future is something I want you to consider *before* you make another big purchase. Can you promise me, that?"

"Yes, I promise."

"I'm serious, Lay. Home ownership is very important for our people. It builds wealth. Why do you think I keep asking you about that? I want you to give it some serious thought."

"Okay, baby. I will." "Now get your fine ass in this car so we can get outta here."

Lay motioned for Dave, the salesman, to come outside. When he was standing next to Lay, he said, "I'm gonna pick the Civic up in a day or so. Is that alright?"

"Well, we usually don't allow cars to just sit on our lot because it takes up too much space."

Lay dug in his pocket, peeled off two crisp one hundred dollar bills, folded them and passed them to Dave with a handshake. "Okay, so I'm gonna pay you $100 an hour to hold the car here until I get back. Now is it okay?"

"Sure is, Brother Lay."

"Thank you, Brother Dave."

Lay patted Dave on the shoulder and walked to his car. All Celina could do was smile at this clown of a man that she loved so much. They got in their cars and drove off the lot.

A couple of weeks passed by as Lay continued to hit bank after bank, piling more and more cash into his stash. All the while, Sammi continued to work, but with a serious chip on her shoulder. Lay noticed the change in her, but as long as she and the girls kept working, he overlooked her attitude.

Sammi's fury came to a head one Saturday when she and her girlfriend, Yolanda saw Celina in Neiman Marcus' shoe section at the Garden State Plaza.

Celina had no idea who Sammi was, nor that she was being watched as she tried on a pair of black crocodile Manolo Blahnik pumps trimmed with a tiny fuschia bow close to the ankle. After paying cash, she then made her way to the handbag section and purchased (also in cash,) a fuschia Nancy Gonzalez clutch to match-, all under the watchful eye of Sammi who was doing her best to remain inconspicuous.

She was no dummy. Sammi knew most chicks didn't walk around with cash like that unless they got it from a man. She knew that money had come from Lay, and it made her even angrier.

Happy with her purchases, Celina made her way to the valet. While waiting for her car, Sammi and Yolanda followed and stood outside a few steps away so she could get a closer look at Lay's woman.

Celina was dressed in a white Gucci sweat suit that hugged her curves, with the sneakers to match. Looking at her figure, Sammi thought, 'hmph that motherfucka definitely has a type. Her ass is almost as big as mine.' Through her Gucci shades, Celina noticed the two women standing off to the side, and that neither one of them went to the booth to turn in their valet ticket.

'They must be waiting for someone,' she thought, and gave a friendly smile as the two women moved closer. Always cautious, Celina nonchalantly put her hand inside of her bag to feel for the pepper spray she carried, just in case.

Sammi didn't say a word, as she side-eyed Celina. Yolanda, however, decided to give her a compliment.

"That's a cute bag, girl. I never saw that one before."

Not knowing whether it was sincere, Celina replied, "Thank you. It came from the Fifth Avenue store."

"Oh, that's why I never saw it. I've never been shopping down there. It must be nice."

"It's not a big deal. Trust me."

Celina smiled as her car pulled up and she reached into her purse with her free hand for the valet's tip. When Sammi saw Celina sitting behind the wheel of her brand new BMW, bearing the temporary tags and the bow still hanging from the rear view mirror, she fumed on the inside.

Her expression must've shown on her face because Celina noticed it as she pulled away from the curb. Shaking her head, she thought, 'I hope her day gets better.'

Sammi stormed back inside the mall, leaving Yolanda outside as she struggled to catch up.

"See! That's the shit I'm talking about! This motherfucka buying bitches new cars and shit! Where's my fuckin' car?!?"

"Sammi, you made plenty of money with Lay. You could've bought two or three cars by now. Why are you so mad at him for doing something nice for his woman?"

"That's not the point. And you'll never get it, either. She makes her own money too! She could afford to buy her own car, but *he* bought it for her. Why the fuck didn't he buy me one?!? If it wasn't for me, he couldn't afford to buy that bitch shit! I got something for that ass, though. Watch!"

"What are you gonna do, Sammi?"

"Don't worry about it, Yo-Yo. Let's get the fuck outta here."

The next Monday, Lay called Kev and Sammi to get them prepared for Wednesday's outing. Sammi gave him three names, not excluding herself for the day's work.

That night he met with Bobby so the work would be ready for pickup on Tuesday evening. Like clockwork, everything was in place and ready to go.

Wednesday morning, Kev sat in front of Sammi's crib and waited for her to come downstairs. Fifteen minutes turned into twenty, and twenty-five turned into thirty, and Lay became more and more annoyed. She wasn't picking up the phone or answering the door when Kev rang her bell. Frustrated, Lay jumped in his car and rode across the bridge to get to the bottom of this bullshit.

When he arrived, Lay didn't bother calling Sammi. He waited for someone to enter her building and went in behind them. Stepping off the elevator, Lay quietly crept down the hall to Sammi's door so he could figure out if she was home. When he reached the door, he heard the TV but no voices or movement.

Lay reached in his pocket, dialed her number and put his ear to the door to hear if her phone would ring. Sure enough, he heard the faint sound of Sammi's cell ringing through the door. 'Oh, this wench is playing games,' Lay thought.

He banged on the door until a guy wearing a red doo-rag, wife-beater, some cheap ass boxers like the ones you get from the African store, and some dirty socks with a hole in the toe, opened it and asked what the fuck he was banging on the door like that for.

Lay looked at the six-foot muscle-bound dude and replied, "I'm banging on the door because Sammi ain't answerin' her phone. I know she saw me calling her. She's messin with my money. And if you don't tell me where she is, you messin with my money too! She knows what she was supposed to do today."

"Like I said, she ain't here."

"Yeah, okay."

Lay looked the dude up and down and thought, if this is the type of nigga she deals with, no wonder she's mad. She's probably taking care of his big dumb ass. He knew that big goofball was lying, but it wasn't worth the amount of showers it would take to get that funky smell off of him if they started tussling. Lay just shook his head and walked away from the door, down the hall to the elevator. He was furious and he knew Bobby would be equally pissed off. All those hours at the computer putting that work together for nothing!

When Lay got downstairs he explained the situation to Kev and asked if he could find some chicks to work. He said he would look into it and get back to him as soon as possible. The two men shook hands and Lay jumped into the Five and called Bobby so he could break the news to him early, hoping they could put their heads together and figure out a way to salvage the day.

They agreed to meet at Pan Pan to have breakfast. On the drive over from the Bronx, Lay wanted to kick himself for not having any of Sammi's girls' phone numbers, but it was a safety precaution he used to insulate him from them in case they got arrested and wanted to rat him out. The only way for them to contact him was through Sammi, and he liked it that way-, until now of course.

He realized how much he needed this chick, and it pissed him off even more.

During breakfast, Lay explained Sammi's behavior to Bobby and as expected, he was vexed. But there was no use crying over spilled milk. He told Lay to put his car in the garage on 132nd Street and ride with him for the day. With nothing on his agenda thanks to Sammi, Lay decided to take him up on the offer.

After eating, Lay dropped his car off and they drove to Stacey's house to get her and Missy. Hopefully, Bobby would have a better day than Lay was having. The girls came downstairs and Bobby drove to the Larchmont, New

York area. Upon arrival he gave Stacey and Missy a check each and watched them go into the bank before driving out of view.

He always found a safe place to sit where he could observe any strange activity, but the girls couldn't see him. A few minutes later, Stacey came out of the bank and walked to her right, passed a Starbucks and ran her right hand through her hair, giving the signal that everything was copacetic.

After a few minutes, Missy resurfaced and mimicked Stacey's movements, exactly. Bobby went to the next corner to scoop them up. Entering the car, they both handed Lay the envelopes while Bobby proceeded to the next destination. About thirty miles away was another HSBC they decided to try. There, the two ladies entered the bank and got in line. Stacey let an older gentleman skip her in place so she and Missy wouldn't be directly behind one another with the same checks.

Missy approached the teller, completed her transaction successfully and made her way to the entrance of the bank. Stacey wanted to go to the young black teller, but ended up with the same teller as Missy because she let the man take her position in line. 'This could mess everything up', she thought.

But Stacey was a pro.

She knew how to handle herself in sticky situations. Approaching the teller, she made small talk as the teller punched numbers in and ran the check through the reader. She looked at Stacey's ID, looked up at Stacey and back at the ID.

This prompted Stacey to ask, "Is everything ok, ma'am?"

The teller replied, "Oh yes, everything is fine. I was just checking something."

Stacey couldn't imagine what that was, because everything went perfectly fine with Missy's transaction. She stood quietly as the teller reached into her drawer to start counting out the $2358.38. Suddenly, for some odd reason, the teller placed the bills back in the drawer, picked up the phone and turned her back to the counter.

"Ma'am is there a problem?" Stacey asked once again.

The teller ignored her and kept speaking into the receiver. Stacey began to get irritated when the teller turned around to pick up her ID but refused to acknowledge her, or respond to her question. She knew shit was about to get funky when the teller turned around, hung up the phone and the manager appeared from the back office. Without hesitation, Stacey jumped onto the counter and down to the floor on the same side as the teller as onlookers gasped in shock and amazement.

She snatched her ID out of the teller's hand and leapt back across the counter and ran out of the bank. The manager grabbed the phone to call 911 as fast as she could, but Stacey was already out of the door. When she hit the street, she desperately looked around for Bobby's rental but it was nowhere in sight.

She immediately called his cell. He picked up on the first ring.

"Where you at?" Stacey asked loudly.

"I see you. Just keep walking to the McD's. Go in and walk through. I'll pick you up on the other side."

"Okay. I got you." Stacey quickened her pace but didn't want to look suspicious by running. She walked through the McD's door straight to the other side as instructed as Bobby pulled up right on point.

Stacey jumped in the back seat next to Missy and ducked down out of sight.

"What happened in there?"

"That fuckin' teller was in there over-doing her motherfuckin' job. Bitch tried to keep my ID!"

"Which one?" asked Missy.

"The same one you had. The old chick with the glasses."

"Oh, she didn't give me any problems. I wonder why she messed with you."

"Yeah, I wonder the same thing."

"Well, you're good now. We're outta here. Buckle up. We're about to do some traveling," Bobby said.

That was a close call, but Stacey was a thoroughbred. She knew the ins and outs of those bank procedures, and could sense the bullshit before it surfaced. They escaped this time, but danger was still on the horizon.

Bobby, Lay and the two ladies managed to salvage the day closing out with approximately $37,000 when it was all said and done. That was good for Bobby, but Lay still had to figure out his situation with Sammi. Without her and her girls, he had no way of generating income. Bobby dropped him off at the garage and Lay drove back to Jersey to figure out what his next move was going to be.

On the way home he called Kev who said he had a chick that was willing to work.

"Did you school her to the game?" Lay asked.

"Sure did," Kev replied.

"Cool, I'll meet you in a few to get her info."

That call gave him a sense of relief, as he now knew he potentially had some source of income to count on.

He hoped she would work out because not everyone is built for this line of work, but at this point he really didn't have a choice.

Hearing Celina's voice always put a smile on his face, so after hanging up with Kev, Lay called her to see how her day went. She was just leaving the office and she said she would call him back when she got in the car.

While awaiting her call, Lay turned on the radio and "I Gotta Be," by Jagged Edge was playing. This was one of his favorite '90s love songs. It made him long for Celina even more. After the day he had with Sammi going AWOL, and the close call with Bobby, he needed the comfort of Celina's love and tenderness. For the first time, he was getting that "marriage feeling" again. Things with him and Celina were going so well, he didn't want it to end.

Lay gave some serious thought to putting a ring on her finger as he envisioned spending the rest of his life with Celina. Just then, his phone rang and she was on the line.

"Hey, Handsome. Sorry I had to cut the call short, earlier."

"That's okay, Babe. How was your day?"

"It was okay, and yours?"

"Mine wasn't so good. I could really use some of you, right now."

"Aww, I'm sorry about that, Babe. I wish there was something I could do."

"You can. All I need is to see and feel you."

"Okay. I just have to stop at my house to get some clothes for work tomorrow, and then I'm on my way to you."

"You have clothes at my crib. Just get over here now. I need you, Boo."

"Okay, okay. I'm on my way, Babe."

When Lay hung up the phone, he gave a sigh of satisfaction. It felt good to know he could count on Celina when he needed her.

At the same time, Celina smiled as a feeling of contentment came over her for realizing she still had that effect on her man.

"He needs me," she said out loud. "And I need him, too."

Before crossing the bridge Lay called Kev and told him to meet at the McD's in Ft. Lee so he could get the new chick's info. He had to get it to

Bobby early so they could be prepared for the next day. Lay also wanted to get all of this taken care of as soon as possible so he could get home to Celina. If he timed it right, they would be walking in the door at the same time and he could start the evening with his lady.

Missing Celina by about twenty minutes, he walked through the door to find her sitting on the couch with her feet under her, watching TV. Lay dropped his keys on the sofa table, knelt down on one knee, threw his other leg on the couch, rested his head on Celina's thigh and wrapped his arms around her waist.

She began to rub his head as she asked, "So, what happened to my baby today?"

It felt so good to be with her, he could stay there in that position forever. Lay shared the day's events with Celina. They ordered dinner, ate, showered, and headed off to bed. That night, the two slept so intertwined, it was if their bodies were one.

Intimacy didn't get much better than that. It was the closeness that he craved. No sex, just closeness. Lay needed that, and Celina provided.

The next day, Lay met Bobby bright and early to get the work so he could try out the new chick. He wanted to test the waters early so if the day went south, he could get it over quickly. Bobby gave him local work because it didn't make sense to go far if no one knew if she would work out.

Kev met Lay by the garage on 132nd Street and 7th Avenue. Lay climbed into the Suburban and Kev introduced him to Cassandra Singletary. She was a short brown-skinned chick with natural short hair, thick in the hips and thighs and probably A-cup sized breasts. She was a cutie, but Lay thought she looked 'green.'

He was afraid she didn't have the heart and know-how to navigate all this game entailed. But, they were there, and he didn't have much of a choice at that point. She was dressed properly, which was a plus. Lay was happy that Kev schooled Cassandra on that part, at least. The only thing left to do was give her a shot.

The three of them rode up to Bay Plaza in the Bronx to an HSBC. Kev knew the drill, so he pulled up several feet away from the front door and let Cassandra out of the truck. Lay had already passed her a check so she was prepared. All they could do now was cross their fingers and hope all went well.

When she reached the front door, Kev drove out of view, but close enough so they could see if anything suspicious was happening. A few minutes went by and there was no activity. Lay began to worry because it usually didn't take that long. He told Kev to call or text her. Kev dialed Cassandra's number and let the phone ring until it went to voicemail.

Lay was definitely on edge, now. A few minutes later, an NYPD cruiser pulled up in front of the bank. The officer got out of his vehicle and rushed inside. 'Oh shit. This shit is about to get ugly,' Lay thought.

"Let's get the fuck outta here", he yelled!

"Wait! We can't leave her," Kev fired back.

"Man, are you serious? We not sticking around to see what the fuck is about to happen. We can hear about it on the news!"

"Yo Lay. I'm not leavin' my chick."

"Okay. I'm getting the fuck out of this truck! And yo' ass is fired!"

Just as Lay opened the door and put his "Icey-Whites" on the ground, Kev said, "Here she comes! Get in!"

Lay looked around and saw Cassandra walking nonchalantly along the storefronts while she dug in her pocketbook for her cell. When she found it she called Kev and asked where he was.

"Don't worry baby. Keep walking. I'm coming to scoop you now."

"Worry? Why would I be worried?"

"Nevermind," Kev said.

When they picked her up Lay asked her what was taking so long.

"Umm, calm down, sir. There was a long line I had to wait on," Cassandra replied.

"Calm down?!? I was worried about *your* safety. If you don't want me to, let me know."

"Kev, your man needs an attitude adjustment."

"Really? And you have a smart-ass mouth!"

"Last time I checked, I was grown and can say whatever I wanted."

Lay was tired of the back and forth. He turned around in the passenger seat to face Cassandra, who was sitting directly behind Kev and said,

"You're right. You are grown, and you can say what you want. But this is *my* show. I run this. So, when you put your ass in this truck when I'm in it, and I hand you one of *my* checks, what *I* say goes. If you don't like it, you can get the fuck out now. Matter of fact, pull over, Kev."

Reluctantly, Kev obliged, but he felt a little embarrassed in front of Lay. He had no idea Cassandra was so headstrong.

"So what's it gonna be? Are we on the same page, or what?"

Cassandra was looking at Kev, waiting for him to say something but he remained silent. When she saw she could get no refuge from Kev, she quietly relented.

"Yes. We're on the same page."

"Good. I'm glad we could reach an understanding."

"Kev said, "The reason we were freakin' out is because you were taking longer than usual and then the police ran inside not long after you did. Now, do you understand?"

Cassandra rolled her eyes and sat back in the seat. "Did it ever occur to you two geniuses that he was cashing his check? *It is payday. Duh.*"

Lay looked at Kev as if to say what the fuck is wrong with your chick? Instead, he turned his head, looked out the window and asked if she wanted to continue.

"Of course. Why wouldn't I?"

"Okay. You perform well under pressure. I like that. But, you forgot the most important thing to do once you get in this truck."

"What's that?" Cassandra asked.

"Give me my damn money!" Lay barked.

"Oh shit. I forgot. If you two wouldn't have been stressing so much, you would've had your money already."

She dug in her bag and passed Lay the envelope filled with hundreds and fifty's. After all that aggravation, Lay was relieved that everything had gone well on her first time out.

Even though he didn't like her smart mouth, he was glad she had that fire in her. He could tell she wouldn't be taking much shit from any of these tellers, and that was a plus. They finished the day with no more hiccups and cleared seventeen checks. Cassandra cashed out with $8,500 when it was all said and done. Her total would've been $10,200 but Kev got $100 off every check she cashed for bringing her aboard. With the $1,700 he already received for driving, his total came to $3,400.

Bobby's cut was $2,550, and Lay walked away with $19,000. 'All in a day's work,' he thought. 'Who needs Sammi?' One question remained was how much of a headache would Cassandra be in the future? Another was, how much love did Kev really have for this chick? He was actually willing to risk his own freedom *and* Lay's to make sure she was ok.

That didn't sit too well with him. Lay wasn't a selfish dude, but he also wasn't a stupid one. He didn't want any of his girls to get caught, but in this game there was no room to use your heart before your brain, either. He explained to every chick that went out that if they got caught to keep their mouth shut. 'I can't get *you* out if I'm locked up too,' was his advice to them, and it made sense. If one of the girls got locked up and snitched on him and

Kev, Lay was only going to look out for *him and Kev*. Self preservation is the first law of survival, a motto he lived by.

The events of the day had him thinking, 'Maybe I should put some thought into the real estate thing like Celina said. She would never steer me wrong.'

Kev and Cassandra dropped Lay off to his car and they went to dinner at Flor de Mayo. Lay called Bobby and asked where he wanted to meet.

He told Lay to meet him in front of Jimmy's on Seventh Ave, which was convenient because it was a block away from the garage. Bobby was feeling good and he wanted to have a drink with the locals that evening. Lay walked over to Jimmy's and stood out front waiting for Bobby to arrive. After standing for a few minutes, he got tired.

Leaning on an old burgundy Buick Park Avenue with his back to the street, he could see everyone going in and out of the lounge. Ladies were dressed to the nines and guys were standing around scoping who they could possibly slide off with when the night was over. There were a couple of stick-up kids lingering in the shadows as well. They were always around looking for a come-up.

Lay tuned them out as he looked at his Rolex and wondered what was taking Bobby so long. Glancing over his left shoulder, he noticed three ladies exiting a cab, looking good as fuck. Two of them spoke as they stepped onto the sidewalk.

"Hey Lay," said one.

"Hey, Yo-Yo."

"How are you feeling?" asked the other as she touched his arm when she walked by.

"Hey, Bruni."

Right away, he regretted Bobby telling him to meet him there because he knew what was coming next. Those were two of Sammi's girls and he assumed she wasn't far behind. Sure enough, Sammi stepped out of the cab and leaned in the passenger window to pay the driver. Her ass was on 1,000.

After paying, she turned and walked to the sidewalk. Lay scoffed and turned his head in the opposite direction to avoid eye contact. As she glided to the front door, someone called her name. She pretended not to notice Lay leaning on the car.

He couldn't deny that Sammi looked good.

The white denim jeans she wore hugged her huge ass perfectly, and the Manolo heels she wore showed off her French-manicured toes which ignited his fetish for nice feet. They pretended not to notice one another as she went to stand with her girls in the short line to enter. The guy who called Sammi left his friends and walked over and gave her a hug.

As he approached, Lay recognized him as E.J., the guy who had schooled Nick to the check game. He was down with another crew from Harlem that was getting check money, but came up short in comparison to Bobby's crew.

Lay shook his head and thought, 'this broad done went and jumped ship.' After the embrace, she looked in Lay's direction to see if he was watching. He was.

At this point, he abandoned the casual attitude and shot daggers at them with his eyes. If looks could kill, they would've been zipping Sammi and E.J. into body bags at that very moment. Just then, Bobby pulled up and exited that big beautiful white S430. All eyes were on him.

He and Lay shook hands and embraced as Lay slid Bobby his cut simultaneously.

"What's wrong, bro?" Bobby asked, as the disgust on his face was that obvious.

"This chick is over there talking to that motherfuckin' E.J."

"What chick? Who the hell is she?"

"That's Sammi, the one who disappeared on me the other day."

"Oh, okay. Fuck it. That's her loss. You got another chick, anyway. One clown ain't gon' stop this circus. Shit, we like motherfuckin' Ringling Brothers out this bitch!"

Lay couldn't help but laugh a little.

"But I just don't want her telling them motherfuckas our business, our methods. You know what I'm sayin'?"

"Well, how much does she know?"

"Shit, she knows everything. That was my bottom chick."

"Oh, now I see why you're upset. You ain't getting no more of that big ol' ass. And she does have a big one. I'm a breast man myself but, I know you had some fun with that."

"Nah bro, it's not that. I stopped fuckin' with her when I got back with Celina. That's why she was all bent out of shape."

"Damn. You're a faithful muhfucka'. I don't know how you do it. I *gotta* play out in these streets. Anyway, don't worry about it. She'll be back. Trust me. We're the best thing moving out here, bro. Now, if you'll excuse me I needs to have some alcohol inside of me and somebody's daughter needs me to be inside of them."

"You're a whore."

"Call me what you want. But you can't call me broke, or desert-dick."

Lay just shook his head at Bobby.

"You need to come inside with me to get some of that frustration off your brain, bro. Stress kills, you know."

"You know that shit is an every now and then thing with me. I don't like being in all those people's faces. And I damn sure don't want them in mine. You go have a good time."

116

"I'm gonna ball the fuck out."

The two men shook hands and embraced again as they parted ways. Bobby left his car double-parked and walked to the front of the line where he was stopped by the bouncer.

"There's a dress code, sir."

"I'm buying bottles."

"How many?"

"How many do I need to get in?"

"It's a $500 minimum."

"Okay, set me up with that and another $500 for my own VIP. Can you make that happen?"

"I sure can."

"Thank you."

Bobby looked at Sammi and E.J., gave a head nod, and walked into the club.

Her girlfriends looked at him in awe as he cut the line and left everyone standing outside. E.J. peered at Bobby with a look of disdain on his face. The two had an unspoken rivalry going on between them but for Bobby it was just competition amongst gentlemen. To Bobby, E.J. was getting some money in this game, but his team was just better at it, was what he thought.

By this time Lay had started to walk back to the garage, shaking off the scene in front of the club. Sammi excused herself from E.J., and walked briskly to catch up to him.

E.J. had a look on his face that said, 'No the fuck this chick didn't!' He was really steaming inside now. 'Two of these muthafuckas in one night?! How much could a muthafucka take?'

"Lay! Lay! You can't speak?"

At first he was going to ignore her and keep walking, but he stopped, hoping he wouldn't regret it.

"Are you serious, Sammi? You walked right past me and didn't say shit. Yo-Yo and Bruni spoke, and you just acted like I wasn't there."

"I didn't see you at first. Then, when I did see you I didn't know *what* to say. I thought you wouldn't talk to me because you were still mad."

"I *was* mad, but I didn't have a choice, so I got over it."

After an awkward silence, as Lay took in how good Sammi looked, he asked, "Is there a reason why you stopped me, 'cause I gotta get home."

Sammi got an instant attitude. "Oh yeah, I don't want to keep you from your precious, Celina."

"She's not *at* my house. There you go, thinking you know everything."

"If she's not there, can I stay with you tonight?"

"You're buggin'. I ain't fuckin' with you. You fucked with my money, and you know I am about my money. I don't know whether you called yourself teaching me a lesson, but that was some wack shit you did."

"I know, Lay. And I'm sorry. It's just...I was in my feelings."

"For what though, Sammi? I didn't do anything to you. We were good. Now you put us in a bad space because of some feelings that don't hold no weight. You were in your feelings and you don't even know why. There's no explanation for that. Shit was just dumb. And now you're over there fuckin' with them other motherfuckas. How do I know you ain't telling him my business?"

"Come on, Lay. I would never do that. You should know me better than that."

Lay scoffed and said, "I thought I did, but you proved me wrong."

"Lay, don't be like that."

"I gotta go, Sammi. You have a good night," Lay said as he turned and walked away, leaving Sammi standing there. She watched Lay walk until he almost reached the garage, then eventually turned and made her way to the club to join Yo-Yo and Bruni, who were already inside enjoying the nightlife.

Once inside, Sammi sauntered past Bobby who was standing at the bar, sipping on a vodka and cranberry juice waiting for his VIP section to be ready. He couldn't help but notice how huge her ass was, again. When he turned his head in the other direction, he saw a tall Hispanic gentleman dressed in a suit approaching, with a bouncer in tow.

'Now what?' Bobby thought. Anticipating them coming to beef with him about the way he was dressed, he got something he wasn't expecting instead. The suited gentleman introduced himself as Jimmy Rodriguez.

"How you doing?" Bobby said. "I paid to get in here like this."

"That's fine. I own the place," Jimmy said.

"Oh, you're *that* Jimmy."

"Yes, that's me. Are you here with someone?"

"Why? What's up?"

"I only asked because those ladies over there would like for you to join them."

Jimmy pointed in the direction of four beautiful young ladies in their own VIP section with a few bottles of their own on the table in front of them. "I didn't want to send you over there alone if you had people with you."

Bobby had noticed a couple of guys from the old Skate Key crew chilling in the corner when he came in. He turned to look at the ladies as one of them stood up with a champagne flute in her hand and raised it to Bobby. She was a tall brown-skinned honey that reminded him of Kisha from "Belly." She was bad as fuck. Bobby turned to look at the Skate Key crew, then back to Jimmy and said,

"Nope. I'm flying solo."

"Good. My security will escort you to their table. Thank you, and enjoy your evening, sir."

When Bobby got to their section, the tall one greeted him with a hug and introduced herself as, Khadijah.

"Have a seat," she said, and introduced him to her girlfriends Dana, Quiana, and Renee. Khadijah poured Bobby a glass of Cris and invited him to have a seat. Bobby sat between her and Quiana on the plush leather sofa and accepted the glass but didn't dare take a sip.

The ladies made small talk as he got comfortable and explained how they were all from Jersey and came to the city to have a little girl's night for no reason in particular. Bobby asked what made them invite him to their section.

"Khadijah said, "When you came in, you looked like you needed to be over here with us."

"Oh, really?"

"Yes. Why? I know you're probably tired of the same old Harlem chicks. Don't you want to chill with some beautiful Jersey girls tonight? Don't you like what you see?"

"I do. I'm just trying to figure out how I became the 'chosen one' tonight."

"You stood out to us. Well to me, really. Trust me it's not a bad thing."

"Damn, you make a nigga feel special."

"Well, aren't you?"

"Am I what?"

"Special."

"I don't know. Am I?"

"There's only one way to find out."

"And how is that?"

Khadijah leaned close to Bobby so she could whisper, "Let's get out of here," in his ear.

Just then, he noticed two bottle girls carrying his bottles to the VIP section that was reserved for him. He asked Khadijah, "What about your girlfriends?"

"It's cool. I drove my own car and met them here. We're all big girls. They'll be alright."

Bobby looked at Khadijah's beautifully bronzed skin and said fuck those bottles, that VIP and the $1,000 he dropped on them both. He wasn't letting this dime get away from him tonight.

"Let's go," he said.

Khadijah said her goodbyes to the rest of the ladies and made her way to the exit with Bobby not too far behind. He didn't want to make shit too obvious.

After all, he *was* still in Harlem, and felt he needed to put some shade on his bullshit for Niecy's sake. That's the least he could do. He watched Khadijah's hourglass figure as she walked outside the club into the night air.

"Where'd you park?" he asked.

"I'm over on 133rd Street."

"Get in. I'll take you to your car."

Bobby's Benz was still double-parked in front of the club un-ticketed and untouched. He let Khadijah in on the passenger side and walked around to get in. Bobby drove around to 133rd Street and she told him to stop when they were next to a grey Nissan Maxima with Jersey plates on it. He got out, walked to the other side and opened the door to let Khadijah out. Bobby told her to follow him to the hotel.

There was no way he was letting her pick the spot, just in case she was trying to line him up for a jux. Before he could walk away, Khadijah grabbed him by the shirt, pulled Bobby close to her and kissed him with the passion of a new bride on her honeymoon. He was a little taken aback by her assertiveness, but turned on at the same time. Khadijah moved her hand from his chest down to the zipper on his jeans and unzipped them.

Bobby was already becoming erect from the kiss, but her playing with his zipper made him hard as a brick. She stopped kissing to say, "Take it out. I wanna meet little Bobby." Fumbling with the button on his boxers, Khadijah finally got her hands on his dick and was pleasantly surprised.

"Oh, Bobby is not little at all."

This put a huge grin on Bobby's face as he stepped back, put his hands on his hips and enjoyed the mini-massage he was receiving. With one hand in his pants, Khadijah grabbed the back of Bobby's head with the other and went in for an even steamier kiss than before. He obliged with his tongue and began to gently squeeze her perky breasts.

Khadijah's nipples stood at attention as she moaned with pleasure from the caress of Bobby's hands. He wanted to feel her flesh, and she wanted the same. Khadijah broke away from the kisses again to whisper, "I want to taste him."

Although Bobby was horny as fuck, he protested, "Not here, baby. We gotta go. Fuck that shit. Get your ass back in this car. You're riding with me."

Khadijah readily obeyed. She immediately unhooked the front clasp of her bra and licked her perfectly manicured index finger as she watched Bobby walk around to the get in the driver's seat. When he saw her nipples protruding through the soft, semi-sheer blouse he nearly drooled on himself. Khadijah's breasts were at least double D's, and this was to his liking because Bobby was definitely a tittie man. He unbuckled his Gucci belt and grabbed her hand so she could rub his dick again.

Shifting the car in drive, they pulled away from the Nissan and rode up the block. When they got to the corner the light was red. Khadijah seized the opportunity to slide her foot out of the Jimmy Choo sandal on her right foot, hiked her denim skirt up and slid her thongs down to the floor.

She put her foot on the dashboard and spread her legs as wide as the space in the S430 would allow. Bobby was trying to remain poised, but everything about Khadijah oozed erotica. As he drove she reached for his right hand and gently placed it on her breast. Bobby loved how she reacted when he gently twisted her nipple like he was opening the combination to a lock, making Khadija's pussy even wetter.

She took his hand and guided it until it was between her legs where her clit was yearning to be played with. Bobby used his ring finger and thumb to spread her labia and keep it open while simultaneously using his index finger to circle her throbbing clitoris. After a few minutes of this Khadijah grabbed Bobby's middle finger and guided it inside of her creamy pussy.

"Fuck," Khaijah moaned.

"Damn, your shit is wet," Bobby said. "Your shit feels thick like I stuck my finger in some warm pudding."

"Enough of this shit. I want you to fuck me."

"Baby, I'm driving."

"Pull over, shit."

By this time, they were already on the Harlem River Drive headed toward the George Washington Bridge and he wasn't about to stop there.

"Nah, I can't stop. That's gonna have to wait until we get to the room."

Khadijah was horny as fuck but she knew he was right.

Instead of letting that kill the mood she did the next best thing. Khadijah reached over to Bobby's already unzipped pants and pulled his dick out. She unbuckled her seatbelt, leaned over and began giving Bobby some bomb ass head. The sucking and slurping sounds she made, and the way she used her hand got Bobby so excited, it made him swerve a couple of times.

There was so much spit, the opening to his jeans was soaked. 'If she keeps this up, I'm not gonna last until the hotel,' he thought. Her head game was so good Bobby leaned back on the headrest and closed his eyes for a second. The sound of a car horn startled him out of his trance. He had drifted out of his lane and almost crashed into a passing vehicle.

"Baby you gotta stop. You gonna make me crash."

"You really want me to?" Khadijah asked as she jerked his soaking wet dick slowly while looking deeply into his eyes.

'This chick is too much,' he thought. Trying to keep his eyes on the road and look at her at the same time he replied,

"No, I don't want you to stop. But I'm not trying to die, either."

"Okay baby. I'll save some for the room."

"Shit, if you don't stop playing with my dick like that we're not gonna make it to the room."

"Aww, am I too much for you, Bobby?"

'Damn, is she a mind reader too?' he thought. Playing it off, he replied, "Nah, you're just what I needed tonight."

"So why did you stop me?"

"Uh, I wanna live to tell my boys about you tomorrow."

"Oh, you a kiss and tell type of nigga?"

"Normally I don't."

That was a lie. He told them everything, especially Lay. "But damn girl, that mouth is serious!"

"You like that, huh?"

"Do I?!?"

"Wait until I get you in that room. I'ma show you something, for real."

Khadijah decided to cut him some slack and sat back in her seat. She rubbed the back of Bobby's head as he continued on New Jersey's 80 West on the way to The Marriott. When they arrived, Bobby told Khadijah to wait in the car while he went to get the room.

On the way inside, he called Niecy to check in before he continued his night of debauchery. It was 12:40, and Niecy was sound asleep with Bobby Jr. lying next to her in the king-sized bed. She picked up on the third ring, with a groggy,

"Hello."

"Hey baby, did I wake you?"

"What time is it, Bobby?"

"It's 12:40."

"Well, what did you think I would be doing at this time of night?"

"I don't know. I was just checking on you and li'l man."

"He's good. I just put him down a little while ago."

"Oh, okay. Well, I'm almost finished work, so I'll be home in a minute. Okay, baby?"

"Yes. But try to be quiet when you come in so you don't wake the baby."

"Okay baby. Love you."

"See you in a minute. Love you too."

As Bobby secured the room and walked back to the car, he realized how much he really did love Niecy. For some reason he still managed to cheat on her. She never did anything to deserve his disgusting behavior, but he continued anyway. Bobby's conscience got the better of him on his walk back and he made up an excuse to get rid of Khadijah.

He called Sean and started talking as soon as the call connected.

"Yo, what's up?" Slow down! Slow down! What happened?!?"

As he was speaking into the phone, Bobby picked up his pace so Khadijah would notice the urgency in his movements. For the first few seconds, Sean didn't know what the hell was going on, but eventually he caught on and remained silent while Bobby ranted.

When Bobby got in the car, he shouted, "Aight, aight, I'm on my way!" then slammed the flip phone shut.

Khadijah asked, "What's wrong? What happened?"

"My brother just got robbed! I gotta go check on him. I'm sorry about this shit. I'ma drop you off to your car."

"Damn baby. Is he okay?"

"I don't know. That's what I'm going to find out."

"Okay, I understand."

Khadijah rubbed his head again as Bobby sped back to the city in silence, thinking about the stack he wasted on the VIP at Jimmy's and the $279 on the room. But more importantly, he thought about getting home to his baby, Niecy. They made it back to her car in record time. Khadijah gave Bobby her card so they could keep in touch.

She touched the right side of his face, guided it to hers, kissed him gently on the lips and said she hoped everything was okay with his brother. Khadijah got out and Bobby stepped on the gas before she had a chance to close the door. He made his way back across the bridge to Niecy and Bobby Jr., showered, crawled into bed behind her and hugged his woman tightly around her waist. He was happy he didn't go through with fucking Khadijah. She made him feel good for those brief moments, but it felt better to be home.

Shit Hits The Fan

Lay, Kev and Cassandra awakened in the wee hours of Tuesday morning to make the four-hour drive to Syracuse, New York. They had had moderate success in the Albany region and wanted to venture further upstate. Lay was used to having at least two girls working at a time but with Sammi and her crew missing in action, Cassandra had to suffice for the time being.

It was now October and the weather was becoming a little brisk. The leaves were turning from green into the beautiful autumn hues of red, brown and yellow. 'New York is a beautiful state,' Lay thought, gazing out of the window while Kev pushed the Suburban up I-84 North. He rarely got a chance to notice it because previously it had only been through the lens of countless trips to and from prisons. Now, it was scenery he could appreciate for what it was.

Cassandra was stretched out in the back seat with a light jacket draped over her head. Her work clothes hung from the hook above her feet on wire hangers from the cleaners, still in the plastic. Air from the cracked window hit the plastic bag and made a sputtering noise like a tiny motor.

They were almost there so Lay organized the MapQuest directions from the farthest point north back down toward the city and then counted the checks to make sure everything was in place. When they were a few miles away from the first bank, Kev found a McD's and pulled into the lot so Cassandra could change into her work clothes. Lay made his way to the counter and ordered a sausage McMuffin meal with a small orange juice instead of coffee.

Kev used the restroom and returned to the truck to wait for Cassandra to finish changing. Lay got his food and met Cassandra at the door at the same time she emerged from the bathroom. They both climbed into the truck, and Kev drove to the first HSBC on the map. When they arrived, Lay had just finished his food and passed Cassandra a check as she exited the vehicle. The walk to the entrance was a little distance but she made it there quickly in her haste to get out of the chilly autumn air.

Inside, the transaction went smoothly and Cassandra walked to the door of the bank and called Kev to let him know where she would be. She told him to pick her up at the CVS at the end of the strip mall.

Following directions, Kev pulled up to the pharmacy as soon as Cassandra got there. He honked the horn lightly to get her attention and she turned around, walked to the truck and got in. She passed Lay an envelope filled with mostly hundreds and fifties and sat back in her seat to relax before her next outing.

Lay counted the bills, then arranged them face front and in the same direction, large bills on the top, smaller on the bottom. He folded the cash, hundreds on the inside and stuffed it in the back left pocket of his jeans. This process went on four more times until he had to move the wad of cash to his front pocket when it became too thick to sit on. At this point the total had reached close to $10,000 as they pulled up to the fifth and final HSBC.

After that, the next target would be Key Bank. This particular branch was located just off of a strip mall with a patch of shrubbery between them. Cassandra looked like she was getting annoyed, but what from, Lay had no clue. He just chalked it up to her less than sunny disposition. Lay handed her the last HSBC check as Kev pulled across the road in a church parking lot and let her out.

From where they sat, they could see the entrance of the bank. When Cassandra reached the door Lay told Kev to leave the church lot and go to the strip mall on the other side of the bushes where the bank was out of view. Kev had to take a leak so he went inside the supermarket to relieve himself.

While sitting in the truck waiting for Kev and Cassandra to return, Lay decided to crawl into the third-row seat. The ride to the first Key Bank was almost an hour away and he could use that time to relax. As soon as Lay got comfortable his cell phone rang. Answering it, he recognized Celina's voice on the line.

"Hey Boo. How are you?

"I'm okay, Mr. Taylor. How's your day going so far?"

"I think you like calling me that because secretly, you want me to call you Mrs. Taylor in return. Is there any truth to that theory?"

"Umm, there might be. But I don't want you to call me Mrs. Taylor until it's officially my name, on paper."

"Oh, really? Are you proposing to me? 'Cause if you are I'ma need you be down one knee while you're doing it."

"I wish I would!" Celina exclaimed loudly in her office, drawing unwanted stares from her colleagues.

"You're always trying to play me, with your smart ass."

"I'm just saying. Mama told me to accept nothing less than the best."

"Okay boy. I had enough of your shenanigans. You sure know how to dance on a sister's nerves."

"Alright baby. My bad. Let's start this convo over. Hello my gorgeous queen, who I love so much."

"That's more like it."

Lay was so engaged in his conversation with Celina, he barely noticed Cassandra approaching the Suburban out of the corner of his right eye. Everything must've gone well, he thought. But then he noticed a short white woman in a tan plaid skirt suit trailing Cassandra. Lay knew something was wrong and quickly told Celina he would call her back as he closed the flip phone while she was in mid-sentence.

Kev hadn't returned from the bathroom yet and Lay was all the way in the third row of the truck. His first thought was to try to get behind the wheel to back out of the space. That notion quickly vanished as an unmarked police car pulled behind the Suburban, blocking it in.

Lay shook his head. "Damn."

Thinking fast, he started tearing up the remaining checks and stuffing them inside a compartment located in the armrest. He couldn't hear the dialogue going on between Cassandra, the officer, and the lady from the bank, but he could tell there was nothing good about it. After a few minutes, the officer walked to the rear driver side window and cupped his hands around his eyes to provide the shade he needed to peer into the tinted vehicle.

He still couldn't see, but he knew Lay was inside. He tried the door handle but it was locked. He then tried the driver door handle and got the same result. After his failed attempts to gain access, the officer tapped on the glass with the knuckle of his index finger and said,

"I know you're in there, Lavian. Open the door slowly and come out with your hands where I can see them."

'How the hell does this motherfucker know my name?' he thought.

The officer hadn't drawn his weapon up to this point, and Lay didn't want the situation to escalate to make him feel that he would need to. Without hesitating, he unlocked, and opened the rear driver side door, stuck both of his hands out, then his feet and stood face to face with Sgt. William Calhoun.

Still holding his hands in the air, Lay automatically turned and assumed the position by placing his hands on the side of the Suburban. Sgt. Calhoun proceeded to frisk Lay. After he was done, he instructed him to turn around.

With Lay's wallet and ID in his hands, Sgt. Calhoun said, "You're a long way from home Mr. Taylor. And that's a lot of money to be carrying around. What are you doing all the way up here? Are you cashing checks?"

Immediately, his blood started to boil. Lay replied, "No. I came up here to buy a car."

"Really? Where's your brother?"

"What brother? I don't have a brother."

Just then, out of his peripheral, Lay saw Kev emerge from the supermarket as another squad car pulled up. The officer driving it got out and made Kev put his hands against the wall to be frisked.

Lay's focus was diverted back to Sgt. Calhoun when he placed his hand on Lay's shoulder and told him to turn around because he was under arrest.

"Under arrest for what? What's the charge, officer?"

The sergeant remained silent and handcuffed Lay's wrists. After he was cuffed, Sgt. Calhoun placed all the money from Lay's pockets along with his wallet on the back seat of the truck.

Lay's cell phone had rung repeatedly throughout this entire process. He knew it was Celina calling to see if he was okay. 'How am I gonna explain *this* shit?' he thought.

Sgt. Calhoun walked Lay to the squad car, sat him in the back seat and proceeded to conduct a thorough search of the Suburban.

Peering out of the window, Lay watched as the search continued. He also noticed Kev and Cassandra being placed in separate cars. When Sgt. Calhoun was done, he stepped out of the truck with the ripped-up checks, money and MapQuest directions, holding them up so that another officer could place them into an evidence bag. Lay could hear his Nextel ringing loudly from inside of the truck and his thoughts shifted back to Celina and what he was going to tell her.

By this time Sgt. Calhoun had made his way to the car so he could drive to the station. They rode the fifteen-minute trip to the station in silence. When they arrived, Kev was already there sitting in a holding cell with his elbows on his knees and hands to his face. Lay walked into the cell and Kev looked up with deep concern on his face.

"What the hell happened," he asked?

"I don't know. I was on the phone with Celina. I looked up and saw Cassandra walking directly toward the truck with this little white lady behind her. She had to notice the lady trailing her, but she just kept walking. And she came straight to the truck! She knows better than that! Now, look at us," Lay replied in a loud whisper.

He realized his whisper was too loud. He didn't want the police to hear their conversation so he stopped talking and sat down next to Kev to continue.

"Didn't you have that talk with her?"

"Yeah, of course I did. I don't know what the fuck is wrong with that chick."

After a brief silence, Kev asked, "Do you think she said anything?"

"Shit, she told them motherfuckas my name. Who knows what else she said?!"

"How do you know?"

"Because when I was still in the truck, the cop said I know you're in there, Lavian. How would he know that shit if he didn't see my ID yet."

"Damn, my bad bro."

"It's not your fault. I blame this shit on that fuckin' Sammi. We would've never had to mess with any new chicks if it wasn't for her pulling that M.I.A. bullshit."

"Yeah, but Cassandra knows better."

"Yeah, well, all that shit sounds good until them boys are all up in your face. Let's just hope she keeps her mouth shut and doesn't do any real damage."

Both men had records so they knew the drill. They each found a spot on a bench and got as comfortable as possible. Lay was trying to drift off to sleep but thoughts of Celina plagued him. He knew he was going back to prison for sure if Cassandra told the police anything inimical.

Even though Josie cheated while he was doing his last bid, she came through like a champ the entire time. Lay didn't know if Celina was cut from the same cloth. Only time would tell.

After what seemed like forever, Sgt, Calhoun unlocked the cell and asked Kev to step outside. Lay expected them to pull this stunt. It's protocol for them to interview those they view as the weakest to the strongest to see if they'll flip. Lay had all the money in his pocket so they definitely believed he was running the show. About thirty minutes passed before Sgt. Calhoun returned with Kev. He unlocked the cell door and Kev stepped in.

When he thought Calhoun was out of earshot, Kev whispered, "That bitch told! She told everything."

"How you know?"

"They told me what the fuck she said. She told them you were the boss and I was just a driver."

"Fuckin' bitch," Lay scoffed.

"That motherfucka' ain't even locked in a cell. She's sitting right out there with the police at a desk like she fuckin' works here."

"Shit. She might as well work here. She did their fuckin' job for them. They should give her a fuckin' badge. She earned that shit." Lay sat back on the bench and shook his head.

"So, what did you say?"

As Kev was about to go into detail, he heard the jingling of Sgt. Calhoun's keys coming down the corridor and stifled his speech. The cell door opened and Sgt. Calhoun said,

"The Secret Service just got here. They want to speak to you, Mr. Taylor."

"The Secret Service?!?" Lay said confused. "Don't they guard the president?"

"Yes, they do."

"So what do they want with me?"

"We're about to find out, aren't we?"

133

Lay had been in some sticky situations before, but nothing came close to this. Every charge he caught prior to this was only prosecuted by the state.

This was some next-level shit that he wasn't prepared for. The walk from the cell to the interview room seemed like the green mile. When Lay reached the opening at the end of the hall, there sat Cassandra at one of the desks just as Kev said. When he saw her she looked away with a scowl on her face.

'What the hell could she possibly be mad at me for?' Lay thought.

Sgt. Calhoun directed Lay to sit down at a table across from Agents Lauren Chambliss and David Nowelle. Agent Chambliss was a short blond haired woman who reminded Lay of Kathy Bates and Agent Nowelle was a tall balding man who looked like the actor John Ashton who played Sgt. John Taggart in the first two installments of the *"Beverly Hills Cop"* series.

Sgt. Calhoun summoned Cassandra and directed her to step inside a room with glass windows so she wouldn't be present while Lay was being questioned. When she stood up, she glared at Lay again and walked into the room.

'That chick has a serious attitude problem,' he thought.

Once Cassandra was inside, Agent Chambliss introduced herself and her partner, second. She advised Lay of his constitutional rights and asked if he understood.

"Yes," Lay replied.

"Do you have anything you want to say before we get started?"

"I don't have anything to say, but I do have a few questions."

"Okay, we might be able to provide some answers for you. Shoot."

"First, what am I being charged with?"

"Nothing, as of now, but that can change quickly depending on your answers to *our* questions."

Lay shook his head and thought, 'I don't have any answers for you.'

"You're with the Secret Service, right?"

"We are."

"And your job is to protect the president, right?"

"We do; as well as other duties."

"So, my next question is, what in the world could you possibly want with me?"

"Well, along with guarding the president, the Secret Service also investigates terrorism and fraud. That's where you fit in the equation."

"I'm not a terrorist. And I haven't committed any fraud."

"We don't think you're a terrorist. But you and your friends have been very busy, Mr. Taylor."

"Busy doing what?"

"That's what we were hoping you could tell us."

"Like I said, I don't have anything to say."

"Okay, you don't want to talk, so we'll help you out. Here's what we know. Dating back about a year, we can place the same grey SUV with New York plates EDL-1997 registered to Kevin Little, at over 200 banks from D.C., Maryland, Virginia and all the way up as far north where we are now in Syracuse, N.Y."

As Agent Chambliss spoke, Lay noticed Agent Nowelle leaning forward in his chair staring directly at him. Up until this point, she was playing 'good cop', so he was wondering when and if the 'bad cop' act was going to come from Agent Nowelle.

Lay's attention to Agent Nowelle was disrupted when he vaguely heard Agent Chambliss say, "$750,000."

Lay said, "You mind repeating that?"

"Which part?"

"That number. What was that number, again?" Lay said.

"We have reports of you and your crew defrauding numerous banks with counterfeit checks totaling close to $750,000. And that's just coming from the institutions that filed reports. There are probably more. Did you hear me that time?"

Lay could tell she was annoyed at this point. "Yes, I heard you." 'Damn! $750,000?!? Did I take that much money?'

"Do you understand the severity of these allegations? That's a lot of money."

"I understand."

"So, what do you have to say for yourself, Mr. Taylor?"

"Nothing. What is there for me to say? You told me things I didn't know myself."

"Well, maybe you can tell us something that could help us help you." This came from Agent Nowelle, who finally decided to join the exchange.

"Help me, how?"

"If you gave us the person who you got the checks from, or showed us how they were being made, maybe we could do something for you."

"Do what for me? I don't need you to do anything for me."

"Where do the checks come from? Where is the information being taken from?"

Lay didn't respond.

"How do you get your hands on this information?"

Again, Lay remained silent. They hadn't asked any questions about Bobby or the rest of the team, so he assumed they only had surveillance on him and Kev. This fact gave Lay a feeling of relief.

If he went down alone, he knew Bobby would take care of him and his family so he wasn't too worried.

The questioning took a different turn. "When it came time for sentencing, we could put in a good word for you being cooperative," Agent Nowelle said.

Lay let out a little chuckle.

"Is there something funny, Mr. Taylor?" Agent Nowelle asked.

"I'm laughing because a minute ago she said I wasn't even being charged, but now *you* have me at sentencing."

"Oh, you're going down for this. Believe me. With the evidence we have against you, there's no getting around it. So, would you like to reconsider?" asked Agent Chambliss.

"Nah, I'm good," Lay replied.

The room fell silent as the two agents and Sgt. Calhoun sat watching him for what seemed like an eternity.

Finally, Lay broke the monotonous silence. "Can I ask a question? And I don't mean any disrespect by this, but if the police has all this information against someone, why do they insist on asking all these questions? I mean, you claim to have all the answers. What do you need from me? There's nothing I can tell you that would make you let me walk out of this door right now, so I don't see the point."

The agents and the sergeant looked confused and frustrated at the same time. When no one responded, Lay said, "If we're done, would it be possible for me to make my phone call now?"

This is when Sgt. Calhoun stood up. "I'll get you that call in a minute. Right now, you can go back to the cell."

Lay rose up and walked toward the hallway that led to the cell where Kev sat, totally stressed out. As he walked past the office where Cassandra sat, he peered through the open glass. Once again she gave him a look of contempt that he couldn't figure. He shook his head and continued to walk until he reached the cell.

Sergeant Calhoun unlocked the cell gate and Lay stepped in. He sat on the bench and listened for the sergeant's footsteps to fade down the hall before speaking.

Kev asked, "You good?"

"No, I'm not," Lay replied. "They know every fuckin' thing about us since last year! That's how far back their investigation went."

"Are you serious?"

"Does it look like I'm playing? Hell yeah, I'm serious."

"So, what did you tell them?"

"I didn't tell them shit." "What did *you* tell them, is a better question?"

Kev hesitated for a moment then said, "I just told them I had lost my job and was just doing this to try to make ends meet for the time being."

Lay looked at Kev like he had two heads. "Are you crazy?!? You just confirmed everything they thought to be accurate. You should've kept your mouth shut. With your statement and what your chick said, they can throw the fuckin' book at *my* black ass!"

"C'mon Lay, you know I would never snitch on you."

"I'm not saying you directly told on me, Kev. But don't you understand? By saying you were involved in any criminal activity corroborates her story and fucks us all?" "You're smarter than that. You gotta *think*, my nigga. If you *say* nothing, they *have* nothing. She made it look like the two of you were working for me. And your statement backs that shit up."

"Damn, Lay. My bad. I wasn't thinking."

Lavian lay down on the bench, closed his eyes and imagined the tongue-lashing Celina was going to give him. In a way, he didn't even want to make the phone call but he knew he had to. She had to be going crazy by now.

Kev sat on the floor with his back against the cell wall, crossed his arms on top of his knees and rested his head on his arms. After a few hours, Lay heard footsteps coming down the hall and sat up hoping it was some news about that phone call. Sgt. Calhoun opened the cell gate and told Kev to step out.

"Excuse me sir. Is that phone call gonna happen any time soon?" Lay asked.

"Yeah, he's first and then you'll go."

"Okay, thanks sarge."

Kev stepped out of the cell and walked down the hall to make his phone call as Lay sat down and waited for his return. Anxiety and apprehension filled his mind about the phone call he had to make to Celina.

He was anxious, because he wanted to know what the bail was going to be so she could post it; and apprehensive because he knew she was going to kill him for putting her through this shit. Five minutes passed. Ten minutes go by, then fifteen. Lay is wondering who the hell Kev could be talking to for this long.

After about twenty minutes, he heard footsteps coming down the hall again. 'It's about time,' he thought. Seconds later Kev and Sgt. Calhoun returned to relieve Lay from the four walls that contained him.

He was already at the gate as the sergeant said, "Your turn, Taylor."

On his way out, Lay asked Kev what took him so long. Kev shrugged his shoulders as if to say, 'I have no clue.' Lay brushed the response off, walked down the hall, and waited for Sgt. Calhoun to tell him which phone he could use.

He directed Lay to sit at a desk in the far corner of the office where he could have some privacy. Lay took a deep breath before picking up the receiver, and then dialed Celina's number. The phone rang six times before going to voicemail. 'I know this woman did not let this phone ring out. She *has* to be expecting me to call.'

Lay pressed the button, waited for the dial tone, and called again. This time Celina picked up on the second ring.

"Hello!" she said frantically.

"Hey baby," Lay said timidly.

"Oh my God, Lay. Are you alright? What happened? We were on the phone and you said were calling me back, and you never did. Then your phone started going straight to voicemail. I didn't know what to think. I was a wreck. I didn't know what happened to you."

Lay sat there with the phone to his ear and let her get it all out before trying to respond. "Babe, Babe, calm down, calm down. I'm okay. I'm good."

"So, what happened? Why did it take so long for you to call me? And please don't tell me what I think it is."

By this time Lay could hear the cracking in her voice.

Celina was about to cry, and that was something Lay promised he would never cause again. This made his next words even more difficult to say.

"Babe, I'm inside. I'm so sorry for leaving you again. I'm so sorry."

Celina sat quietly on the phone in disbelief as a tear formed in the corner of her chestnut brown eye.

She slid off the bed and onto the floor, shaking her head from side to side.

"Babe, are you there?" No answer. "Babe. Hello?" No response.

Celina had let the phone drop by her side. It hung limply from her hand while she cried silently. She wiped her tears after a few minutes and placed the phone to her ear to hear Lay pleading, "Babe, please answer me so I know you're alright."

Trying to conceal the pain in her voice as best she could, Celina said, "I'm okay, Lavian. What do you need me to do?"

'That's my girl,' Lay thought. "Hold on for a minute."

He turned to Sgt. Calhoun and asked, "Excuse me sir, do you have any idea what time we're gonna see the judge?"

"*You* won't see a judge tonight but your case will go before him and he will set a bail."

"Thank you. Babe?"

"Yes, Lavian?"

"Okay, they're probably going to set a bail for me tonight so I need you to look in your closet in my black suede Gucci loafer box. I don't know what the bail is going to be, but that should cover it. If not, then I'm gonna have to... nevermind. I'm not even gonna think like that."

Celina held the phone and waited for more instructions. "Who are you going to get to ride up here with you? I don't want you driving alone at night."

"I'll ask Sasha to ride with me."

"Okay, I guess that's it, Babe. They'll probably let me use the phone again after the judge sets bail. I'll let you know what to bring, then."

"Okay, Lavian. I understand."

"Okay, Babe. I gotta go now. You okay?"

"I'm fine."

"You sure?"

"Yes, Lavian. I'm sure."

"Alright. And, Babe, we're going to get through this, together. I promise you, okay?"

"Okay."

"I love you, Celina."

"I love you too, Lavian."

The two hung up. Lay walked back to the cell with his head hung low as he thought about how disappointed Celina was with him. He had let her down once again. No matter how many times she said she was okay, he knew she really wasn't, and that bothered him even more.

When he reached the cell, he lay on the bench and put his arm across his eyes to block out any possible light. He felt dark on the inside and that's all he wanted to see. Kev asked Lay if he was okay. Lay said yeah, but Kev could tell by his tone that he wasn't. He also knew it wasn't a good time to try and hold a conversation with Lay, so he reclined on the opposite bench and stared at the ceiling.

An hour or so passed and another officer came down the hall to the cell where Lay and Kev had fallen asleep. He told them their bail was set at $10,000 each and that they would be transported to the county jail in a little while. Lay asked if he could use the phone again so he could tell Celina how much money she needed to bring.

The officer told him he would be able to use the phone after they were processed into the county lockup.

Lay said, "Thank you, sir. What about the girl?"

"She doesn't have a bail," he replied.

When the officer walked down the hall out of earshot he asked Kev if he could cover his bail.

Kev said, "I got the ten, but I don't have much more than that."

"What are you doing with your money, Kev? You should have way more than that saved."

"I know, Lay. I try to save. That paper feels so good when it touches my hands. Then I see something I want and I just gotta spend it. Or I end up helping Mom Dukes out. You know how it is."

"I know how it goes. I do. Don't worry about it. I got you this time."

"Damn, for real Lay?"

"Yeah, my nigga. I'm not gonna leave you in here. You know I got you. Don't I always?"

"You do, bro. I can't front. You definitely do."

Kev reached out to shake Lay's hand and when Lay extended his, Kev grabbed it and drew him in for a hug. As the two men embraced it dawned on Lay why bail hadn't been set for Cassandra. That further confirmed the fact that she had snitched.

This gave him a disturbing feeling in his gut because in all the years he spent hustling, this was the first time anyone ever actually told on him. He tried to shake the feeling off and just relax until he was able to call Celina again. Thirty minutes later Lay, Kev, and Cassandra were transported to the Onondaga County Justice Center in three separate vehicles. The crazy part was Cassandra was actually free to go with a desk appearance ticket to return to court the following month. The only reason she couldn't leave was because she didn't have any money.

When they arrived, Kev and Lay were brought into the huge detention center and told to sit in a couple of chairs that were against a waist-high brick wall in a carpeted circle with two phones in the center. There was a TV hanging from the ceiling, playing of all things, COPS.

Two sheriff's deputies sat behind the desk that separated them from the carpeted circle by a large bricked wall that stood about chest high. After the two men were processed in the county system they were allowed to use the phones to make collect calls only. Lay dialed Celina's number and waited for her to pick up.

On the third ring she answered sounding wide awake, even though it was after midnight.

"Hello," the recording narrated, "You have a collect call from…, Lavian Taylor, an inmate at the Onondaga County Justice Center. To accept this call, press five, now. To block this and all future calls of this nature, press eight, now."

Celina immediately pressed five and waited for the call to connect.

"Hey Boo. How are you feeling?"

"I'm okay, Lavian."

She only used his government name when she was pissed.

"You sound wide awake. Did you get any sleep since we spoke last?"

"How could I, with all this going on?"

"I understand. But you're going to need some sleep to make the drive up here." "Did you get a hold of Sasha? Is she riding with you?"

"Yes. She's coming with me. She's just waiting for my call."

"Okay, good. My bail is $10,000, but I need you to bring twice that amount so I can bail Kev out too. It's where I-"

"I know where it is, Lavian."

"Okay, baby. Did you speak to Bobby?"

"Yes. I called him as soon as I hung up with you. He obviously told everyone else because they all called to check on me, which is another reason why I couldn't get any sleep if I tried."

"Well, that's family, Babe. They're just looking out for us."

"I understand. I'm not upset about that. It's just that I had to have the same conversation over and over with all your brothers. Then Yvette and Niecy called, and I had to do it again. I appreciate their concern but it was annoying after a while. I'm definitely going to have to explain to Sasha why

144

we're driving to Syracuse in the middle of the night. So, that's yet another time I'm going to have to relive this nightmare."

"I know, Babe. And I'm sorry for putting you through all of this. I never meant to leave you again. I promise I'm going to make it right. I promise."

"And how are you supposed to do that?"

He really didn't have an answer, but before Lay could think of something to say, Celina abruptly said, "It doesn't matter at this point, Lavian. Besides, Sasha's waiting for me. We have a long drive."

"Okay baby. I'll see you when you get here."

"Okay."

Before he could thank her, Celina hung up the phone. 'Damn. I really fucked up. She hasn't been this mad at me in a long time,' he thought.

Lay hung his head as he looked at the phone, and then hung it up. He walked to the side of the circle where Kev was sitting, sat two chairs away from him and told him Celina was on her way with the bail.

"Thanks again, bro," Kev said.

"Don't worry about it." Lay folded his arms and sat back in the chair to try and get comfortable while he waited for Celina to arrive.

He looked up at the TV. A Pizza Hut commercial went off only to reveal that COPS was still on. Lay hated that show, so he closed his eyes and tried to focus on how he was going to adjust to this new situation. His entire life just got turned upside down. Little did he know shit was about to get even thicker.

He now had an open charge, so that was an automatic violation of his parole. Although Lay was on inactive reporting status he still had to notify his P.O. about this arrest. More importantly, the dilemma with Celina weighed on his brain heavily and he needed to figure out a way to make things right with her.

'But fuck all that. The motherfuckin' United States Secret Service came to see me! Me, the little black boy from 139th Street.' He couldn't believe it, but it had definitely happened. That shit had Lay's mind racing. They had been watching him for over a year and had built a federal case against him and his crew. He wondered if they knew about Bobby and the others. 'They had to. If they were on me, they had to see me meet with Bobby.'

Lay got a hollow feeling in the pit of his stomach as he imagined his whole team being taken down because of him, even though he didn't do anything to make himself hot. He stood up, walked to the other side of the circle, put his hands on the wall and stared at the floor. The severity of the whole situation finally hit him.

'If they knew anything about Bobby and the others,' he thought 'they would've asked me about them. Maybe they *didn't* know about the rest of us. They can't.' Lay's mind began to relax a little as he found some comfort in this rationale. He pushed off from the wall and slowly walked back to his seat. Kev had dozed off.

Lay didn't know how Kev could have possibly fallen asleep because it was so cold in there. He sat down and once again looked at the TV in disgust. After a few minutes, his eyes drifted back to the screen, but his mind was a million miles away. He thought of Celina again and hoped she and Sasha would be okay driving up there in the middle of the night. 'My baby, Celina. I have a damn good woman.' Those thoughts comforted him as fatigue overcame him despite the cold, and he slowly drifted off into a light sleep, as well.

Meanwhile, Celina and Sasha snaked along the highways of New York State in the dead of night. Celina drove and Sasha fell asleep after a couple of hours. This gave Celina time to think about the entire situation. She loved Lay dearly, but at the same time didn't know if she was cut out for all this extra madness he'd heaped onto her plate.

And although he provided her with an extremely comfortable lifestyle, it didn't overshadow the mayhem she now faced. Besides, Celina had a promising career in real estate and was very capable of holding her own in this world without a man. Everything Lay brought to the table was an added bonus and she treated that luxury as just that-; a luxury.

'Hmph, I don't need this shit in my life', she thought. There was no way she was going to leave him stuck in jail, but there was a lot to be considered once he was out. She had some serious pros and cons to weigh.

Before she knew it, Celina had approached the Syracuse exit and made her way off the interstate.

She woke Sasha up so she could read the MapQuest directions and guide her to the Justice Center. It was exactly nine-thirty eight when the two ladies entered the building. The sun was shining brightly, and a new day of business had begun for the good people of Syracuse. 'I should be just getting to the office to start my day, but instead I'm all the way in East Bubblefuck, New York, doing this dumb shit,' Celina thought as she approached the deputy sitting behind the desk.

Off to the side, she noticed a row of four chairs, and a woman sitting in the first seat on the far end.

Sasha sat at the other end of the row while Celina handled the business at the desk.

"Good morning officer. How are you? I'm here to post bails for Lavian Taylor and Kevin Little."

"Good morning ma'am. What is your name and relationship to the inmates?"

"My name is Celina Barnett. I'm Lavian Taylor's fiancé."

The deputy looked at her left hand and noticed that Celina didn't have a ring on her finger.

She said, "I'm not wearing it today," before the deputy attempted to make the inquiry.

He turned his attention to the computer. After a few keystrokes, he came back to Celina and said, "Their bails are set at $10,000 each."

"That's fine."

"That's fine?" he asked, not trying to mask his cynicism even a little bit.

"Yes, it is." Celina reached into her Louis Vuitton Damier Speedy and pulled out two stacks of $100 bills wrapped neatly in paper bands labeled $10,000 on each of them.

"That's a lot of money for you to be carrying around ma'am. Can you account for that large sum?"

"I sure can."

Anticipating some resistance, Celina made a stop at Chase Bank before going to the courthouse. She didn't hesitate to withdraw that chunk from her savings because she knew Lay would replace it as soon as he got out. Celina reached into her bag once more and presented the bank receipt with the date, time, and location of the withdrawal.

After examining the receipt he asked, "You live here in Syracuse?"

"No."

He looked the paper over once more and said, "Give me a second."

He stepped from behind the desk and walked through an office door that was located on the right. Celina turned to look at Sasha and shook her head in disgust as the officer returned with a sergeant.

"Ms. Barnett?"

"Yes?"

"I see you're here to post bail for a Lavian Taylor and Kevin Little."

"Yes. Yes, I am. Is everything alright?"

"It certainly seems that way. Deputy Kent will process everything and you'll be on your way."

Celina never bothered to notice what his name was. She was just so ready to get this over and done.

"Thank you, sir."

"You're quite welcome."

The sergeant returned to his office and Deputy Kent proceeded to count the $20,000. With one Louis Vuitton driving glove already off, Celina pulled off each finger of the other glove one by one without taking her eyes off the deputy while he counted.

She then stood there with her arms folded until he finished.

"How long will it take for them to be released?"

"It's early, so it shouldn't be more than a couple of hours.

Deputy Kent turned back to the computer, typed some more, then grabbed Celina's receipt from the printer. As she signed, he placed the money in a safe that was located in the sergeant's office.

Now, the wait begins. Celina sat down next to Sasha crossing one leg over the other. She had put on a brave front up to this point but inside she was crumbling. Now that she knew her man was about to be released, Celina breathed a sigh of relief. Unable to hold it in any longer, she rested her head on Sasha's shoulder as a tear formed in the corner of her eye and slowly made its way down her cheek.

Sasha put one arm around her friend and rocked back and forth in the hard plastic chairs where they both sat. The woman sitting at the end of the row looked at Celina and Sasha and dropped her gaze down.

It seemed like forever, but around two and half hours later Lay and Kev stepped from behind the heavy electric sliding door located behind the desk where Deputy Kent sat.

Two deputies escorted them around to the front of the desk where they signed their release papers and the notices to appear in court. In those couple of hours Celina and Sasha waited, they had each dozed off. They were awakened when the woman sitting at the end of the row leapt out of her seat and headed straight to the desk towards Lay and Kev.

The deputies told her to stand back until they were finished signing their paperwork.

Celina looked on in astonishment as Sasha whispered, "Who the hell is this chick?"

"I don't know, but she's definitely happy to see one of them."

When the forms were signed Lay turned and walked in Celina's direction while the woman gave Kev the biggest hug and kiss. "Well, she obviously knows Kev," Sasha noted.

Lay knelt in front of Celina, took her hands in his and kissed them. "I thank you so much for being my queen, my rock. I love you so much."

Celina was a little embarrassed, as passersby stared at Lay down on one knee, but she didn't care. She was just happy he was out. He stood up, threw his arms around Celina and squeezed her tightly.

She pressed her face against his chest and the tears began to fall again.

"I am so sorry, Boo. I promise I will make it up to you."

Lay kissed Celina repeatedly on her lips, simultaneously tasting the salt from her tears and wiping them from her eyes. Between kisses he whispered the words, "Please forgive me."

After a few minutes into Lay's apologies Sasha asked, "Can we please get out of here?"

Pulling away from Lay, Celina said, "Yes, I forgive you. Now, let's go Babe, please."

The five of them stepped out into the crisp autumn air and walked to Celina's car. During the walk, Kev introduced the ladies.

"Celina, Sasha, this is my girl, Cassandra."

"Nice to meet you," Cassandra said.

"Nice to meet you as well," Celina responded.

Sasha remained silently side-eyed. There was something she didn't like about Cassandra, and she chose not to hide it; not even a little bit.

Kev and Cassandra needed a ride to pick up his truck from the station where they'd first been transported after their arrests. They climbed into Celina's car as Lay got behind the wheel to drive. He had no idea how to get to the station so he asked for directions.

There was some underlying tension in the air, so for the most part they rode in silence. When they reached the station Kev and Cassandra got out and he leaned into the window to kiss Celina on the cheek.

"Thanks for coming all the way up here, sis. Love you for that."

"No problem, Kev. You know I wasn't leaving y'all in there."

He and Cassandra walked inside the station as Lay pulled out of the parking lot. Celina's window wasn't halfway up before Sasha yelled,

"What the fuck was wrong with that bitch?!? Her energy was so stank! I don't like chicks like that. Mad for no reason. Her attitude was just, yucky."

"I don't know about all that, Sasha, but it was kind of rude of her not to say thank you for getting her man out of jail."

Lay just shook his head. They had no idea what kind of disposition Cassandra had. Celina also had no idea it was because of Cassandra their asses were in the slammer in the first place. She was going to flip when he told her. Lay knew this so he waited until they were on their way home to reveal that info.

Now that it was just the three of them in the car Lay began to share his account of what actually happened. Celina was tired from being up all night but she was still amped to hear what caused all of this bullshit, and her body wouldn't let her sleep.

When Lay reached the point about Cassandra snitching, Sasha leaned forward excitedly, grabbed the back of Celina's seat and yelled, "I knew it! I knew it was something about that no-good bitch!"

Celina just stared at Lay in disbelief.

"So, the whole time I was up there bailing you out, she sat on the side and didn't say a word to me. Then we end up giving this woman a ride. You knew she put you in jail and you neglected to tell me?"

"Because I didn't want you to be more upset than you already are."

"Yeah, thanks for thinking of me, but you can save that, Lavian!" "Are you sleeping with her?!?"

"Me?!? Babe, are you crazy? Do you really think I would do something like that? That's Kev's girl."

"I know you Lavian. You're kind-hearted even when you shouldn't be. But I also know you wouldn't tolerate snitching. Am I right?"

"You're absolutely right."

"So why didn't you tell me what she did, Lay?!? You must have some soft spot for her!"

Celina was beyond annoyed and upset at this point. Tears were forming in the corners of her eyes, and she clenched her fists as if she were ready to punch Lay while he was driving. Celina wasn't the type to fight at the drop of a dime like Sasha, but if pushed she would definitely get it popping. Although out-weighed, and probably out-classed as far as fighting goes, she badly wanted to get her hands on Cassandra.

"Babe, calm down for a minute. Did you forget that Kev was in the car, too? He needed a ride back to the station. I couldn't leave him out here because of her."

"I know you couldn't leave Kev, but you could've left *her* ass!"

"But *he* wasn't gonna leave her, Babe. C'mon. You know better than that."

"So basically he chose a bitch that put him in jail over you? Is that what you're telling me?"

That last question struck a chord with Lay.

Those thoughts had crossed his mind a few times in the past few weeks, but he dare not share that with Celina.

"Never that. Kev wouldn't go against me for no one," he replied.

"You sure about that, Lay?" Sasha finally chimed in. "Hmph, I'm glad you *didn't* tell me that bitch snitched because I would've whipped her stankin' ass!"

"My point exactly. That's the other reason I didn't say shit until they were out of the car. I knew your violent ass was coming."

"Shut up, Lay," Sasha retorted. "You know I'm right, this time, though. That bitch needs her ass beat!"

Celina had had enough of this conversation. She was emotionally and physically drained. She pulled the sun visor down to look in the mirror and noticed the puffiness under her eyes. Flipping the visor up, she sat back, threw her jacket over her shoulders and closed her eyes.

Lay reached under her jacket, grabbed her hand, and held it as he drove. This very small gesture comforted Celina. She knew Lay loved her and was always trying to make sure she was okay in every situation. The warmth of his hand was soothing, and after being awake for almost twenty-four hours, Celina finally drifted off to sleep.

Lay turned around to see if Sasha was still awake. She was looking out of the window, deep in her own thoughts.

"Thanks Sash," he said, breaking the silence.

"Huh?"

"Thanks for riding with my baby."

"Oh. Don't worry about it. You know that's my girl."

"I know, but I appreciate you."

"Try not to stress her out so much. That's how you can thank me."

"Trust me Sash. This was not in the plans."

"I know, but you better make it right with her. She's a good woman."

"You're right, sis. I will." Lay thought hard and heavy on the drive home how exactly he was going to make that happen. He had no idea at the time but it was a mission he was determined to fulfill.

Upon returning home, Lay called Bobby and the team to inform them of his ordeal with the United States Secret Service and Syracuse's finest. Although it was a serious predicament, they knew Lay would hold up under the pressure. Malcolm was furious about Cassandra snitching and wanted to take care of her *and* Kev but Bobby strongly advised against it.

Violence was always a last resort and only engaged if absolutely necessary. Malcolm didn't care too much for Sylvia's, but the three of them agreed to meet there the next morning to discuss the latest situation. While Lay was on the phone with Bobby and Malcolm, Celina got in the shower to wash off the day's events.

She had slept almost the whole ride back, awakening only when they dropped Sasha off at her house. Even then she remained silent until they reached Lay's apartment.

As soon as he hung up the phone, Lay got undressed and joined Celina in the shower. He knew she was still upset and didn't know if she might protest but he made the attempt anyway.

When he pulled the curtain back, Celina turned and glanced at him but continued showering like he wasn't there. Lay stepped close to her wrapping one arm around Celina's waist. With his other hand, he moved Celina's hair to the side and began gently trailing kisses down the back of her neck repeatedly to her shoulder and back up to her ear.

"I'm so sorry, baby," he whispered. "I'm so, so, sorry."

Without uttering a word, Celina turned to Lay, buried her face in his chest and wept like a baby. Her arms fell to her sides, and she dropped her wash cloth onto the shower floor.

He could feel Celina's anguish with every sob and whimper, and did his best to console her. Lay held Celina in the shower until she got herself together and bathed her from head to toe. When he was done, she stepped out of the shower, dried off and got ready for bed. Lay did exactly the same thing, crawling into bed next to Celina when he was done. He held her snugly in his arms until they both drifted off to sleep.

Celina woke up before Lay the next morning and decided to work from home that day. She saw a little puffiness lingering around under her eyes in the bathroom mirror and didn't want to go into the office that way.

She pulled one of Lay's wife beaters from his drawer, and grabbed a pair of boy shorts from her own.

She put them on and went into the kitchen to make some coffee. Celina sat on a barstool with her leg folded beneath her, waiting for the coffeemaker to do its job. By this time Lay had awakened, brushed his teeth and joined her in the kitchen. The two greeted each other briefly and he left to shower before meeting Bobby and Malcolm in the city.

Bobby felt that the whole team needed to hear the news about Lay's mishap first-hand, so Sean, Tony, and Stacey were all present at the breakfast meeting. Bobby cautioned everyone about suspicious vehicles and to always be aware of their surroundings because things had definitely changed. Their activity had received unwanted attention from the big boys, and that was nothing to play with.

Sean, being his typical self, said, "Man, fuck them motherfuckas! We getting so much money, we can *pay* them to leave us alone."

Bobby rarely got upset but he slammed his fist down on the table, startling everyone, and said, "I'm not fuckin' playing, Sean! This is some serious shit! They could be on all of us as we speak. You may not value your freedom, but I value mine. We don't know what's going on with their investigation so be careful out there."

"It's either that, or we shut everything down until we can figure out what's going on."

Murmurs of "no's" and "we don't want that's" sounded from the group.

"Okay then. Be on your P's and Q's and we'll see how things play out."

Realizing the severity of the situation, the team finished their meals in subdued silence for the most part. When they were done, everyone left except for Bobby, Malcolm, and Lay.

The three of them discussed what their next moves were going to be after leaving Sylvia's.

"I'm going to take some personal time for myself," Lay said, "at least for a couple of days."

"You do that," replied Malcolm.

Lay excused himself from the table, stood up, dug in his pocket and dropped $200 on the table for the check. He felt it was his fault the meeting had to be called in the first place. The least he could do was pay the bill.

After breakfast, Lay drove to Celina's office to surprise her. He stopped to pick up some flowers thinking that might possibly cheer her up. When he arrived, he was told that Celina had called out sick. 'Damn,' he thought. 'My baby must really be fucked up. She never misses days from work.'

Immediately he called her cell phone and got no answer. He then called the house phone and got the same outcome. Lay's mind started racing.

"Where the hell are you?" he said out loud.

He threw the flowers in the back seat and raced home to check on Celina.

Meanwhile, Bobby and Malcolm went to the barbershop after breakfast. Stew was there waiting with an envelope containing copies of checks from new banks for the team to hit. Malcolm took a seat in the barber's chair while Bobby and Stew remained outside in the Denali to discuss the contents of the envelope.

When they were done, Stew then began asking Bobby questions that he had never asked before. This made him a little uneasy so he offered very vague answers. Stew noticed how uncomfortable Bobby was and ended the conversation. He gave him some dap, exited the vehicle and assured Bobby he would check him later. Bobby closed the envelope, placed it in the center console and went inside the shop. He gave Malcolm a head nod to indicate everything was good.

A smile flashed across Malcolm's dark brown face. Usually Bobby would have had the same reaction, but that wasn't the case this time.

Malcolm knew his brother, and he knew something transpired when he met with Stew. Or maybe Lay's situation was starting to sink in. Either way, Bobby's demeanor was a little off. He had switched from normal to having a deeply concerned expression on his face. One way or another Malcolm was going to get to the bottom of it.

When Lay made it back home he found Celina under the covers sound asleep. He was tempted to wake her, but decided against it. If she didn't go to work or answer the phone, she must have really been tired. Instead he sat on his side of the bed and rubbed the back of Celina's head.

"Yesterday must've really done a number on you," he whispered.

The gentle stroke of his hand made her stir, but not enough to be awakened. Celina switched positions but remained asleep. Lay quietly stood up and left the bedroom so she could continue to rest. He walked into the living room, placed her flowers into a vase, and called Milton Chase, his lawyer, to discuss his newly found acquaintance with the U.S. Secret Service. Mr. Chase assured him he would be okay, and that he could easily get them to drop the charges to a state-level matter. Lay's mind was at ease for the moment, but he wouldn't believe it until it was in writing or guaranteed in court.

After hanging up with his attorney Lay turned on the TV and watched some daytime bullshit until it started watching him. He was awakened by the faint sound of Celina moaning in the next room. He went into the bedroom only to find an empty bed. When he moved closer he realized the moans were coming from the master bathroom.

He opened the door to find Celina kneeling on the floor holding her abdomen with her right hand and gripping the side of the vanity for support with her left. Celina heaved once more. She abandoned the vanity, placed both hands on the toilet seat and vomited what looked like water into the open hole.

Lay stepped in and rubbed her back as she convulsed one more time but nothing came out.

"Damn baby. Are you okay?"

Celina turned and looked at Lay as if to say, 'does it look like I'm okay, genius?' Instead she turned her face back to the toilet and waited for the next round of God knows what to be ejected from her stomach.

When it appeared she was all done, Lay helped Celina to her feet. She threw water on her face and began brushing her teeth as Lay rubbed her back. Noticing how good her ass looked in the boy-shorts made him feel a little frisky, so he let his hand drift all the way down to the bottom of her butt cheek.

As soon as he did, Celina paused from brushing her teeth, looked in the mirror and gave Lay a death-stare, until he moved his hand up to her back. She rolled her eyes for what seemed like an entire sixty seconds, and resumed brushing. When she finished, Celina wiped her mouth and left Lay standing in the bathroom like he had never been there. He leaned on the sink with both hands, looked in the mirror and thought, 'negro, you fucked up big time.'

Celina sat on the sectional with her laptop and tried to get some work done. After a few minutes, Lay sat next to her and tried to muster up the courage for a conversation. Still not acknowledging his presence, she searched for properties on the laptop.

Lay looked down at a glass of water that sat by her feet. He reluctantly asked, "Did you eat some bad food, baby?"

"No. I only drank a cup of coffee after you left."

"Coffee made you sick like that?"

"No. I don't think it was the coffee."

"You think it's something worse? You wanna go to the ER?"

Annoyed by the interrogation, Celina finally said, "I'm pregnant, Lavian."

"Wait... what? Are you sure?"

"Yes, I'm sure." "I took two tests and they both came back positive. I was sick like this a few days ago but I didn't know what it was at first. I had an appointment for my gynecologist yesterday, but I was in Syracuse, thanks to you and all this mess. I took another one after I threw up this morning, and it was positive as well. It's in the guest bathroom garbage can. You can see for yourself."

Lay took the laptop from Celina, sat it beside her, got down on one knee and kissed her hands. His reaction was priceless.

"Damn, baby. I'm so happy."

He looked up at Celina in tme to notice tears beginning to well in the corners of her eyes.

"I'm not keeping it, Lavian."

He unclasped his hands from around hers.

"What do you mean, you're not keeping it? Why wouldn't you keep our baby?"

Seeing the confusion and disappointment on his face, Celina's anger began to subside. She wiped away her tears and grabbed Lay's hands.

"There's nothing in the world I would love more than to be the woman to give you your first child. When I took the first two tests I was ecstatic. That's when I made my appointment for the GYN because I wanted to be sure. But when you got locked up…" Her voice trailed off. "I can't lie. I wished they were negative. I can't have this baby by myself, Lay. I *won't* have it by myself."

"But you won't have to. We're gonna beat this thing, Babe. You and me, together. We'll get through it. I know we will."

"You can't guarantee that Lavian, and you know it."

No matter how much he wanted to believe the opposite, he knew she was right. There was no way his freedom was secure at this point.

"You're right, Babe. I'm sorry. I was being selfish and thinking only of myself. At this point I can't guarantee my freedom. And to put that extra burden on you would be dead wrong on my part. I won't put any pressure on you. I'll support whatever decision you make."

It killed him inside to say those words, but he had put Celina through enough already.

Celina gazed into Lay's eyes and questioned how she could love him so much. He stood up, and pulled Celina from the couch so he could give her a proper hug. Kissing her gently on the lips, Lay asked, "Are you hungry? Do you think your stomach can hold any food down?"

"If I eat anything it has to be something light."

"You name it, you got it. Your wish is my command."

"I don't want you to go out. Stay in here with me. Let's just order something."

"Will do," said Lay. The two ordered takeout and spent the evening in, enjoying each other's company.

Lay spent the next few days catering to Celina's every whim as she worked from his house and hardly went outside except for an occasional ride with him to the store. To get her out of the house, he planned a day at the spa. The next day he made an appointment for her hair. The day after, he scheduled mani-pedis for the two of them and chauffeured her to every single session. Every day they ate breakfast lunch and dinner together by way of delivery or dining out.

Celina didn't have to lift a finger. 'If having his baby is going to get me all of this on a daily basis, I may have to reconsider,' she joked. But she knew it was just wishful thinking because the reality had settled in very quickly.

While Lay was busy taking care of home, Bobby still had a team to look after. He wore the crown and therefore bore the responsibility of ensuring everyone's well-being. Although his last exchange with Stew was shaky, Bobby went against his gut and continued to do business with him until something else proved to be more fruitful. He sent his team out to several states, and into various financial institutions in quest of the almighty dollar-; those small pieces of paper that drew them in like a moth to a flame. It was the allure of monetary gain that made one overlook the perils that lurked ahead.

Sean headed back to Connecticut, where he had prior success. Tony ventured out to the South Jersey-Philly area. Malcolm, Bobby and Stacey remained close to home while Lay sat at home in Fort Lee, New Jersey, and drove Celina crazy. All the attention and pampering was cute at first, but Lay began plucking at her every nerve after a while. Besides, she was getting stir-crazy, being cooped up in the house all day, so she decided to go back to work in the office.

With Celina gone all day, and the rest of the team out working, Lay became restless. He sent flowers every other day and randomly popped up at her job, to take her to lunch.

One evening, she sat him down and said, "I understand that you're sorry and I recognize the effort you're putting in to make amends, but you're smothering me, Babe." "I know you mean well, but please don't send any more flowers to my job. My desk looks like The Brooklyn Botanic Garden."

She paused and smiled to soften what she was saying. "And we don't have to eat out every night. I do remember how to cook, Lay."

"Are you sure, Babe? I was just trying to make you smile every d-..."

"Lay."

"Yes?"

"I'm smiling."

"Okay, good. So am I out of the doghouse?"

"You were never in any doghouse, Lay."

"You know what I mean. Are you gonna stop being stingy?"

Celina shook her head, looked to the ceiling and replied, "Yes, Babe. I'll stop being stingy."

Lay slid off the couch onto his knees, pulled Celina's Fendi pumps off and kissed her perfectly manicured toes.

"I can't stand you, you know that, right?"

Ignoring her, Lay continued to kiss her feet until Celina protested.

"Get your ass up off the floor! You don't have the good sense God gave you."

Rising from the floor, Lay replied, "I was smart enough to get your fine ass back, wasn't I?"

"That wasn't because you were smart. It was because I still loved your crazy ass."

"Whatever it was, I got you back, and that's all that matters."

"Anyway, we both know who the intelligent one is in this relationship."

"Yeah, me," Lay said as he plopped his body down on the couch and crossed his legs on the ottoman.

"I wanted you to get me a glass of cranberry juice before you sat down, Babe."

"I thought you were tired of me waiting on you hand and foot. I'm off duty, lady."

"Oh, really?"

"Yes. You said you wanted me to chill out on the Benson shit. Be careful what you ask for."

"You're right. I did say that."

Celina reached into her purse to retrieve her cell phone while Lay flipped channels on the TV remote. A few seconds later, the phone on the wall in the kitchen rang. Lay ignored it as he sat forward to pay closer attention to the TV screen.

"Aren't you going to answer the phone?"

"No. You get more calls here than I do."

"Yes, but it's your house, Mister."

Realizing Celina wasn't going to answer the phone he got up and walked into the kitchen carrying the remote with him so she wouldn't be able to switch the channel. Snatching the receiver off the wall, Lay said,

"Hello."

"Hello handsome. Since you're in the kitchen you can bring me that cranberry juice. Now, who's smarter than whom?"

Without uttering a word, Lay hung up the phone, removed the juice from the refrigerator and filled a wine glass.

Lay couldn't help but crack a defeated smile as he sat the glass on a coaster on the end table. "You definitely got me with that one, with your sneaky ass."

"What ever are you talking about, Mr. Taylor?"

Lay sat on the couch and Celina draped her legs over his thighs. She knew he wouldn't be able to resist so she asked, "Could you rub my feet, Babe?"

"I would, but I'm off duty."

Celina lifted her foot up and put her big toe under Lay's chin and begged, "Please, Babe? I've been working hard all day."

"You don't play fair."

Celina pouted like a spoiled two-year old as Lay began to rub her pretty little feet. She reclined on the arm of the sofa, reached for her glass of cranberry juice, and sipped as she smiled, 'Got him again.'

The next morning, Celina went to work leaving Lay at home to fend for him self. With the team off earning and Celina back to work, he would have to find something to occupy his time. There was only but so much daytime television and video games he could tolerate. He went downstairs to the gym for about an hour, came back, showered and got dressed. It took him thirty minutes just to select an outfit.

"This house is driving me nuts. I gotta get outta here," he said aloud.

Donned in black Sean John jeans, a white Versace crew neck sweater, black Mauri sneakers, and a black Pelle Pelle leather baseball jacket, Lay finally left the house. Where he was headed he had no idea. It was almost lunchtime so he hopped into the car and made his way to The Crab House in Edgewater.

As the hostess seated him he scanned the establishment to acclimate his surroundings. Along the wall were a row of tables that were scarcely occupied by various patrons. He noticed a familiar face seated at the very first table. There she was, the lovely Monique Peele, one of Lay's old flames. She worked as a personal assistant to Mr. Dalvin from the group, Jodeci.

Being the typical man that he was, Lay's mind immediately drifted off to all of the sexual escapades they'd shared together. There were some steamy, passionate ones and some wild adventurous ones as well. She was dining with a gentleman so he dare not impose on their meal. Lay held the menu up to his face as if he was trying to hide, but couldn't really concentrate because his mind was clouded by all the reminiscing that was going on.

Sex with Monique was the bomb! She was definitely in his top five. 'You need to get your life together,' he thought.

In an attempt to do just that, he finally decided on the Chilean sea bass with grilled asparagus and garlic mashed potatoes.

When he placed the menu down on the table, Lay was shocked to see Monique standing before him in a black knee-length pencil skirt that hugged every voluptuous curve. The Louboutin pumps she wore complimented her shapely calves that she'd neglected to shave for a couple of days, so the stubble was on display for all to see. That didn't bother him at all because he loved every inch of her body, and Monique had a pair of the sexiest legs Lay had ever seen. Her white blouse with black microdots covered her ample 36DDD's. The sleeves were mid-forearm length and revealed a presidential Rolex that looked exactly like the one Lay had bought for Celina.

"Hello Mr. Taylor. How have you been? And an even better question is *where* have you been? You seemed to have vanished from the face of the earth."

Lay couldn't believe Monique was standing in front of him within arms reach, looking as gorgeous as ever. He hadn't realized it but his bottom lip was hanging, revealing his straight semi-white teeth.

Snapping out of his mini-daze, Lay replied, "I've been better, but I'm okay now that I'm looking at all of *you*. How have *you* been?"

"Do I have to remind you how to greet a lady, Lavian? Where are your manners?"

Lay pushed his chair back and stepped around the table so he could give Monique a hug. Her body was so soft, and she smelled fantastic.

Monique's breasts pressed against his torso and excited Lay a little too much, so he released her from the embrace.

"You look well, Mister."

"And you look even better than I remember. What have you been up to?"

"Well, after Jodeci I got my Bachelor's in Communications from N.Y.U. while interning at Universal. When I graduated, they hired me as an A&R and I've been there ever since."

"Do you like it?"

"It's okay. It pays the bills so I can't complain. But you know a sister is always looking to advance."

A light bulb went off in Lay's head. "You probably come across a lot of the starving artist types, right?"

"I have. Some of them have their shit together and some don't. Why?"

"I might have a way for you to make some money on the side, if you're interested."

"I'm not afraid of a little side hustle, Lay, but you know I don't mess with your line of work."

"It's a totally different line, and a totally different me."

"I hope some things are still the same."

"You're so nasty, girl."

"And you loved every bit of it."

"I did."

In the not-so-far back of his mind he knew he *still* did. "I don't want to be rude to your date but I would like to discuss this further, Ms. Peele. Is that possible?"

"Umm, I'm not on a date. It's a business lunch. And yes, you can meet me at my office and we'll continue it then. I have to admit, I'm intrigued."

Monique turned to walk away so she could retrieve a business card from her purse. Lay didn't take his eyes off her body as he watched her take every single step. Even her *walk* was sexy as hell!

Monique returned with her card and said, "It was nice to see you Mr. Taylor. Make sure you use that card."

Lay accepted the card and replied, "Likewise." He stood up again to give Monique another hug.

As he released, he held on to her left hand so he could kiss it. "Nice watch, by the way. I bought my girl the same one."

"Oh, that's so cute. But mine is platinum. Step your game up, Chief. Talk to you soon. Toodles."

Monique returned to her table to resume her lunch.

'Did this motherfucka just try to play me? How the hell does she know the watch I bought Celina wasn't platinum?'

That last statement almost gave Lay an attitude. She just shit on both his and Celina's watches, put together.

By this time, the waitress had come to take his order, and he spent the rest of the lunch thinking of how he was going to utilize Monique in his operation. The day had proven to be productive after all. 'Monique Peele. It was indeed good to see her again,' he thought, while staring down at her card. Only time would eventually tell *how* productive.

An Unintentional Indecent Proposal

The morning of November 13th started like any other normal autumn day for the team. It was a Wednesday, and Bobby was at Jimbo's on 145th and Lenox Avenue waiting for everyone to pick up their envelopes. He ordered three eggs sunny side up, home fries and turkey bacon. He sipped occasionally from a large plastic cup of orange juice that sat next to a cup of coffee while he waited for his food to be cooked. Malcolm was the first to arrive with about six women in a minivan he had rented.

He headed to Bobby's table all the way in the back, thinking about how it always seemed to be available whenever Bobby decided to meet there. Malcolm made small talk, grabbed his envelope and made his exit. Next, Tony and Sean entered almost simultaneously. By this time, Bobby's food had arrived and he began to eat.

Tony and Sean only sat across from him long enough to grab their envelopes. Sean, in typical fashion, snatched a piece of Bobby's turkey bacon off the plate before he dashed out of the door. Disgusted, Bobby set his silverware down and pushed the plate away. A few minutes later Lay pulled up and was getting out of the car when Bobby stepped outside.

"Whatchu know good, Lay? You ready to come out of retirement?"

"Nigga, I *never* retired, but I figured out a way to continue getting some bread if you're willing to help me."

"Of course, bro. What is it? Talk to me."

"You remember Monique that I used to fuck with?"

"Monique, Monique, Monique, from down...."

"Yeah, *that* Monique."

"I remember. What about her?"

"I ran into her last week at The Crab House. We chopped it up for a few, and I figured I could use her to get me a few girls to go out. If you wouldn't mind splitting the profit with me, I could continue to earn without going out myself. I'll share the expenses with you and we'll split the rest. Whatchu think?"

"Shit nigga, I don't care. The more chicks that go out, the better it is for us. Hell yeah! Let's do it. When is she gonna be ready?"

"I haven't finalized everything yet. We're supposed to meet at her office this week to get her on board, officially."

"Okay. Well, you know the drill. When she's ready, just shoot those names to me and you'll be back in business."

"Bet."

"What you about to do?"

"I just came across the bridge to talk to you about this. I ain't doin' shit."

"Ride with me to drop this work off to Stacey. She's going out with my white chick today."

"Okay, cool."

Lay parked his car in Bobby's spot and the two men hopped into the Benz and rode down to Stacey's. When they were five minutes away Bobby called Stacey so she would be downstairs when he got there.

Stacey was in front of her building when they pulled up. Bobby got out of the car, gave her a hug, kissed her on the cheek and slipped an envelope full of checks into Stacey's Louis Vuitton Speedy bag all in the same motion. Bobby asked if Maureen was in place and she responded affirmatively.

"Okay baby. Go do your thing. Make me proud."

"Shit, fuck proud. I'm gonna make you some money!"

"Okay, well get to it, then."

Bobby turned to walk back to the driver's side of the car. Stacey approached the passenger side, so Lay let the window down.

"Hey Lay. How you been with your chocolate self?"

He blushed a little. Lay smiled and replied, "I've been okay, Stace. What's up with you?"

"I'm chillin. About to go make my captain richer than he was yesterday."

"You do that. And be careful out there."

"Shiit. *They* better be careful. I don't play no games when I'm doin my thing. You know that."

"Oh, I know."

Stacey leaned into the window and gave Lay a kiss on the cheek, then turned to walk away.

"Hit me when you're on your way back," Bobby yelled out of Lay's window. Stacey threw up the peace sign and kept walking to her truck.

Bobby and Lay spent the rest of the day riding around and killing time until Stacey called. In the midst of that they stopped at Staples to restock on some necessary supplies. A few hours later, she hit Bobby's phone and instructed him to meet her at Ottomanelli's on the eastside. They were already on the eastside but further downtown so it took only a few minutes to get there. When the two men walked in, Stacey was enjoying a Caesar salad topped with grilled shrimp and a chilled glass of Riesling.

"Are you ordering something?"

"I'll have the same thing you're having," Bobby said.

"I'll eat when I get home," Lay responded.

"How was it today? Everything go smooth?" Bobby asked.

"Everything went great, except at one spot Maureen said they acted a little funny so she tore the check up when she came out and we just started using the other ones. All of those popped like clockwork."

"Did you see her tear the check up," Bobby asked?

"Yes. She ripped it up as she was walking back to the car and threw it in the garbage. I saw her."

"Okay, good. So how did we do?"

Having already taken her cut, Stacey said, "See for your self," as she passed Bobby two stacks of hundreds in the amount of $26,000 each.

Bobby flipped through all of the bills making it sound like he was shuffling a deck of cards.

"This looks good. I'll count it later."

"You good, baby?"

"I'm always good," Stacey replied.

"Get that waitress over here so I can order this food."

The two of them enjoyed their meal and relished in the day's work while Lay sat mostly in silence. He joined in the conversation occasionally but his thoughts were a million miles away.

The next day Lay woke up and sat at the edge of the bed trying to decide whether he would make the trip into the city to Monique's office or not. He was barely out of hot water with Celina and didn't want to risk getting thrown back in the pot. He knew his history with Monique, and how they'd never been able to keep their hands off one another.

Meeting her in her office was not such a good idea. 'She won't try to fuck me at her job, would she?' he wondered. Then again, he remembered Monique giving him some in the parking lot of an ice cream shop in broad daylight. 'I gotta get her to meet me in a public place for my own safety. If I fuck up again, my baby will kill me.'

Celina had already left for work so he was able to be alone in his thoughts for a while. Deciding not to put it off any longer, Lay pulled Monique's card from his wallet to make arrangements to meet that afternoon. He typed in her number and waited for her to answer as the phone rang until her voicemail picked up.

Lay left a message asking if they could meet. He closed his phone, set it on the nightstand and went into the bathroom to start his day. As soon as he turned the water on to start brushing his teeth, his cell phone rang. Lay dashed back into the bedroom and flipped it open, answering it on the fourth ring.

"I was about to hang up, Mr. Taylor. Good morning," Monique said in a sultry voice.

Lay shook his head. 'How does this woman manage to sound this sexy so early in the day?'

"Good morning Ms. Peele. I was wondering if today was a good one for us to have that meeting."

"I don't see why not. Let me look at my schedule…. Umm nope, I'm free after lunch. Let's say 1:30. Is that good for you?"

"One thirty it is."

Lay was apprehensive about being alone with Monique so he asked, "What restaurants are close to your office. Do you want to meet at one of them?"

"No, my office is fine, Babe. Besides I already have a lunch meeting. That's why I'm meeting you after. Pay attention. Let me find out you're afraid to be alone with me, Lavian."

Feeling embarrassed for being exposed, he quickly shot back, "Girl, ain't nobody scared of you."

"Okay, well stop acting like it and have your ass here at 1:30. Not CP 1:30, either."

"I got you."

"Okay, I'll see you then, handsome."

Lay closed his phone and shook his head again all the while hoping this wouldn't turn out to be a mistake.

After getting dressed, Lay had time to kill so he stopped by Celina's office for a minute. She was just finishing up on the phone with a client when he knocked on the door.

"Hello, gorgeous. How's your day going so far?"

"Hey. It's a little busy. How about you? What are you getting yourself into today?"

"I actually have a meeting at Universal at 1:30."

"Oh, okay. Magazine stuff?"

"You can say that."

"Well, I hope all goes well for you."

"Yes, pray for me."

Celina let out a little chuckle. "Why am I doing all that? Is it that serious?"

"I mean, not really. Okay, wish me luck. Maybe that's better."

"Sure sounds better. You make it seem like you're going on trial or something."

'If you only knew,' he thought.

Celina stood up, adjusted her skirt, grabbed a folder off her desk, and hit Lay in the chest with it.

"Well, I have work to do, and you don't want to be late, so shoo."

She placed the folder inside of her bag and smacked Lay on his ass as he stood up. She knew he hated that, but she also knew that would make him leave quicker.

Although he was reluctant to go into the city, he left Celina's office and pointed his car in the direction of the Lincoln Tunnel. It was probably futile, but Lay figured if he stopped by Celina's office first, it would somehow deter him from any deviant behavior once he got next to Monique. There was just something irresistible about that woman.

Lay pulled up to a nearby parking garage and retrieved a ticket for the car. As he exited the garage he noticed a black man leaning at the entrance smoking a cigarette. When Lay passed, the man dropped his cigarette on the ground, stepped on it and walked in the opposite direction. Lay noticed all of this out of the corner of his eye, but didn't give it a second thought.

He entered the Universal building and found the elevators. When the elevator came he stepped in and pressed the button for the eleventh floor. Stepping out, Lay approached the receptionist and asked for Ms. Monique Peele.

"Do you have an appointment?"

"Uh, yes. Yes, I do."

"Your name, sir?"

"Lavian Taylor."

"Okay. I'll see if she's in. Give me a moment. You can have a seat while you wait."

"Thank you."

Lay wasn't seated for more than two minutes before Monique came out of the door on the right side of the receptionist's desk. He noticed how shapely her legs were in the skirt she wore with the Yves Saint Laurent pumps. She extended her hand as Lay stood up to shake it.

"Mr. Taylor?"

"Yes."

"You can follow me."

Lay did just that as Monique glided down the hall past several offices, hypnotizing him with her every step. When they reached her office Lay stepped inside and took a seat in the chair in front of Monique's desk. She closed the door behind them and locked it. Lay's heart began to race a little as Monique walked around his chair, sat on the edge of her desk directly in front of him and crossed her legs. 'What is this woman trying to do to me?' he wondered.

"Okay, let's talk business," Monique stated.

"Really? You expect me to concentrate on business with you doin' all that sexy shit? Why don't you go sit your ass behind your desk?"

"Because I'm comfortable right here, that's why. Relax, Lavian. If I want something to happen, it will. And there'd be no way for you to stop it, trust me."

He knew she was one hundred percent right, but he knew he needed to keep his composure as well. Lay swallowed and said, "Tell me more about these starving artists you deal with."

"What's to tell? Like I said, some of them have their shit together more than others." "My question to you is, how you're interest in them is going to translate into dollars in my bank account."

"Funny you should say, bank. My line of work is completely different from what you remember. I'm into white-collar shit now, and I need people, preferably females to go into the banks and cash corporate payroll checks for me. For us, rather. I'll give you $100 off every check that gets cashed."

"And all I have to do is provide you with girls who are willing to go into the banks?"

175

"Exactly. You know their personalities and their financial situations so you'll be able to determine who's willing to do something strange for some change and who's not."

Monique uncrossed her legs, walked around to the other side of her desk and sat down as if she put her figurative thinking cap on.

This was a relief to Lay, because her legs and the fragrance she wore had become intoxicating to him. It was a small miracle he was able to concentrate long enough to finish his thoughts.

"This sounds like something I can do. I have a couple of girls in mind. Actually, I have something better than the artisits."

"Who?"

"Strippers, or dancers, better yet."

"Since when do you hang out in strip clubs? I didn't know you were into chicks."

"I'm not. I just spend a lot of time there because that's where records are broken nowadays, not in the clubs like they used to be. It's the new wave. Pay attention. You'll see what I mean in a couple of years."

"So you think the dancers would be better?"

"Why not? They're already doing something strange for change."

"But this is illegal."

"I know. And I'll let them know, too. If they bite, they bite. If not, so be it. But I think I have a couple who'll be with it."

"Okay, sounds good to me."

"Okay. I'll get back to you with their names when I've had a chance to groom them."

"Sounds good to me," Lay said as he stood up and reached across the desk to shake Monique's hand.

She extended her hand and obliged, then asked, "What's in it for me besides the money?"

Lay was almost out of there but he should've known that it was too good to be true.

"What do you mean? You're getting $100 off every check. What else do you need?"

"Money is not and never will be an issue with me. And, I don't *need* anything, Lavian. It's what I *want.*"

"And what might that be?" Lay asked trying to conceal a slight tremble in his voice.

"I don't know what this new chick has done to you but you're acting all nervous around me and I don't like it. I had hoped you didn't think you were going to get away with *only* doing business with me but I see things have definitely changed between us. So I"ll be on my best behavior. For now."

Lay sighed and said, "C'mon Mo'. You know I got mad love for you and I always will. I'm in a relationship, and I'm just trying to be better than I was before. It's nothing against you, baby." He pulled Monique around the desk and hugged her while caressing her ample butt cheeks.

"Lay, you were always in relationships whenever we fucked. You had them, I had them. It never made a difference before. What's so special about this new one?"

"Well, actually she's not new. It's Celina. We got back-..."

"Celina?!?" Monique interrupted as she pushed herself from Lay's embrace and placed her hands on her hips.

"Oh, I see. You're back with your precious little Celina. How cute is that?"

Lay became annoyed instantly. "Really, Mo'?"

"Yes really, Lavian."

"And what's so wrong with Celina?"

"Hmph…, nothing, if that's what you're into. Taking care of broke bitches," Monique scoffed.

"Oh, a lot of shit changed since back then. She's not the timid little chick I used to cheat on and mistreat, anymore. She's all woman."

"A woman that can't even buy her own watch," Monique retorted.

Lay just happened to look down at her wrist which now donned a yellow gold Bertolucci, flooded with diamonds. 'I can't stand this motherfucker,' he thought.

"She *can* buy her own shit. She's just lucky enough to have someone who can buy it for her."

"You call it luck, I call it a handicap. I never needed a man for anything but dick."

Thoroughly ticked off, Lay stepped in Monique's personal space.

"Ain't nothin' handicapped about my woman. She's capable of doing whatever you do, and probably better."

"And yet here you are in *my* office, asking *me* for help, and defending her. That shit is pitiful. Pitiful and pathetic."

Lay was equally irritated and aroused at the same time. He pushed Monique back onto the desk, pulled her skirt up to reveal she wasn't wearing panties. She offered no resistance as she watched, with a tiny smirk of satisfaction, Lay throw his face, tongue first into her already wet pussy. He sucked on Monique's enormous clitoris as her eyes rolled into her head from receiving his oral pleasure.

Lay pushed her legs into the air as Monique fought to keep her balance on the cluttered surface. Realizing her efforts were futile, she lay back and let Lay go to work on her vagina that was now dripping with her juices as well as his saliva. Monique unbuttoned her blouse and unhooked the front clasp of her bra so she could rub her erect nipples while her pussy was being devoured by a horny, aggravated man.

She reached for and found Lay's hand and pulled it to her breast so he could play with her other nipple. Monique was almost close to climax, but when Lay let go of her nipple and stuck his index finger inside of her ass, this pushed her over the edge. Her body began to tremble and convulse as she grabbed the back of Lay's wavy head and pulled his mouth deeper into her vagina.

"Mmmmotherfucker!" she squealed as her orgasm reached its pinnacle.

Monique struggled to catch her breath and sit up at the same time, knocking her telephone to the floor. But Lay didn't let up. He sucked on her clit until she couldn't take it anymore. She pushed his head away and kicked him in the shoulder with her four-inch heel. Lay stood up and wiped his mouth as Monique fell back onto the desk looking at the ceiling, and breathing like she just ran six miles.

Eventually Monique managed to clear her head and sit up. Lay gazed at her luscious breasts while she stood up to adjust her skirt. He grabbed one of them and sucked her nipple like a newborn baby. Monique let him enjoy it for a few seconds, before pushing him onto the chair. She could see his rock- hard dick bulging through his jeans, but ignored the urge to suck it.

She walked around the desk, putting her 36DDD's back into their rightful place, reached into the drawer, pulled out a toothbrush and a travel-sized tube of toothpaste. She walked back around to the door, opened it and said,

"There's a restroom down the hall on your right. I"ll call you when I'm ready with what you need. Now get your nasty motherfucking ass out of my office."

She held up the toothbrush and toothpaste as he walked past her on the way out. When he was in arm's reach, Monique grabbed his face and said,

"Let me taste my pussy."

She proceded to kiss Lay deeply and passionately in the doorway while in clear view of her colleagues.

He was taken aback, but enjoyed every bit of her antics.

"Now you can go," she said, and pushed Lay down the hall.

"I can't stand your ass," Lay said.

Monique closed the door, leaned against it, sighed and said, "Nigga, you love this bitch."

Lay opened the bathroom door, rinsed his mouth with water, looked in the mirror and said out loud, "Damn, I love that bitch."

After brushing, Lay left the bathroom and did the walk of shame down the hall past Monique's co-workers. Some paid him no attention while others glared at him to the point where it made him quite uncomfortable. One young lady even winked at him as he made his way out the door to the reception area. Waiting for the elevator, all Lay could think about was getting home to shower before Celina made it there.

As he descended the eleven floors to the ground, he felt the wave of disappointment come over him. 'I can't believe I let her get me that fuckin' mad and horny at the same time. I gotta stay away from her and keep it strictly business from now on. Yeah right, motherfucka'. That's what the fuck I said when I took my dumb ass in there in the first place. Fuck it. What's done is done.'

When the elevator reached the ground floor Lay stepped out into the fall New York City air and walked back to the garage. He gave the attendant behind the bulletproof glass his ticket. Lay paid the man and noticed a line of nearly a dozen people had formed behind him like a concert had just ended. When he stepped to the side to wait for his car to be brought up, he noticed the same black man who had been standing at the entrance of the garage from earlier. He was now two people behind him in line, waiting to pay.

When the two made eye contact, the man, dressed in a dark grey business suit gave Lay the traditional head nod a lot of black men tend to do instead of actually speaking. Lay returned the same greeting. Grey suit tried his best to conceal it, but when he reached back to get the wallet from his back pocket, he revealed a .9mm neatly secured in a shoulder holster.

Lay instinctively kept his distance and wished his car would arrive sooner than later. He didn't have anything against the police, but elected not to be around them all the same, if he could. Just then, a parking attendant pulled up in his shiny black car. It made him feel a little self conscious in front of the man with the grey suit.

He reached in his pocket to give the attendant a tip, as he normally did, but didn't want to pull his money out in front of grey suit man. Fortunately, Lay kept the small bills on the outside of his folded knot. He quickly peeled off whatever bill was there, which happened to be a twenty. That was way more than he wanted to give, but he wanted to get out of there far more.

The attendant looked at the twenty and said, "Thank you! Thank you, sir!"

"No problem. Thank *you*."

As Lay stepped inside the car and adjusted his seat, grey suit man approached and said, "That's a nice car. What year is it?"

"Two thousand one," Lay replied.

"It must be nice."

"It's okay. I have no complaints."

"Have a good evening."

"You do the same," Lay shot back as he rolled the window up and pulled out of the garage.

He couldn't figure out if that exchange was a sincere compliment or if the officer was being weird on purpose. In any event, he had a more

181

pressing matter to deal with. He called Celina to see what time she would be home to see whether he had time to make it there before her. She said she would be home her normal time of around six-thirtyish. 'Good,' he thought. That gave him enough time to get his life together before she got there.

Lay put the pedal to the metal and pushed through the New York traffic, back to New Jersey where he belonged. The meeting with Monique was a success and the evening with Celina was uneventful. She didn't suspect a thing. Now, all he had to do was wait for Monique to call so he could start earning again. Aside from his oral transgression earlier, it proved to be a good day.

The Alphabet Girl

Assistant United States Attorney Silvia Ryan rode the Long Island Railroad into work, feeling anxious and a little nervous at the same time. She had been given the lead on an investigation for the first time in her short three-year career with the federal government. The case was small compared to some of the other cases that she sat second chair to, but it was big enough to make a name for herself if she got the job done swiftly and correctly.

Silvia Ryan was small in stature but proved to be extremely large in presence when necessary. Standing only five feet two inches tall, slim built and very pretty, she was often overlooked in the male-dominated field she chose for her career. Most people, including other women, thought she was a pushover until she opened her mouth. Contrary to the popular saying, Silvia's bite definitely measured up to her bark.

Upon arrival at One Saint Andrews Plaza in lower Manhattan, AUSA Ryan headed to a briefing with the U.S. attorney. The next task on her agenda that morning was visiting a female who had been sitting in lockup for the past two weeks. She had her driver take her to 150 Park Row to have a chat with the suspect in custody.

Wearing the standard prison jumpsuit and white skips with no socks, the female in question waited in the interrogation room. She was a tall, beautiful blonde with supermodel looks and a physique to match. Her hair was pulled back off of her face and pinned into a neat bun on the top of her head.

She sat in the room quietly for what seemed like hours with her hands folded on the table in front of her and her feet crossed underneath the chair she sat upon. She'd become preoccupied with a small stain on the wall in front of her when the door opened. AUSA Ryan walked in with a mugshot stapled onto the front of a folder.

"Good morning Ms. Kowalski. My name is Silvia Ryan. I am the Assistant United States Attorney assigned to your case. I presume you know why you've been detained."

"I do."

"Okay good, we're off to a good start. So, you want to tell me what's been going on with you for the past year?"

"No. I want to speak with my lawyer."

Silvia had elected to remain standing thus far to show she meant business.

"And here I thought we were going to get along this morning. Silly me. Okay, Ms. Kowalski, you don't want to tell me anything, so I'll tell you a thing or two."

Silvia opened up the folder, pulled out a black and white surveillance photo of Ms. Kowalski at a bank counter and placed it on the table. She repeated this process over and over until the table looked like a collage.

The last piece of paper Silvia pulled out of the folder was a check that Ms. Kowalski had attempted to cash when she was picked up by NYPD two weeks prior. A day later, the case was then handed over to the feds and placed into the hands of AUSA Ryan.

Until then, Ms. Kowalski had only glanced at the photos that were laid before her. When Agent Ryan placed the check on the table in front of Ms. Kowalski it got her attention.

"Do you know what this is?"

"It's a check."

"It's the check you attempted to cash two weeks ago."

Ms. Kowalski sat silent.

"Ms. Kowalski, how many photos are on the table?"

She surveyed the table and said, "Around fifteen, maybe."

"That's close enough."

Agent Ryan opened the folder again, this time pulling the small rectangular pieces of paper from the center and placing each one on top of a photo that had already been laid on the table.

"Each photo has a corresponding check that I can attach to it. That's fifteen checks with a photo of your face at a bank counter cashing it."

"You can get up to five years for each check in front of you. Seventy-five years in total, in case you were wondering. But that's not all. Do you see how thick this folder is?" "It's filled with pictures and checks that you've been cashing for the past year."

Ms. Kowalski sat in silence.

"You still have nothing to say?" "To say you've been busy is an understatement. But, I've been equally busy," Agent Ryan stated as she cleared the table of its contents.

"I detected a slight accent when you spoke. Where is it from?"

"Poland."

"I thought that's what I heard. How long have you lived in this country?"

"I was born here, so you can save your threats of deportation. That doesn't frighten me."

"Ahh, *you* were born here, but your parents weren't. I know their immigration status is coming up for renewal. I also know your father's health is not the best and he's getting the best care he can get here in the States-; the type he can't get back home." "With one phone call I can make their renewal process a nightmare. Or it can go as smooth as butter. The choice is yours."

Ms. Kowalski's demeanor softened and the expression on her face gave her away. The thought of being separated from her parents made Ms. Kowalski sick to her stomach. Agent Ryan knew she had her.

"What do you want from me?" Ms. Kowalski asked, with tears welling up in the corners of her eyes.

"That wasn't so hard, was it?"

Agent Ryan placed photos of Sean, Malcolm, Tony, and Lavian in front of Ms. Kowalski.

"Do you know any of them?"

"No, I don't." Agent Ryan scooped up the four photos, set them aside and placed a photo of Stacey on the table. "What about her?"

"Yes."

"Okay, what about him?" Agent Ryan asked as she placed a photo of Bobby next to the one of Stacey on the table.

"Yes, I know him too."

"Who are they?"

"Her name is Stacey Mack. I met her at my place of work. His name is Bobby. I met him through her. That's all I know about him."

"All you know is his name is Bobby?"

"Yes. That's all I needed to know."

"How did you get mixed up with these two?"

"Like I said, I know Stacey from work. She and I would talk sometimes. She asked me if I wanted to make some extra money aside from my poor excuse for a paycheck. She told me what I had to do and that was that."

"So, this Bobby is the go-to guy?"

"Yes. He called the shots. He decided where we went, how often we went, and how much we got paid."

"Okay, that's what we figured. See, we don't want you. We want the source. The problem is, up until this point, you're the only person I can prove has committed a crime. But if you tie them in, I can go easy on you. Unlike the other two, you have no priors so you're eligible for probation."

She paused before continuing. "Of course, you'll have to plead guilty and have a felony on your record but it would take jailtime off the table for you. The two weeks you've spent in here will be the last time you'll be behind bars and you can walk out of here today if you so choose." "Do you need time to think about it?"

"What do I have to do?"

"First, you'll have to get them-, well Bobby specifically- on tape talking about the operation."

"But he doesn't talk to me about anything like that. Once I received my instructions from Stacey there wasn't much for us to talk about."

"Just wear the wire. We'll do the rest."

"A wire?!? Are you trying to get me killed?!?" "Can't you just tap my phone line? A wire is too risky. I would be too afraid that something will go wrong."

"I guess a phone tap will do. How often do you speak with him?"

"There's no set time. Either he calls, or Stacey lets me know when to be ready."

"Okay. The tap on your phone should suffice."

"I'm going to get the paperwork together for you to sign for your consent to participate. In the meantime, is there anything I can get you? Coffee, tea, anything?"

"I thought you were supposed to offer that in the beginning of all of this."

"You watch too much TV."

"All I need is a pen."

"Very well. I'll be back in a minute," Agent Ryan said. She gathered the photos and placed them neatly back into the folder.

"I think you made the right decision, Maureen," Agent Ryan stated before walking out of the door and closing it behind her.

"I *know* I did," said Maureen.

AUSA Ryan had a cooperating participant in the investigation she would call "Charles in Charge."

In her office she placed a three-by-five photo of Bobby at the top of the board and used a magnet to hold it in place. Next to it she wrote out the name, Robert "Bobby" Charles. She drew two small lines under the photo and placed photos of Maureen and Stacey at the ends of each line. After writing their names on the board she then lay out the photos of Sean, Lavian, Tony, and Malcolm trying to piece together where they belonged. Somehow, she knew they were all connected and she was determined to prove it.

It was business as usual for the next couple weeks as Bobby's team continued to fill their safes with cash and also add to the growing kitty that had climbed into six figures. Malcolm, Tiecy and Little Malcolm had moved to The Avalon to be close to Bobby and Niecy. Tony and Yvette had moved up to The Avalon on the Sound, in New Rochelle because she wanted to stay close to her parents who lived in the Bronx.

Celina had decided to keep the baby. Lay wanted his child to grow up in the same home so he gave up the two-bedroom and upgraded to a three bedroom in the Atrium so Celina and her son Barry could live with him. Sean was still being the same old irrtating person he was expected to be. Moving from one woman to the next, he was in no hurry to nor had any intention of settling down.

Lay and Celina were the last to move so the ladies decided to throw an intimate housewarming/baby shower for them. It was nothing fancy, and for the most part, included family only. The only outsider there was Celina's best friend, Sasha. She stood about five foot four inches tall and mostly resembled Shar Jackson from the show 'Moesha'. Celina had always wanted to hook Sean up with Sasha but Lay strongly advised her against it, so she left the idea alone.

Tonight was different, however. Celina knew that Sasha was six months into a breakup with her ex and there was no chance of them reconciling at that point. She saw this as an opportunity to try her matchmaking skills once again.

Surprisingly, Sean was kind of quiet this particular evening, but it never took much to get him going.

He was sitting on one end of the sectional watching TV as he sipped from a glass of Moet Rose. Bobby and Malcolm were trying to figure out how to cheat Niecy and Tiecy in a game of spades they had going on at the dining table. Yvette had fallen asleep in Tony's lap from exhaustion and perhaps having one too many.

Lay had what he considered the best seat in the house. He sat in the middle of the couch directly in front of the TV with his feet on the ottoman and the remote by his side. Sasha was in the kitchen making a drink.

Celina left her there, went into the livingroom, sat between Lay and Sean and said, "Sasha told me to ask you if you were tired of messing with all those birds and ready to get with a real woman?"

Sasha had just stepped into the living room and caught the tail end of Celina's comment. After taking a sip of her drink she said, "Don't listen to her. I didn't say shit about you."

"Oh, 'cause I was about to say; don't play with me li'l girl."

"I got your little girl. You don't want none of this, *li'l boy*."

"You're right. I don't want none of it. But if I did, it would've happened already."

"Oh, you think so?"

189

"Think?!? I know. Girl I'll have you butt-naked in the Bahamas by tomorrow night."

Sasha had never paid Sean any mind in the past for two reasons. One, was because she had been in a long-term relationship. The other was because she knew Sean was a player, and could never be taken seriously. But tonight felt a little different for some reason.

The banter between them fed her ego in a way that she hadn't felt since her breakup. Actually, she hadn't received any attention from a man of substance since then. Not that Sean had much either, but he was definitely ten steps above all of the weridos who hit on her on a daily basis. She was flattered, to say the least.

"Oh really? Well, talk is cheap, nigga."

"Oh, you think I'm bullshitting. Sis, where's your laptop? I'm about to change your friend's life. It's about time she stopped fuckin' with them RN's anyway."

"What the hell is an RN, Sean?" Celina saked.

"A Regular Nigga."

Everyone laughed except for the women.

"Um, excuse me, but my ex had a good job with benefits, thank you! Ain't nothing wrong with a working man!"

"Ain't nothing right with him either," Malcolm said under his breath. Tiecy heard him and kicked him under the table.

Lay shook his head and gave Celina a look. She read his mind and could almost hear him asking her, 'Why did you get that motherfucka started?' She stuck her tongue out at Lay and got up to retrieve her laptop. When she returned, she plopped down on the couch next to Lay, opened the laptop and asked Sean where he wanted to stay.

"Ask her. I don't care where we stay."

"You're the man. You plan the trip," Sasha shot back.

"Okay. Tone, where did you and Yvette go on your first trip?"

Without lifting her head from Tony's lap, Yvette said, "The Atlantis resort on Paradise Island."

"You've been ear hustling all this time?" Tony asked.

"I heard enough," Yvette said.

"Yeah, that Atlantis spot looked dope. Book that one."

"First class?" Celina asked.

"Of course, Sis; I'ma show her what a real motherfuckin' trip is supposed to be like."

"How long are you staying?" Niecy asked from across the room.

"We can stay for a month! I don't give a fuck!"

"You talk so much shit, Sean. You probably can't even afford to stay for a week," Sasha scoffed.

"Celina, book that shit from Sunday to Sunday. Your friend must think it's a recession over here. You just make sure McD's will let you off fries for a whole week. And bring an empty suitcase. We gon' buy new shit everyday out there. You do have a suitcase, right?"

"Don't play your self," Sasha retorted.

"I'm just making sure. You never know."

Adding more fuel to Sean's fire, Tony said, "Y'all must think we ain't getting' money around here. Bro, go empty-handed, take her shopping every day *and* cop the luggage to bring it back in, nigga!"

All the women started clapping and screaming. Yvette finally sat up and asked, "What you got to say to that? They have Gucci, Louis, Versace, and all that shit out there. Go with no luggage and bring our girl back with a new wardrobe, Big Baller!"

"Yo, Tone. Who side you on, my nigga?"

"Sis, you ain't said nothin' slick. That's even better. Baby, don't bring nothin but your ID and the clothes on your back. I got something for all y'all."

Celina broke into all of the commotion, quieted everyone down and said, "So there you have it. Two first-class round-trip tickets to Paradise Island Bahamas, Atlantis resort for seven days seven nights. Will there be anything else, my Big Baller Brother?"

"Nope, thank you, Sis. I got it from here."

"And how will you be paying for this?"

"Put it on your card. I'll give you the cash right now. What do I owe you?"

"That will be nineteen hundred sixty-seven dollars and twelve cents."

Sean dug into his right pants pocket and placed all the money he had onto Celina's laptop without counting it. Celina fanned through the bills and asked, "Is this enough?"

"You doubt me, Sis? Count it and tell *me* if it's enough."

Celina counted the twenty-five hundred dollar bills and said, "This is over, Sean."

"I know. It's a li'l something extra for your travel agent skills."

"Shit, anyone else need to go on vacation? I could do this all day."

"You gave up all your money, showing out. Now you can't even pay the toll to get back across the bridge," Sasha scolded.

Sean chuckled and said, "I live on this side of the Hudson, sweetheart. You should try it."

Then, he reached into his left pocket, pulled out another wad of hundreds and fanned them in front of Sasha's face.

"The word broke is not in my vocabulary, Love."

"Get out of my face, fool."

"It's too late for that, Sash. He's gonna be all up in your face for an entire week," Celina said.

"That ain't all I'm gon' be all up in."

"Boy, please. Whatever."

"Nine months from now we're gonna be having our *own* baby shower."

Just the thought of finally having sex was making Sasha feel a little tingly inside. But she kept her composure and said, "I hope you can back up all that shit you talk."

"Ask around, baby. I'm certified."

"Certified crazy," Lay said, finally speaking up.

Sean grabbed his jacket, turned and said, "Bobby, clear my schedule until I get back."

An amused Bobby chuckled and replied, "No problem, my brother. Enjoy."

"I'm about to get out of here. I got shit to do before I blow Sasha's mind for a whole week. Goodnight, everybody."

Sasha was sitting on the arm of the sectional watching Sean act a fool. After sliding his arms into the North Beach leather jacket, Sean approached her and moved so close to Sasha that, his crotch pressed against her hip. She was slightly turned on by his assertiveness, and offered no resistance. His cologne served as an aphrodisiac as she inhaled all of his masculinity.

'Damn, this nigga smells good.'

Sean gently grabbed Sasha's chin, kissed her on the lips then said,

"And I'll see you tomorrow, lady."

Sasha's eyes remained closed seconds after the kiss as she had to catch her self from being caught in Sean's spell.

"You definitely will."

"Good. Tomorrow it is."

Lay got up to lock the door. As Sean walked through the doorway he said, "You're an asshole. You know that, right?"

"Yeah, but you love me, though."

"Get out of my house,"Lay replied, and shut the door behind him.

The rest of the evening flowed smoothly as the couples laughed, drank, and socialized. Lay was content. 'I love my little family,' he thought.

The Takedown

The next morning Sean picked up Sasha from her house and drove toward JFK so they could begin their week of fun and sun. He called her as he was pulling up. She came down five minutes later wearing a black velour Christian Dior sweatsuit with a pair of leather and suede sneakers to match. All she carried was a Christian Dior pocketbook with her ID, passport, cell phone, and whatever else women carry in their handbags.

"Good morning. I see you know how to follow orders," Sean said.

"Instructions. I follow instructions, not orders. Don't confuse the two. And, a very good morning to you, Mister," Sasha replied.

She opened the door and got inside of Sean's Benz. As she buckled her seatbelt she added, "Chivalry is dead around here, I see."

"My bad. I was supposed to get out and open the door for you, right?"

"That's okay. You just earned your first strike."

"I don't play baseball."

"Neither do I. But don't worry. You won't be playing with *anything* over here if you don't learn how to act."

"Oh, I like you! I need a woman that can try to keep me in line. Notice, I said try."

"Well, to try is to fail. I got this."

Her last statement put a smile on Sean's face as he steered through the New York City morning traffic en route to JFK. When they arrived, Sean left his car in long-term parking, and the pair walked to the Delta counter to pick up their boarding passes. After reaching the gate they had some time to spare so Sean tried to make amends for the car door debacle by offering to get Sasha some breakfast.

She declined, but asked for a tea with lemon and three sugars. Sean granted her request and then they made small talk until it was time to board the plane. As they waited, Sasha noticed an interracial couple sitting in the next row from them. They were taking turns snapping shots of each other and posing for the camera.

At one point, the man stopped the photoshoot to adjust the lens and accidentally hit the shutter, making the flash go off. He almost blinded Sean in the process because at that moment Sean happened to be looking directly at it. The man noticed what had happened and apologized to Sean.

"It's okay," Sean replied, as he rubbed his eyes.

The man resumed the photo session with his wife as Sean's eyes regained their focus. He turned to look at Sasha and noticed that her nose was turned up at the couple.

"What's wrong, baby? Don't tell me you're one of those sistas that don't like to see brothas with snow bunnies."

"Please. I don't care where a nigga sticks his penis. That motherfucker is acting like he's taking pictures of her, but I swear he's taking some of us too."

"What?!?"

"Don't make a scene. Just pay attention. There's something fucked up about them. I can feel it."

"You're paranoid baby."

"Call me what you want. I don't like them."

"Okay."

Sean felt a little uneasy after that, but he didn't want it to spoil their vacay so he changed the subject to lighten the mood. Sasha played along but still had reservations about the couple.

A few minutes went by, and the announcement was made to start boarding. They were in first class so Sean and Sasha got up to stand in line. With only one couple ahead of them, they boarded immediately after, and settled into their seats as the rest of the passengers followed suit. Sasha had the aisle seat and watched every person that boarded the plane.

Sean ordered some champagne so they could relax a little. Sasha sipped, but stayed on point the entire time. When the last passenger boarded and the door was closed she grabbed Sean's arm, almost making him spill his drink.

"I told you there was something shady about that couple," she whispered excitedly. "They sat in our section the entire time we waited to board but their asses are not on this plane!"

"Maybe they're not going to the Bahamas."

"Everyone *else* that was sitting in our waiting area is on this plane; on their way to the fuckin' Bahamas."

"How the hell could you remember all those people, Sasha?"

"I'm a woman, Sean."

"Yeah, a woman with a pornographic memory."

"Photographic."

"That's what I said."

"You're playing and I'm serious, boy."

Trying to ease Sasha's suspicions, Sean said, "Maybe they were on standby."

After thinking for a second, Sasha agreed, "You may be right but I still didn't like all that picture-taking shit. Who takes that many flicks in the damn airport? You haven't even gone anywhere yet."

"I don't know either, but we're here and they're not. Let's just enjoy this week."

"Okay," Sasha relented.

Sean sipped his champagne and stared out of the window for a few minutes, trying to think about the week ahead, but everything Sasha said was still in the back of his mind.

She grabbed his hand while the flight attendants gave their pre-flight speech and said, "Even though you were being an ass about it last night, I want to thank you for this trip. I needed this after my breakup."

"No problem. If nothing more comes out of this, I would hope that we could at least be friends."

"I'm cool with that," Sasha said.

Unknown to her and Sean, the interracial couple from the waiting area watched through the enormous window as the plane eased away from the gate.

Monday December, 2nd

Bright and early Monday morning, Agents Christopher Bradley and Sarah Belgrave sat in the office across the desk of AUSA Ryan waiting for her to end her call so they could bring her up to speed on their investigation. When she hung up Agent Bradley spoke first, telling Ryan how they had tailed their target, Sean Prescott to various banks in Connecticut for the past several weeks.

"The target used several female accomplices to enter those branches to cash forged payroll checks. A full report from HSBC has him and his faction defrauding several companies out of close to one million dollars-; $927,000, to be exact." It was Agent Belgrave's turn to speak. She told Ryan that, "We planned to resume surveillance this Wednesday, as his M.O. is to only move from then until Friday. However, there's an issue.

"He left yesterday to go to the Bahamas for a week," said Bradley.

AUSA Ryan sat forward, leaned on her desk with both elbows.

"I'm confused. You mean to tell me you let a known target in a criminal investigation leave the country with a passport?!? Are you kidding me, agents?!?"

"With all due respect ma'am, there was no way for us to take him without breaking cover."

Trying to maintain her fury, Ryan asked, "Was he alone?"

"No. He's with a, Sasha Raymond."

"Is she one of his accomplices? Does he use her to cash the checks?"

"We don't know, but it doesn't look that way. She's not on any of our surveillance." She's actually friends with the girlfriend of another target, Celina Barnett."

"Which target?"

"Lavian Taylor."

Ryan opened a folder, flipped a couple of pages and said, "Okay. Kirkland and Gadson are on that detail. When does he return?"

"His itinerary has him arriving Sunday evening at JFK."

"Okay. I have to wrap this up before he gets back. We'll move on the other five this Friday. I don't want to take them early because it will spook Prescott if he can't get in touch with his co-conspirators while he's away. I don't want him taking flight from there and ending up on the other end of the planet, slipping through our fingers again."

"Well, the two of us could fly out there and take him on the beach."

"You'd like that, wouldn't you?"

A huge smile formed across Agent Bradley's face.

"The answer is no, Bradley. You'll meet him at the airport when his flight lands."

His smile disappeared immediately.

"Okay. You have your assignments. You have a little less than a week to prepare. Make sure your people are ready for this apprehension, and no dropping the ball this time. My name is riding on this."

"Yes ma'am," both agents replied as they stood and left Ryan's office.

When the two were gone, AUSA Ryan walked to her board, placed a photo of Sean under Bobby's and drew a diagonal line from the bottom right corner. At the end of that line she placed a photo of Sasha that was taken in the airport and wrote her name on the bottom with a question mark next to it. She then placed a photo of Lay on the board next to Sean's and drew a horizontal line between the two of them. Ryan didn't have a photo of Celina so she just drew a line from the bottom right corner of the photo and wrote her name with a question mark next to it.

After that, AUSA Ryan took a step back, folded her arms and admired the way her board was shaping up. Satisfied, she walked to her desk and sat down with a smile on her face. Almost simultaneously the silence was broken by a female voice on the intercom.

It said, "Ms. Ryan, Mr. Morgan needs to see you in his office."

"Okay. I'll be right there."

Conrad Morgan was her boss, the U.S. Attorney for the Southern District of New York. He was a tall and lean, but muscularly built man with salt and pepper hair. Mr. Morgan started his career in law over thirty years ago as a young prosecutor. Having graduated from Columbia University, he made his bones downtown in the courtrooms of 100 and 111 Centre Street in the state division before making the jump to federal. From there he rose in the ranks until holding one of the top seats in New York City where he has sat for the past eleven years.

AUSA Ryan stood up, adjusted her suit and walked out of the door down the hall to where her boss' office was. On the way she hoped he hadn't heard about Sean's little vacation. She would never hear the end of it if he did. She was nervous, but anxious to report that she was almost at the end of the investigation and was ready to close the case.

Arriving at the door, she made sure she looked presentable before knocking. As Ryan reached up to knock on the door, Mr. Morgan's deep baritone voice told her to come in. She opened the door and asked, "How did you know I was at the door, sir?"

"I know everything, Agent Ryan. Please, have a seat."

"Yes sir."

"A few months back this department investigated and took down a criminal organization similar to the one you're investigating now."

"Yes, I remember, sir."

"Good. The main target in that case, an Edwin Johnson, known on the street as 'E.J.', gave up his source of the stolen info. It was a Stewart James who works in a clearing house. He provided copies of payroll checks to that crew which helped advance their enterprise. Mr. James in turn agreed to become a C.I. to avoid prosecution and jail time, and spoke of another crew who he had sold information to. Guess who sits at the helm of that crew?"

"Robert 'Bobby' Charles."

"You guessed it."

"So what does this mean for my case?"

"Because Mr. James was so eager to cooperate, we've arranged that he remain employed at the same clearing house he so willingly stole from in order to assist in the apprehension of your crew." "To answer your question, this is just an ace in the hole in case Mr. Charles' underlings decide to remain loyal. I understand you have a wiretap on another C.I."

"Yes, I do."

"Now you have my authorization to access the wiretap that Mr. James already has on his. Two confidential informants against him will be too tight of a squeeze for him to wiggle out of."

"In fact, I'm having Mr. James brought in this afternoon so you can instruct him on what you need."

"Okay, sir. Thank you. I won't let you down."

"No problem, Ryan. Just make sure Mr. Prescott gets a friendly welcome home from the U.S. government. When he lands, I don't want his feet leaving the borough of Queens."

"Sir, how did you-...?"

"I told you I know everything, Agent Ryan."

Mr. Morgan picked up a pen and started writing on a piece of white paper.

Sensing the briefing was over she stood up and turned to leave the office. Mr. Morgan picked up the phone to make a call and AUSA Ryan walked out of the door. When she got on the other side, Ryan let out a sigh of relief that she didn't get chewed out for letting Sean leave the country. She walked down the hall to her office and closed the door behind her once she was inside.

On her desk was a folder with a photo of Stewart James stapled to the front. AUSA Ryan opened it and skimmed its contents just to get some background on the C.I. She picked up her phone and called Stew to instruct him not to come into the office that day, because everything could be handled over the phone. He recognized the number but when he answered he was shocked to hear a woman's voice on the line because he was used to dealing with AUSA Tracy Kemp, who prosecuted E.J. and his crew.

Ryan introduced her self, notified him that he would be dealing with her from now on, and how she needed his assistance in the Bobby Charles investigation. She asked for a rundown on his prior dealings with Bobby to see if what he told her matched what was in his file. Pleased with what she heard she told Stewart to set up a meeting over the phone with Bobby for Wednesday.

"What banks are they asking you for now?"

"Lately he's only been asking for HSBC and Commerce copies."

"Okay. Before you meet with him I want you to make duplicate copies of everything. Save the duplicates and bring them to me Thursday morning. Got it?"

"Yes, I got it."

"Okay. I'm counting on you, Mr. James."

After hanging up, AUSA Ryan called all of the agents on the case and set up a meeting for the next morning to make sure everything was in place for the takedown. Then she called Maureen to have her schedule a work day with Bobby for Friday. AUSA Ryan took no chances and wanted to use every advantage available.

Later that evening, Bobby and Niecy were in Garden State Plaza doing some shopping for Bobby Jr. when his phone rang. It was Maureen. She asked when she was going out to work again because she needed some money. Bobby told her to get with Stacey and call him back when she locked down the dates she was available to take her out.

"I thought you and I were going out. I haven't seen you in a while," Maureen said.

"It doesn't matter who you go with as long as the outcome is the same," Bobby replied.

"You're right. I'll call Stacey now. Bye Bobby."

"Bye."

Niecy was giving Bobby the side eye because she could tell he was talking to a woman, but she never bothered him when she knew he was handling business. Bobby immediately called Stacey and told her to expect Maureen's call. Having gotten that out of the way, he focused on family time with Niecy and his son.

A few minutes later, his phone rang again. This time it was Stew on the line asking what copies he needed for the week because he was already sitting on some H's and C's he had put to the side. That was music to Bobby's ears but he was spending time with Niecy at the moment. He told Stew he wanted them, but was going to try and see if Malcolm could pick them up.

Stew felt it was a good idea because now he could get Malcolm on the wire as well as Bobby. He seemed to be enjoying his life as a snitch.

"Okay. I'll call him now."

"Cool."

Stew immediately called Malcolm to see if they could meet that evening. Malcolm was on his way to the George Washington Bridge when he received the call, but turned around and met Stew at the barbershop. He gave Malcolm the copies and sent him on his merry way. The duplicates were in his glove compartment waiting to be passed to AUSA Ryan on Thursday morning.

All was going smoothly on both sides of the law, but only one would be victorious in the end. Maureen called Stacey to set up work for Friday just like AUSA Ryan instructed her to. Stacey agreed and the trap for Bobby was set.

Maureen called Ryan and explained the details of Friday's proposed outing. After hearing Maureen out, AUSA Ryan hung up the phone and smiled on the inside because she knew the Bobby Charles organization would be no more, come Friday evening. Even though they all couldn't be taken at once, she was delighted with how things were playing out. 'Sean Prescott would be the last fish to fry and his ass will be seasoned, floured, and dropped in the pan on Sunday.'

Friday couldn't come soon enough.

Tuesday December, 3rd

Tuesday was a normal uneventful day for the team. That was the day they usually spent preparing for the Wednesday through Friday work week. The team brought all the names of the ladies who were going to work to Bobby so he could begin printing the checks. This process was very time-consuming, so Bobby would set aside an entire day to get his part of the job done. Turning it into green was up to his colleagues.

For AUSA Ryan, this Tuesday was a day for organization and strategizing. She scheduled a meeting for the ten agents assigned to the case to go over procedure for Friday's takedown. Bill Mansfield and Jeffrey Black were assigned to Bobby. They were seasoned veterans with the most experience, even more than AUSA Ryan. Angel Castro and Michael Stanton were designated to Malcolm. And, Joseph Perez and Alton Walker got Tony.

The meeting went well, and everything was in order for the apprehension of the organization. AUSA Ryan could already picture the suit she would wear when she received her commendation. After the meeting she dismissed the agents and decided to leave for the day. There was no sense hanging around the office when there was really nothing for her to do until Friday morning.

Wednesday December, 4th

That Wednesday was business as usual for the team. Tony took his girls back to Philly which up to this point had proven successful. Bobby and Lay sent Stacey and a few of Monique's girls out to New Jersey. Malcolm tried his hand in Connecticut since Sean was on vacation. The day was fruitful for them all as they pulled in around $30,000 each. They each set aside money for the kitty as always, before going their separate ways for the rest of the evening.

Lay met Monique at Jezebel's to drop off her cut of the day's take. Secrectly, he was glad they met in a public setting because he definitely didn't want a repeat of the last encounter they had. Lay kept it strictly professional by not ordering, and concentrated on the names of the girls that would be going out the next day. Monique was on her best behavior as well, and had been since the tryst they shared in her office.

Having received the names, Lay passed Monique her cut under the table in his folded cloth napkin, excused himself and headed to his car which was parked down the street. Sitting across the street three cars behind Lay's BMW was a black Chevy Impala with tinted windows that contained Agents Jerry Gadson and Mickey Kirkland. They were the agents assigned to keep tabs on Lay's daily activities. They knew he would probably be headed home after the meeting so Agent Kirkland wanted to switch the tail to Monique instead.

Previous surveillance of Lay leaving her office led them to question her boss about any extracurricular activities she may have been involved with. That inquisition came up short and they figured the connection to Lay was strictly social. Agent Kirkland scared her boss to death with an obstruction of justice charge if he warned Monique about their conversation.

Still, something didn't sit right with Kirkland. He felt there was something off about the meeting Lay and Monique just had and expressed those thoughts to Agent Gadson. "If they're screwing, why would he meet her for dinner and not stay long enough to eat?"

"Maybe they really are just friends. Or maybe they had an argument. She pissed him off and he left. Who knows when it comes to women?"

"But he didn't look upset when he came outside."

"I think you're reading too much into her. *He's* the target. He'll be taken down on Friday and we'll be done with them both. But if you wanna bring her in too, we can. It can't hurt."

"Of course I wanna bring her in. She's dirty. I can feel it. Besides, I definitely want to get a closer look at those knockers."

"You're a fuckin' perv."

"No, I'm a fuckin' man. You should try it some time."

"Shut the hell up. I *am* a man. A man who happens to be a husband. You should try *that* some time."

Agent Kirkland didn't have a comeback so he put the conversation to bed. It was settled. Monique would be picked up on Friday along with the rest of the Bobby Charles team.

Monique had no idea that she was now in the crosshairs of the U.S. government as she sipped on her Chardonnay and waited for her dinner to arrive.

Lay pulled out of the parking space and headed toward the Lincoln Tunnel. He listened to WBLS as the smooth sounds of Marvin Gaye's "I Want You" caressed his ears on the drive home. Lay often compared himself to "The Trouble Man", especially when he went through problems with women. That hadn't been the case for a while now, since he found himself back in the loving bosom of Celina Barnett.

Lay knew Celina wasn't cooking much these days so he took the liberty of calling ahead to The Cheesecake Factory to order dinner for his family. Although there was an an extensive menu, the three of them almost always ordered the same thing. He ordered the shrimp scampi with Angel hair pasta for Celina, the Roadside Sliders for Barry and the Pasta Da Vinci for himself.

Celina had just finished helping Barry with his homework and opened her laptop to check some emails when Lay walked through the door.

208

She instructed Barry to put his books away and wash his hands for dinner. Lay placed the food on the kitchen counter and walked back into the living room to kiss who he felt was the most beautiful pregnant woman in the world.

"Hello Georgous. How was your day?"

"It was okay, and yours?"

"My day was productive."

"Well, productive is always good."

"How's my other baby?"

"Your other baby is fine, but this pregnancy feels different from Barry. She has me using the bathroom every five minutes, it seems."

"Leave her alone. A little pee ain't never hurt nobody."

"I can't stand you."

"And how do you know it's a she, anyway?"

"Because I said she is. That's what I want, so that's what I'm going to get. Is there a problem?"

"Whatever. Do you want me to put your food on a plate?"

"No. I'm starving. You can give it to me now. Please and thank you."

By this time Barry was seated at the table, waiting to tear into his mini burgers. Celina stayed on the couch watching CNN while Lay sat at the table discussing Barry's day at school as they ate. After dinner, Barry got ready for bed as Lay cleaned up, showered, and got ready for the next day. Celina had already retired to bed so he kissed her on the back of the head before turning off the light and snuggling up behind her. Before long, he was asleep as well.

Thursday December, 5th

On the eve of closing the biggest case of her career to date, AUSA Ryan reached her office bright and early to go over any last-minute details with all of her agents. She reached out to the ten that were assigned to the case for any updates or concerns; there were none. She then gave a call to Stew and scheduled a time for him to bring in the copies of all the checks he gave to Bobby this week.

Stew said he would be in her office no later than seven. He felt it was best he came after meeting with Bobby or Malcolm again so they wouldn't be suspicious of his whereabouts. Stew was never missing when it was time to collect his bread, so his absence would've raised an unnecessary flag. AUSA Ryan agreed and said she would be there waiting for him.

After hanging up with Stew she placed a call to Maureen who didn't answer but returned the call a few minutes later. She gave AUSA Ryan the time Stacey would be picking her up and assured her that she was still fully on board with cooperating.

"I'm glad to hear that. Now remember, we need to catch Mr. Charles with the checks in his possession. When Ms. Mack picks you up does she usually have them with her or does she have to meet him?"

"If he's riding with us he'll have them, but if *she's* taking me out she'll meet him prior to picking me up."

"That's a problem for us."

"I know. I hadn't thought about it until now."

"Okay, let me think. Let me think. I got it! Here's what we'll do. I'm going to give your number to Agent Mansfield tonight. He's going to text you his number. Tomorrow when Stacey picks you up you're going to ask her if the two of you are heading right out or does she have to meet Bobby first. If she has the checks already, we're going to have to improvise. Either way you're going to relay this info to Agent Mansfield. Got it?"

"Yes, but I'm a little nervous now. Are you sure this is going to work? I'm not tying to get killed."

"No one is going to get killed. Don't back out on me now, Maureen. You got this, girl. And besides, Agent Mansfield will be tailing your every move from the time you step out of your door. I told you I would take care of you, didn't I?"

"Yes."

"Okay, well you have to trust me," AUSA Ryan reassured Maureen, even though she wasn't sure of anything herself at this point.

"Get some rest. Tomorrow this will all be over and you can get back to your normal life. Good night Ms. Kowalski."

Before Maureen could reply, AUSA Ryan had hung up the phone and the line went dead.

Overlooking that small detail could throw her entire case off track, and she wasn't about to let that happen. AUSA Ryan immediately picked up the phone and called Agents Mansfield and Black to meet in her office to discuss strategy as soon as possible.

While the feds were dealing with their issues, the team geared up for another day of work. Bobby wanted a quick breakfast at Jimbo's so he got there around nine and ordered at the counter before having a seat at his favorite booth, only to find it to be occupied by a couple of teenagers who were probably cutting school. The cashier came from behind the counter and asked the boys to switch booths so Bobby could sit in his usual spot. They were finished eating so they didn't protest.

Bobby sat down in the adjacent booth to wait for the boys to vacate, then slid into his booth and sipped his coffee. A few minutes later Malcolm walked through the door and ordered a breakfast sandwich and orange juice to go, at the register before sitting with Bobby.

Bobby passed him his envelope under the table and made small talk until his sandwich was ready. Tony and Lay walked in almost simultaneously as Malcolm was paying for his food at the register. He gave them dap and left. Tony sat down, grabbed his envelope under the table, and pulled out his cell phone to make a call. He had a seriously worried look on his face.

As Bobby's food arrived, he asked Tony what was wrong. With the phone still pressed to his ear, he replied, "One of my girls is not answering her phone."

"Which one," Lay asked?

"Crystal. She's my main chick. I need her. Shit always goes right when she goes out."

"How many do you have on deck," Bobby asked, before shoving a forkful of eggs in his mouth.

"I have three in the van now, but I need my bottom chick. You know how I am."

"Well, keep calling her. She'll answer ev-..."

Tony's cell rang in the middle of Bobby's statement. He answered on the first ring.

"Hello!" Tony barked. "Damn. Where you been, baby? I've been calling you all morning." Tony paused, listening. "But she's okay now, right? Good. I'm on my way to get you now, baby." Tony ended his call, and let out a sigh of relief. "I got my baby back."

"What was her issue," Lay asked?

"Her broke ass baby daddy didn't want to watch their daughter, so she was trying to find a babysitter. Then, the motherfucka just decided to change his mind at the last minute. And that was only after Crystal promised to pay him."

"She had to pay him to watch his own child?" Lay asked in a disgusted tone.

"Yeah, that muhfucka don't do shit all day, but wanna stop her from eatin'. I hate niggas like that."

'I definitely been there before,' Lay thought.

"You're good now, bro. So, make it happen," Bobby urged.

"I'm better than good. I'm great!" Tony gave both men dap and trotted out the door.

"So it's just me and you. What's going on, Lay? How's Celina and the kids?"

"Everything is cool on my end. What about you?"

"Everything is soave bolla."

Lay looked at Bobby with contempt. "You do know that's a wine, right?"

"Yup."

"Lying ass nigga. You ain't know shit."

"What's up with Stacey? Is she meeting us here or we going to her crib?"

"We gonna shoot down there as soon as I finish this food."

"Cool. Yo, how has that white girl been working out for you and Stacey?"

"She's cool. I mean, she's just like any other chick, just white. She has the same issues as any of the other ones."

Bobby was finished his breakfast and sipped his now semi-hot coffee as Lay stood up to stretch his legs. He walked outside into the crisp December air, took in the heat from the blinding sun and waited for Bobby to pay for his food. Lay looked down and noticed a small scuff on the toe of his brand new Tims and bent down to wipe it away.

What he didn't notice was Agents Mansfield and Black sitting in an unmarked car across the street in front of Esplanade Gardens' building 5, carrying out their daily routine of tailing Bobby's every move. Lay pulled out his cell phone to check on Celina as Bobby walked out of the door and tapped him on the shoulder.

"Let's go, bro."

Lay closed his flip, walked to the car and got in on the passenger side. Bobby climbed in, started the car and pulled off without putting his sealtbelt on.

When he got to the light, Agent Black, who was driving pulled out of the parking spot and eased directly behind the Benz. Bobby noticed him but brushed it off. The light turned green and Bobby went through the intersection, driving southward on Lenox Ave. Agent Black made a right and went up 145th Street toward Seventh Avenue. When Bobby was approaching 144th Street, a black Impala pulled out of its parking spot and made its way south on Lenox as well. Inside were Agents Gadson and Kirkland. They stayed a couple of cars behind Bobby and Lay so as not to get made.

It worked, because neither Lay nor Bobby had a clue they were being tailed. The two drove to Stacey's house and dropped her checks off without incident. All of this took place under the watchful eye of the U.S. government, who had agents strategically placed around Stacey's home. After making the drop, Bobby and Lay rode out to Jersey and killed time at Riverside Square Mall until it was time for lunch. There, they would dine at The Cheescake Factory while waiting for the calls to come in about the day's progress.

A couple of more hours passed. Another day was done, and the team had taken their slice of the pie. Bobby and Lay waited in the office for Malcolm, Tony, and Stacey to return with the day's results. After everything was collected, Bobby gave Lay his cut and dropped him off at his car. Once alone, Lay called Monique to set up a time and place to meet so she could get paid. She informed him that she would be stuck at work for a couple of hours so she wouldn't be available until late.

Lay agreed and promised to hold her cut until tomorrow afternoon. He told her to let him know where she wanted to meet for lunch. She said okay, and they said their goodbyes. He pointed his car toward New Jersey and headed home.

Friday December, 6ᵗʰ

Yvette's alarm went off at 6:30 a.m. as it did every weekday morning. She wiggled out from under Tony's arm which was draped across her neck to silence the blaring noise. He was sound asleep and hadn't budged an inch. Yvette shifted in the king-sized bed, trying to get comfortable so she could catch a few more zzz's.

"Thank heavens for that snooze button," she said softly.

Yvette closed her eyes and tried to doze off for a few. Nine minutes later the alarm went off again and Yvette reached over to turn it off. She sat up, adjusted the scarf on her head, scratched her left breast and yawned before pushing her husband's leg off of her thighs.

"Why do you sleep so wild, Tony?" she asked as she slid her feet into her slippers.

Tony let out a low groan as Yvette walked into the bathroom. She threw some water on her face and was brushing her teeth when there was a loud banging at the door. Befuddled about who could be knocking so loudly and so early in the morning, she stepped out of the bathroom and yelled,

"Babe! Get up and see who's banging on the door like the police!"

Tony didn't move a muscle.

"Anthony!" she barked.

Finally showing some signs of life, he rolled over and opened one of his eyes to view his wife's beautiful cocoa-complexioned naked body now standing over him with a mouthful of toothpaste.

"You hear me calling you. Go get the door, Babe."

The banging had gotten louder by this point.

"The door?" a thoroughly confused Tony asked.

"Yes, the door. Don't you hear that shit?"

"Why don't you get it?"

"Because I'm getting ready for work, and you ain't doing nothing but sleeping. *And* I don't have any clothes on."

Yvette walked back into the bathroom just as the knocking stopped and a loud boom came from the living room. That jolted Tony completely awake.

"What the hell was that?!?" Yvette asked as Tony jumped up and stumbled into the living room to find six federal agents with guns pointed at his head.

"Get down on the floor and keep your hands where I can see them!" one of them yelled.

Tony obeyed as Agent Walker put his knee in his back and cuffed him. He then grabbed Tony by the arm, lifted him to his feet and sat him on the couch.

"Is there anyone else in the house we have to worry about, Mr. Brown?" Agent Perez asked.

"My wife is in the bathroom getting ready for work. I don't know what this is about, but please don't arrest her."

By this time Yvette had heard all the commotion and locked herself in the bathroom.

"What's your wife's name?"

"Yvette."

Agent Walker motioned for two of the agents to search the apartment as Agent Perez drew his weapon and cautiously entered the bedroom to find it empty. He knocked on the bathroom door and asked, "Mrs. Brown, are you in there alone?"

Yvette sat bare-assed on the toilet lid, toothbrush still in hand with toothpaste dripping out of the side of her mouth down to her chin, still too shaken to respond.

Agent Perez didn't want to break the door down, so he knocked and asked again.

Collecting herself, Yvette managed to say, "I...I'm by myself but, but I'm not dressed."

"Do you have something in there you could throw on?"

"No. My robe is hanging on the back of the bedroom door."

Agent Perez looked to his right and saw the white Ritz Carlton robe hanging exactly where Yvette said it would be.

"Okay. I'm going to pass you the robe through the door so you can put it on. But before I do that, I need you to tell me if you have any weapons in there."

"All I have is my toothbrush."

"Okay. Listen to me very carefully. I don't want anyone to get hurt. I need you to open the door very slowly and stick both hands out where I can see them. I'm going to hand you the robe. Put it on, open the door all the way and sit on the floor with your hands on top of your head. Can you do that for me?"

"Yes."

"Okay, go ahead."

When Agent Perez heard the door unlock he raised his gun eye level with his right hand and waited to see both of Yvette's hands emerge from behind the door.

When she did, he passed her the robe with his left hand and waited for the door to open all the way. Yvette slid both arms into the robe, tied the belt then sat on the toilet and opened the door like she was instructed to do.

With his gun pointed at her head Agent Perez stated, "I told you to sit on the floor, Mrs. Brown."

"Shit. That floor is too cold to be putting my ass on it."

"Okay, do me favor, put your hands on top of your head and go sit on the sofa next to your husband, please."

Yvette followed his orders and joined Tony on the couch where he sat, in his boxers.

"Okay, Mrs. Brown, you're probably wondering what all of this is about," Agent Walker said.

"That and why you felt it necessary to break my damn door down."

"One, we have a warrant which you will be able to see in a minute. Two, we gave you an ample amount of time to answer. We knocked for at least five minutes."

Yvette shot a look at Tony. "I told you to get your lazy ass up and open the door."

Tony looked back, rolled his eyes up to the ceiling. "Not now, Babe."

Agent Perez said, "Mr. Anthony Brown, according to Title 18 U.S. Code section 1344 you are charged with multiple counts of conspiracy to commit bank fraud."

"Did you know what your husband was up to, Mrs. Brown?"

"No, she doesn't. And I'd like to keep her out of it," Tony blurted, before Yvette was able to respond.

"That's fine, Mr. Brown. While agents search your apartment do you have anything you want to tell us?"

"No."

"That was quick. Nothing you want to tell us about Mr. Charles," Agent Walker asked?

"Nope."

When he asked about Bobby, Yvette's eyes opened wider like she saw a ghost. She wondered if any of this was happening to the other wives.

218

As the search and interrogation continued, Tony stood his ground and remained silent. Yvette was beside herself because strange men were tearing her house apart, looking for God knows what, and at the fact that she had to sit in her bathrobe with nothing on under it while it all took place.

The agents who searched the apartment were finished and entered the living room empty handed. "Nothing?"

"No sir."

"Okay, Mr. Brown, Agent Perez is going to let you get dressed so you can go downtown."

"Alright. What about my wife?"

"She's fine. You'll be able to speak to her later on today."

"What about my door?" Yvette asked.

"It'll be fixed today, Mrs. Brown."

"Good."

As Tony got dressed Agent Walker tried his best to calm Yvette about the situation but it wasn't working. All she could think about was how she was supposed to take Tony out tonight to celebrate her good news. She had found out she was with child a couple of weeks prior, and wanted to surprise her husband.

Yvette's thoughts then ventured off to how much time he may have to do and if she wanted to raise her baby alone. In the bedroom, Agent Perez told Tony to instruct the agent where to find his clothes. After that, Agent Perez removed the cuffs from Tony's wrists while another agent kept his gun drawn as he got dressed.

When he was done, Agent Perez grabbed Tony's and Yvette's cell phones off the nightstands. He put the cuffs back on and they led Tony back to the living room.

"Which one is your phone, Mrs. Brown?"

"That one," Yvette replied, pointing at the Nextel in his right hand. He gave Yvette the cell phone and nodded to the agents to take Tony.

When Yvette saw him dressed and cuffed, the reality hit her smack in the face. Tears started to form in the corners of her eyes as she stood up and asked,

"Can I at least kiss my husband?"

The two agents flanking Tony looked at Agent Walker for approval. Walker nodded his head and Yvette ran to Tony, threw her arms around him and kissed him.

After a few seconds, she released him and sat on the sofa again. The two agents led Tony out of the door, down the hall and to the elevator.

As he walked out of the door Agent Walker turned to Yvette and said, "Don't bother trying to warn the rest of the crew. The same thing is happening to them as we speak."

By this time Bobby was already in the city waiting to meet with the rest of the team. Niecy and Li'l Bobby rode in with him this morning because her mom was going to babysit while she did some running around. Bobby dropped her and the baby off by her mother's building, then drove down 125th to M&G's to grab some breakfast while he waited.

Bobby called Stacey to see if she could pick Maureen up and meet by Grant, but her phone rang out and went to voicemail. It was weird for her not to answer but he shrugged it off. While Bobby waited for his food, Malcolm walked in to grab his envelope, pausing to answer a call from Stew.

"Can we meet by the barbershop?" Stew asked.

"For what?"

"I have something for y'all but I'm not gonna be around later. I'm going away for a few days. You can just see me when I get back, but I wanna get these to you now so we won't be held up."

"Aight, but don't have me waiting. I'm trying to get my day started."

"I'm here already. I'm waiting on you."

"Okay. I'm on my way now." Malcolm closed his phone and said, "I'm about to go see this nigga Stew to grab some more copies. He said he's not gonna be around for a few."

"Okay, hold them and I'll see you tonight. Also, call Tony and tell him to meet me here."

"Aight, home team. Got you."

Malcolm walked out of the restaurant, hopped into his truck and pulled off.

At 8:55 Bobby's phone rang and he answered. It was Maureen.

"Ive been calling Stacey and can't get in touch with her."

"Yeah, the same thing happened when I called. I don't know what her story is but I'll figure that shit out later. You ready to rock and roll?"

"Yes."

"Good. Do me a favor. Take a cab to Amsterdam and 123rd Street and I'll be wating for you there."

"Okay. I'm getting myself together now."

Bobby hung up and tried to reach Stacey one more time, to no avail. When his food arrived he threw some eggs on his toast and made a quick to-go sandwich so he could meet Maureen. Bobby wrapped the sandwich in a napkin, left a dub on the table, gulped down some orange juice and walked out of the door. He hopped in the truck, dropped his sandwich on the passenger seat and drove to the light on Amsterdam Avenue. When the light turned green Bobby made the left and pulled up in front of Associated Supermarket.

He called Niecy and told her she was going to have to take a cab to run her errands because he had to take care of something.

"Well, I'm going to need some more money if I have to do all that, Babe."

"Okay, I'm downstairs in front of Associated. Come get it. But hurry up, because I have to go."

"Okay, I'm coming now."

Bobby hung up and began to devour his sandwich before Niecy could get to him. He definitely didn't want Maureen to see his wife so he hoped she wouldn't take long.

Niecy arrived a few minutes later and opened the passenger door of the Denali.

"How much more do you think you're gonna need?"

"A couple of hundred should do."

Bobby dug in his pocket, peeled off three C-notes and handed them to Niecy. She took the bills and climbed into the truck to give her man a kiss.

"Thank you, handsome."

"You're welcome, baby. Have a good day."

"You too."

Niecy climbed out of the truck, put the money in her purse and hailed a cab. Bobby finished his sandwich and was in desperate need of a beverage. He left the truck double-parked and went inside the supermarket to grab something to drink. After paying for his Snapple Apple, he stood out in front and waited for Maureen to pull up.

Just then, four black Suburbans with flashing lights and blaring sirens flew past his truck and stopped a couple of blocks away. He was so focused on the action down the street he didn't notice Maureen get out of the cab until she was right in his face.

"Hey, Bobby."

"Oh shit. Hey, Maureen."

"Are you okay?"

"Yeah, I'm just trying to see what the hell is going on down there."

"You ready?"

"Yes."

"Okay. Go get in the truck."

Maureen followed his instructions as Bobby's attention was again diverted to the activity down Amsterdam. He saw two of the agents running up the street toward him as his phone rang. 'Damn, these motherfuckers about to snatch *somebody's* ass,' he thought. Never taking his eyes off the agents, Bobby answered the phone to a frantic Yvette on the line.

"Bobby, the feds broke our door down and took Tony this morning!"

"What?!?"

Repeating the words actually made tears form in Yvette's eyes again. As soon as she finished her statement, one of the agents that was running, stopped in front of Bobby while the other kept going. The agent who stopped drew his weapon, placed his other hand on Bobby's chest and told him not to move. The other agent came back with his gun drawn and made Bobby get on his knees.

The four SUVs made u-turns. One pulled up in front while the other two pulled in back of Bobby's truck, blocking it in. Two agents jumped out of one of the SUVs, drew their weapons and approached Bobby's Denali. Agents Mansfield and Black exited their vehicle wearing blue windbreakers with the letters FBI emblazoned on the back in bright yellow. Bobby noticed the shiny gold shields that swung from the chains around their necks as Agent Black approached and asked,

"Is there someone inside your vehicle, Mr. Charles?"

"What vehicle?" Bobby asked as the last Suburban arrived.

AUSA Ryan exited the vehicle wearing a blue windbreaker with the Department of Justice seal on the chest, and a body armor vest underneath it. She walked over to Bobby and instructed the first two agents to stand him up. After doing so, she asked,

"Do you know who I am?"

"No. Should I?"

"Don't worry, we'll get better aquainted a little later."

She told Agent Mansfield to secure Bobby's phone and make sure the power stayed on. By this time two other agents had taken Maureen out of the truck, cuffed her and put her in back of one of the government SUVs.

All of this happened in a matter of seconds and Bobby never got a chance to end the call, so Yvette heard all of the chaos. Not understanding what was happening she hung up and immediately called Niecy who was almost out of Harlem by then.

When she answered, Yvette yelled, "Niecy, I was just on the phone with Bobby trying to tell him the feds raided my house this morning and took Tony and it seemed like something bad was happening to him too. I heard a bunch of noise; then his phone went dead and now I'm calling you. What the fuck is going on today, Niecy?!?"

"Calm down, Yvette. Let me call Bobby and see what's going on. I'm going to call you back, okay?"

"Okay. Hurry up, please." Niecy tried to remain calm as she called Bobby's phone. It rang out and went to voicemail. From her experience, when someone got locked up the police turned their phone off, so she wasn't too worried at that point. To be sure, she called him three more times with the same result.

Niecy told the cab driver to turn around and take her back where he picked her up. Then, she called Yvette back to gain some clarity about Tony's situation. After hearing the details, Niecy told Yvette to get dressed and meet her at her mother's house. Yvette wanted to, but declined because she had to wait for her door to be replaced. She assured Niecy she would be there as soon as it was done.

9:00AM

At the same time Bobby and Maureen were being detained, Malcolm was pulling up to the barbershop to meet Stew. He had called previously to make sure Stew was out front when he arrived. Sure enough, he was. Malcolm left his phone in the truck when he got out of it to speak with Stew. The two men shook hands and he tried to pass Malcolm an envelope in plain view of anyone who may have been looking.

"You know we don't move like that," Malcolm protested as he pushed Stew's hand away.

"Get in the whip, my nigga."

Both men entered the vehicle to find Malcolm's phone ringing. He was still conversing with Stew so it got ignored. After Stew told Malcolm how long he would be away and made other small talk, he exited the truck. His phone kept ringing but Malcolm decided not to answer until he was off of Seventh Avenue.

He pulled away from the barbershop, made a u-turn on 143rd and drove to a red light on 142nd Street.

"Hello. What's up, sis? What's wrong?"

"The feds took Tony this morning and now I can't get in touch with Bobby."

"What the fuck?!?"

Just then, Agent Castro lit him up and hit the siren for Malcolm to pull over.

"Damn, these motherfuckers fuckin' with me early in the morning," he stated out loud.

Malcolm thought he was being pulled over for his cell phone but he was in for a rude awakening.

Before pulling over he drove to the middle of the block when two black Suburbans pulled in front of him coming up from Lenox. 'Oh shit. This

226

ain't about no cell phone,' he thought as he stepped on the brake and brought the truck to a complete stop. Agent Stanton told Malcolm to turn off the ignition, drop the keys on the ground and stick both hands out of the vehicle over the loudspeaker in the SUV.

"Oh my God, Malcolm!" Niecy exclaimed.

"Shit! Sis, I gotta hang up. Call Tiecy and tell her I love her."

Malcolm did as he was instructed and dropped the keys to the ground.

"Using one hand, open the door, step to the front of the vehicle, and get down on your knees with your hands on top of your head," Agent Stanton shouted.

Once again, Malcolm obeyed the commands coming from the Suburban. When he was on his knees all six agents jumped out of their vehicles and swarmed Malcolm.

Agent Stanton and Castro told two other agents to search Malcolm's truck while they cuffed him, then lifted him from the ground and guided him to one of the government vehicles. They sat him in back of the SUV then closed and locked the doors. A few minutes pass and one of the agents that searched Malcolm's truck approached Agents Stanton and Castro holding two envelopes.

"We got him, sir," she said.

"Good. Let's wrap this up," Agent Castro said. All eight agents climbed into their respective vehicles and rode down to headquarters.

9:20AM

Meanwhile, Lay was in the shower daydreaming about the morning sex he and Celina had before she left for the office. She was barely showing, so the little baby bump didn't inhibit her from any activities, including making love to her man. When he was done, Lay dried off and sat on the edge of the bed watching the news with a towel wrapped around his waist.

His cell vibrated on the nightstand and he got up to see who it was. Picking up the phone, he saw it was a text from Monique. He also noticed that he had missed several calls from Niecy. He tried calling back, but Niecy's line was busy. The problem was, Niecy had both of her lines tied up with Yvette and Tiecy.

When they couldn't get Lay, they immediately called Celina and asked her if Lay was okay. She told them he was fine when she left for work earlier, so they left it alone. Niecy found it peculiar that Lay was the only one who hadn't been locked up, so she didn't mention what happened to the others. She urged Tiecy and Yvette to do the same. With no luck reaching Niecy, Lay texted Monique to confirm that he would be bringing her change in a little while.

He went into the living room, turned on the stereo and proceeded to get dressed. When he was done, he went downstairs and waited in the lobby while his car was being brought up by the valet. His cell phone rang. It was Celina. She told him that Niecy had called asking if he was okay.

"If I'm okay?" a confused Lay asked. "Why wouldn't I be?"

"I don't know, Babe. You have to ask her."

"I tried calling her but it was busy."

"Oh. I don't know what it was about, but I just wanted to let you know she called."

"Okay. Thanks, Beautiful. Call me as soon as you leave the doctor. Have a good day."

"I will. Love you."

"Love you too."

By this time Lay pulled out of the arc-shaped driveway and onto Palisade Avenue. Two cars behind, a black SUV with tinted windows containing Agents Gadson and Kirkland trailed his every move. They followed Lay across the George Washington Bridge, down the West Side Highway all the way into midtown without even coming close to blowing their cover. When he got to the garage Lay parked his car, got the ticket and walked to the building as he always did. He went to the eleventh floor, asked the receptionist for Monique, and sat in the waiting area until she came out to get him.

She emerged a few minutes later, and they went back to her office. Monique had no idea that the floor above and below had federal agents posted, who were poised to storm her office at a moments notice. Lay sat in the chair opposite Monique, with the huge mahogany desk separating them. He placed an envelope filled with hundreds and fifties on her desk and she quickly scooped it up to put it away.

As Monique returned to her desk, there was a knock on the door. She walked around Lay to open it and her boss was standing there with Agents Gadson and Kirkland behind him.

A stunned Monique asked, "Hey, Jason. What's going on? Who are they?"

By this time, Lay had turned around to see what Monique was talking about and caught a glimpse of the activity at her door.

"These gentlemen have some questions to ask you," Jason replied nervously.

"Me?!? What do they want to ask me? And exactly who are they?" asked Monique, sounding extremely annoyed.

"They can tell you exactly what's going on. I'm out of this." He scurried away from the door.

Monique shot a look toward Jason. 'You fuckin' coward,' she thought.

Kirkland and Gadson had now stepped past Monique and occupied her office along with the other agents. Lay rose from the chair, and stood face to face with Agent Kirkland. He instantly recognized him as the man in the grey suit from the garage.

Monique closed the door and turned to Agent Gadson. "So, is someone going to tell me what the hell is going on?"

"It looks like you got some shit going on, Mo'. You need me to call a lawyer?" Lay asked confidently.

"You're going to need a lawyer of your own, Mr. Taylor," Agent Kirkland retorted.

"Have a seat. Both of you."

Monique and Lay looked at one another with expressions of complete confusion written all over their faces.

"What would I need a lawyer for?"

Agent Kirkland looked at Lay. "I said, sit down. Now, if you don't mind, I'm going to ask the questions from now on. Is that okay with you?"

Without waiting for a response, he turned his attention to Monique, who sat behind her desk with a look of disgust and agitation in, both of equal measure.

"Well Ms. Peele, Mr. Taylor is correct. It seems that you do have some *shit* going on, as he so eloquently put it. Do you care to tell us about it?"

"I have no idea what you're talking about, Agent whatever the fuck your name is."

Lay was amazed at how women were always able to get away with speaking to the police any way they felt.

"Ms. Peele, I'm only going to warn you one time to watch your language. Am I clear?"

Monique rolled her eyes and replied, "Whatever."

"Okay, let's try this from another angle. Monique Peele and Lavian Taylor, you both are being charged with conspiracy to commit multiple counts of bank fraud, according to Title 18 section 1344 of the Federal Criminal Code," Agent Gadson said.

"Bank fraud?!? I haven't engaged in any criminal activity, especially in any banks. So I don't know where all this is coming from," Monique fired back.

"Oh, you haven't? Well, *he* has. Isn't that right Mr. Taylor? That's why it's called conspiracy. Can you spell prison, boys and girls?"

"I don't know what you're talking about, either," Lay replied.

"Well, you don't have to know what we're talking about, because we do."

Agent Kirkland motioned for two of the agents to cuff Monique and Lay.

"Please stand and place your hands behind your backs," the agents requested almost simultaneously.

"You can start your search," Agent Gadson instructed to the other two agents.

Lay and Monique stood in the corner handcuffed while the agents tore her office apart looking for evidence.

A few minutes later, one of the agents pulled the envelope Lay gave Monique earlier from the inside pocket of her coat hanging in the closet. He passed it to Agent Gadson who asked,

"Do you always walk around with this much cash on your person, Ms. Peele?"

"That wasn't on my person. You didn't find that on me."

"It was in your coat pocket."

"That's what your mouth says. I didn't see where it came from."

"No problem. We'll let the jury decide where it came from. Let's get them out of here."

When the door was opened, Monique's colleagues stared, as she and Lay were led out of her office, down the hall, and to the elevators. Some of the women even had tears in their eyes. When she was passing his office Jason told Monique he would get his lawyer on the phone, immediately. She said,

"It's the least you can fucking do."

As they rode down in the elevator, Lay's thoughts took him back to Syracuse, and the fiasco with Kev and Cassandra. He remembered how angry and hurt Celina was back then, and didn't want to imagine how she was going to handle this shit. Lay wondered if this was the reason Niecy had called asking if he was okay. 'Did she somehow know about this?' he thought. 'Nah, how could she? She doesn't know Monique.' 'Maybe she asked because something happened to Bobby and the rest of the crew.' 'Nah,' he thought again, 'she wouldv'e told Celina if it did.'

'Maybe...'

His thoughts were interrupted when the elevator door opened and the flash from a news camera almost blinded him. A team of news reporters had been notified about Lay's and Monique's arrest and began bombarding them with questions, only to be ignored. Monique didn't try to conceal her identity, but walked throught the lobby and out of the doors with conviction.

Lay squinted his eyes from the flashes, but never dodged the cameras as he was led to the government SUV awaiting him. The ride downtown seemed like it took forever, as the vehicles transporting Lay and Monique moved through traffic with the sirens blaring and lights flashing. The only thing going through Lay's mind was the thought of facing Celina with this mess, again. With Agent Gadson in the back seat sitting next to him, Lay looked out of the window, sighed, and then closed his eyes.

Although Tony was picked up first, Bobby and Maureen arrived before him, because the agents had to come from New Rochelle, and the traffic was heavy during that time of day. Next to show up was Malcolm, followed by Lay and Monique. Tony was brought in shortly after. AUSA Ryan was notified of the news that the four main targets were all detained. They were held in separate cells in order to prevent any attempts to collaborate on their stories.

Upon learning that the targets were in custody, AUSA Ryan headed to 500 Pearl Street to oversee the intake process of her detainees. When she walked through the door, Tony was being uncuffed and placed in a holding cell. All eight of the agents working directly under her gave AUSA a standing ovation, but she quickly silenced them.

"We did an excellent job out there today. I'm proud of you all. However, we're still not in the clear. It's up to Agents Belgrave, Bradley and their team to close the show on Sunday. In the meantime, prep the targets we do have in custody for interrogation. Once again, great job out there. I appreciate you all."

AUSA Ryan removed her jacket and body armor and turned her attention to a file and plastic evidence bag that read Robert "Bobby" Charles written on it. She picked it up and walked into the interview room where Bobby sat cuffed to the table in the center.

"Hello Mr. Charles. How are you?"

"I've seen better days."

"I can imagine. Can I offer you anything? Water, coffee, coke, food, anything?"

"No, I don't need anything except some answers."

"Okay, you want to get right to it. I appreciate that." My name is Sylvia Ryan. I am an Assistant United States Attorney for the Southern District of New York. We met earlier in the field. I know you're wondering why you're here, so let me not keep you in suspense. For the past year and a

233

half, several banks have been reporting a string of fraudulent checks being cashed in their institutions up and down the northeast region of the U.S. and for some reason, we weren't able to get a handle on any of it. Until now, of course. I have to hand it to you Mr. Charles. You managed to elude us for a long time. And I have to admit, we didn't get on your tail because of something *you* did wrong."

"If that's the case, how did I end up here?"

"That's a good question. You didn't slip up Mr. Charles. Your only mistake was the people you had around you."

Her last statement made Bobby's heart drop. His first thought was who amongst his crew was a rat. He couldn't believe his ears. Bobby's thoughts were interrupted when AUSA Ryan continued, "I know my agent read you your Miranda rights so I can ask, do you have anything you want to say?"

"No."

"Okay. Here's the situation. You and your crew are charged with multiple counts of conspiracy to commit bank fraud under Title 18 subsection 1344. Bobby knew exactly what he got picked up for, but couldn't figure out how they got on to him and the team in the first place. The first thing that came to mind was Lay's situation in Syracuse. 'Did he bring heat to the rest of us? But that shouldn't be it, because Lay hasn't been out since he caught that case. So where did this shit come from?'

It was all about to be made clear to him without having to ask. AUSA Ryan opened the folder and placed a check that Maureen tried to cash on the table in front of Bobby. He ignored it and instead opted to look Ryan directly in her eyes.

Unshaken by his stare, she asked, "Do you know what this is?"

"No."

"You haven't even look at it, Mr. Charles."

"I don't have to look at it to know I don't know what it is."

234

"Okay. This is a check that was intercepted when one of your underlings tried to cash it at an HSBC branch. She was arrested and subsequently decided to cooperate with the government."

AUSA Ryan reached into the evidence bag, pulled out the envelope containing copies of the checks she received from Stew and placed them on the table.

"These are copies of all the checks you cashed this week, courtesy of Mr. Stewart James. These corporations all coincide with the checks at the banks that you and your crew defrauded. The numbers are all off by a few digits, but just similar enough to make the connection. We even have copies of the checks Malcolm picked up from Stewart today. So you sir, are backed into a corner. We have you Mr. Charles. You, and your entire organization. And because you sit at the top of the pyramid, we don't need your cooperation."

Bobby kept a serious poker face the entire time, never once looking at all the evidence presented before him. But on the inside, he was fuming. 'That stinkin' bitch! And that motherfuckin' Stew! I'ma pop his top off when I catch him,' he thought.

As AUSA Ryan was gathering up the paperwork on the table she said, "I'm going to let you sit on all of that while I go speak with your co-conspirators."

When she was done AUSA Ryan walked out of the room and smiled with satisfaction. Although Bobby didn't break, she could tell she made an impact on his psyche as he sat in the room with his head in his hands. Upon reaching one of the interview rooms down the hall from Bobby's, AUSA Ryan knocked twice, then entered without waiting for permission.

In there sat Stacey, who had been picked up from her home around 6:30 that morning. Ryan's strategy was to eliminate Stacey from the equation before Bobby had a chance to pass the checks off to her. Agents Black and Mansfield had been unsuccessful in getting her to turn against Bobby no matter what tactics they used. AUSA Ryan remained silent and observed the interview for a few minutes. Realizing their efforts were futile, she decided to move to the next interrogation room.

The same held true for the rest of the detainees, as they remained steadfast in their loyalty to Bobby. Her last chance was to get some information out of Monique, who had remained strong until this point. This also proved to be fruitless because Monique wasn't moved by their interrogation tactics. Agent Kirkland could've possibly been more effective if he wasn't so fixated on her breasts.

"Why are you protecting him?" Agent Gadson inquired.

"I'm not protecting anyone but myself, and I don't have to speak about anyone else's business to do that. I already told you my relationship with him is strictly social."

"Strictly social," Agent Kirkland scoffed in disbelief. "You do know he has a girlfriend."

A thoroughly irritated Monique stated, "Once again, not my business. My only concern is how he eats my pussy and how his dick curves to the right."

Having heard enough, AUSA Ryan pushed away from the wall she was leaning against and walked out of the room. She didn't feel the need to check on any of the others so she let her agents do their jobs and focused her attention on Maureen. She walked down the hall to a row of cells that were secluded from all the rest. The last cell in the row contained a very nervous Maureen sitting on the bench hugging her legs so tightly that her chin rested on her knees.

Looking up as Ryan reached her cell, Maureen stood up and walked to the bars. Ryan held her finger up to her lips so Maureen wouldn't speak, and silently mouthed the words, "You did good."

A soothing sense of relief came over Maureen as she returned to the bench and watched AUSA Ryan walk away from the bars that separated the two of them. She left the holding area, went to grab her belongings, made sure all of her detainees were prepped to see the magistrate, and headed back to her office.

On the ride back, she received a call from U.S. Attorney Morgan congratulating her on the success she had in the field. She thanked him and when they hung up a pleased AUSA Ryan crossed her legs in the back seat of her government SUV and gave her self a figurative pat on the back.

11:55AM

Celina walked into her doctor's office arriving five minutes early, signed the appointment sheet and took a seat in the waiting room. She picked up the December issue of Essence with Halle Berry on the cover and flipped through it while waiting for her name to be called. Trying to decide whether to read the article about Halle or "The Five Minute Talk That Can Save Your Marriage," Celina's attention was drawn to the TV when she heard a familiar name come from the speaker.

She looked up at the screen and saw Monique being brought out of the Universal building in cuffs. Her thoughts instantly went back to the days when she and Monique would beef over Lay. That situation had her mind so fucked up that Monique once told Celina she was with Lay the previous evening and she questioned him about it, even though he had been with *her* the entire night.

Celina shook her head as she watched Monique being led to the black SUV. She wasn't the type to wish harm on anyone, but no tears would be shed for the predicament Monique found herself in. Celina listened to the reporter tell the story of how Monique was suspected to be involved in an elaborate check fraud ring, when the camera cut to the footage of Lay being brought out of the building in cuffs as well.

Celina stood up, dropping the magazine to the floor as she gawked at the television in disbelief. Her knees weakened and she fell back into the chair as the camera cut to a mugshot of Lay while the reporter spoke of his extensive criminal history, as the media often does when it comes to black men. She covered her mouth in shock as some of the patients looked at the news and others noticed her reaction to the TV.

A woman sitting next to her touched Celina's arm and asked, "Are you okay? Do you know those people?"

"No..., no I don't."

She shook it off, gathered her things and approached the young lady sitting behind the front desk.

"Please tell Dr. Hobgood I have to reschedule."

Celina was already walking through the door before the receptionist had a chance to respond. She immediately called Lay's cell knowing he wouldn't answer but still hoping somehow what she just saw on TV was part of a bad dream.

When it rang and went to voicemail the reality set in once again. Celina's mind raced as she called Bobby to find out if he knew anything about what happened to Lay.

Same results. Voicemail.

Feeling light-headed, she got in the car and started driving with the windows down so the air could hit her in the face. 'I can't believe this shit is happening again. And what the fuck was he doing with *that* bitch?!? Always talking about how much he's changed. He's better off in there because I'm going to kill him when I catch him,' were all the thoughts going through her mind as she drove through the N.Y.C. streets.

Celina looked through the call log to find Niecy's name so she could call her. Niecy felt bad for not warning her about the other arrests so she didn't answer the phone. Celina called right back, and Niecy reluctantly answered on the second ring.

Trying to keep her composure, Celina spoke shakily into the phone.

"Niecy, have you seen the news?"

"No, but it's all in the streets so I already know what's going on. They all got picked up this morning."

The word about the team being snatched was buzzing all through Harlem, especially after Lay was on the mid-day news.

"Is that why you called and asked me if Lay was okay?"

"Yes."

Celina felt the rage begin to rise in her gut. "So why didn't you tell me *then*, Niecy?!?"

"I'm not gonna lie. I didn't tell you because I didn't understand why Lay was the only one that didn't get snatched, and I thought-..."

"You thought what?!? Why in the world would you think that about my man, Niecy?"

"I don't know. It just seemed funny to me that he was the only one who was still free. I didn't know what to think."

"But why would that be the first thing that popped into your head? If you would've told me, I could've warned Lay and maybe he could've helped the rest of them. Did you ever stop to think about that?"

"I know, Celina, and I'm sorry. But put yourself in my shoes. How would you have felt if everyone was locked up except Bobby? Y'all would've been looking at him sideways, too."

Celina paused and thought about it for a second. Maybe she did have a point.

"Besides, this is not the time for us to be going at each other. We have to stick together to help our men."

Celina was still fuming, but deep down she knew Niecy was right.

"Meet me at my mother's house as soon as you can. My sister is here and Yvette will be here later."

"Where am I going?"

"She lives in Grant, 124th and Amsterdam."

"Okay, I'm downtown by my doctor. I'll be there in a minute."

The two women hung up and Celina pushed through traffic until she made it to Harlem. Arriving at their mom's thirty minutes later, Celina sat down with the twins and waited for Yvette to get there, which was taking entirely too long. Tiecy's eyes were still red from all the crying she did earlier. Niecy was holding Little Bobby across her lap while he slept. Celina sat on the sofa and watched as News 1 aired the story again.

Tiecy broke the silence by asking Celina if everything went okay at the doctor.

"I never saw her. I was in the waiting room when the news plastered Lay's face across the TV. I had to get out of there. Thanks for asking, though."

"I don't blame you, girl. I was a wreck when Niecy called me. I still am."

"I wish Yvette would hurry up. I'm trying to get home in case Bobby calls."

It hadn't dawned on her until she said it but Celina needed to do the same. Besides, it was almost time for the kids to get out of school by then, and Celina was getting antsy from just sitting around. 'If she doesn't get here in the next thirty minutes, I'm leaving,' she thought.

Just then, Niecy's phone rang and it was Yvette on the line saying she was there but couldn't find a parking space. That worked in everyone's favor because they were all ready to get home anyway.

Celina and the twins met Yvette downstairs by her car and they agreed that the best thing to do was stay off the phones and not to speak about what happened to anyone except immediate family until they hear from the men.

"We'll set up a meeting again after everyone has spoken to their husbands," Niecy said. The four women agreed, hugging one another before going their separate ways for the evening.

Celina picked Barry up from school and tried to explain once again why Lay was not going to be home that night, a speech she was tired of having to recite. She got him home, fed him dinner, and let him play with his Playstation. She kept the phone by her side the entire night, even taking it with her while she showered, hoping to hear from Lay. When she was done, she relaxed by rubbing shea butter on her belly.

"Your daddy is driving me crazy, little girl."

The day's events got the best of her and she found herself becoming weary. With heavy eyes and drained of all of her energy, Celina curled up in as close to a fetal position as she could and cried herself to sleep.

8:47PM

After the entire crew pleaded not guilty in front of the magistrate, they were separated again, and transferred to the Metropolitan Correctional Center. When Lay reached his cell, he immediately made up his bed. When he was done, he lay down staring up at the top bunk in the cell that would be his home for the next few weeks. Every kind of graftti and form of profanity imaginable had been scrawled across the makeshift canvas. Once again he was inside of another jail cell, forced to ponder the situation he found himself in. Although he knew he was facing a significant amount of time, he was more concerned with Celina, Barry, and the baby.

He couldn't imagine the look on her face when she found out what had happened. 'Here I am putting her through some more bullshit. And this was her biggest fear, to have this baby alone. I told her we would get through the last situation. Now, look at this shit. Damn, Lay. Damn.' There was nothing he could do but wait to see how much time they were going to offer him.

With the feds having a 97% conviction rate, there was no way to get around this, except to become a snitch, and that definitely wasn't going to happen. So his plan was to accept the first offer they presented, and then see what kind of magic Mr. Chase could work for his Syracuse case.

Lay's thoughts drifted from his dilemma to what was going on with his brothers. While in the interrogation room, Agents Gadson and Kirkland informed him that his entire crew was in custody, so he wondered how everyone was holding up. He wasn't too worried about them folding under the pressure, but what about Monique?

'All that shit talking could've been a façade because she knew I was there. She could've been singing like Whitney Houston when they had her under that bright light.' That would've fucked everything up for the team if he introduced a snitch into the fold. 'Knowing her, she's probably gonna blame me for all of this shit.'

If that's the case she defintitely had no reason to be loyal to Lay or his crew. 'Damn, she must have been mortified to get arrested in front of her co-workers that way, especially when those news cameras practically

243

jumped us. The news! Shit! Celina *had* to see me get arrested with Mo' on the fuckin' TV! I'm a fuckin' dead man. How the fuck am I gonna explain *that* shit? I'll be lucky if she doesn't leave my black ass. But after that episode in Mo's office I was chillin; I wasn't trying to fuck up again. I'm not a praying man but I seriously need God on my side for this one.'

After hours upon hours of stressing, Lay's anxiety continued to get the best of him until his brain couldn't take it anymore. His eyes got heavier and heavier, and he eventually drifted off to sleep.

In the morning, Lay was awakened by a CO tapping on his cell door for the count. He was supposed to be up, standing by the door when the CO passed his cell. Lay had never been in the federal prison system so he didn't know all of the rules. He stood up and walked to the door as the CO asked if he was okay. Lay nodded his head up and down and he moved on to the next cell.

Instead of lying down again Lay washed his face and brushed his teeth as best he could with the tiny brush he was issued. He waited until his cell was unlocked for chow so he could ask someone about the phones because as reluctant as he was to have the conversation, he knew he needed to check on Celina. After barely touching the cold oatmeal he was served, Lay asked a guy sitting at his table what time the phones came on.

"They came on at six, as soon as they pop the cells, homie."

"Thanks."

Lay quickly emptied his tray and went to the phone so he could make the dreaded call. He entered his ID number, dialed Celina's cell right after, and waited for her to accept his call. Celina was awake but still in bed watching the news when out of the corner of her eye she noticed the screen light up on her cell phone.

'This *better* be him calling and not someone else being nosey.' Her phone had rung so much the night before that she turned the ringer off to avoid all of the questions. She found it a little difficult to sit up, so she leaned on her elbow and reached over to get the phone off of her nightstand. Celina finally answered on the fourth ring and waited for the prompt to accept.

"Hello," Celina stated dryly.

"Babe?"

"Yes, Lavian?"

"How are you? How's Barry and the baby?"

"Everyone is fine."

"I know this looks crazy, Babe, but-..."

"I know. We'll get through it. That sounds so familiar."

"Babe, I know I've done my share of bullshitting you in the past, but this time is totally different. I promise you."

"How, Lavian?"

"Because Babe, after my last mishap I was chilling. I wasn't doing anything. This investigation came out of nowhere, and it didn't start with me. I guarantee that."

"Okay. So I have one question. Actually I have a few, but this one sticks out in my mind the most. If you were so-called chilling, why in the world did I see you being paraded across the TV with Monique, Lavian? What part of what you call chilling did she play?"

"Babe, I can explain that, but I promise you, it's not what you think."

"It's not what I think? How do you know what I think, Lavian?"

"You think that I'm fucking her, but it's not like that at all. It was strictly business with me and her. I swear."

"Strictly business, huh? So, all of a sudden you're in the music business now?"

Lay had to think of something quick, because he was about to go under.

"No, I'm not. Nor am I trying to be. I was only using her connections in the industry to get subjects for the magazine. That's all."

He wasn't a very good liar, but managed to come up with that one fairly quickly.

"So, out of all the people in the world, you mean to tell me you had to use *her*, knowing the history the two of you had? You couldn't think of

246

anyone else? Bobby couldn't think of anyone else? I find that hard to believe, Lavian. I just do."

"I know Babe. I know my track record has not been good with her, but I promise you it wasn't like that this time. Not at all."

In her mind, Celina knew there was a possibility that he could be telling the truth, and began to soften. Lay had definitely been on his best behavior the past few weeks, and she wanted to give him the benefit of the doubt. She wanted desparately to believe that he and his friends were finally trying to transition into legitimate enterprises.

But the fact that this whole situation was the talk all over Harlem, and Lay's messy ass was on the news was too much for her to handle. Celina's ego and embarrassment wouldn't let it go that easily. She also knew that it wasn't the time to dwell on the negative, so she changed the subject to the more pressing matter.

"We'll revisit the Monique discussion later. What do you need me to do, Lavian?"

"I appreciate that, Babe, but I need to know that you're okay, too."

"I'm as okay as I'm going to be, given the circumstances."

"Well, the first thing I need you to do is call Chase to find out when he can come see me. Get with the other ladies, especially Niecy to find out what's up with Bobby and the rest of the team. I don't know if I'm going to see any of them before we got to court, so let them know I'm going to sign up for the library every day. And..., I know I said this before, but we're going to get through this, Babe. I need you to know that."

"Okay, Lavian. I believe you."

"Good. What happened at the doctor? Is everything okay with my little princess?"

"I had to reschedule after all of this happened, but we're fine."

"Okay Babe. I'm not gonna hold you too long, but you know where everything is if-..."

"I know, Lay. I don't need anything but for all of this to be over."

Knowing he had let Celina down once again, his only reply was,

"Okay Babe, I understand."

"Kiss Barry for me, please. I love you."

"I love you too, Lavian."

As they hung up the phone, Lay couldn't believe how calm Celina had been throughout the whole conversation. He knew she was furious, disappointed, and fed up. Maybe she was trying not tyring to stress because of the baby. Either way, he knew they were dealing with some serious shit.

Lay walked away from the phone over to the CO to ask how to sign up for the library. After doing so, he went back to his cell until breakfast was over. He tried to mentally prepare himself for everything that loomed ahead. He lay down on his bed once again, consumed with stress as he stared at the bed above him.

Sunday Dec. 8th

Agent Bradley was sitting at his desk checking on the status of flight 712 from Nassau because Sean Prescott was on that plane and he was the last piece of the puzzle he and Agent Belgrave needed to close this investigation. The flight was scheduled to arrive at 6 p.m. in Terminal 5, but the gate was still unclear. Bradley immediately called the airline to get that information while Agent Belgrave arranged for the other four agents to leave for JFK ahead of time. She wanted every detail to be in place so this apprehension would go down perfectly.

After hanging up with Delta, Agent Bradley phoned ahead to the Port Authority Police to alert them of their arrival and of their intended target. Once all of the arrangements were made to accommodate them, Agents Bradley and Belgrave headed to JFK. Upon arrival, they saw their four agents strategically positioned in the waiting area.

With some time to kill, Agent Belgrave went to the newsstand and helped herself to a Vanity Fair magazine while they waited for the plane to touch down. Agent Bradley looked at his watch and noticed the time read five-fifteen. 'Almost showtime.' He walked to the enormous window to wait for the forty-five minutes to lapse.

Sean held Sasha's hand as the captain made the announcement for the passengers to fasten their safety belts and prepare for initial descent. The past seven days they shared on Paradise Island had been heavenly. Sadly, it had come to an end. Sasha hadn't been doted on and showered with that much attention from a man in quite some time, and she didn't want it to be over. Contrary to what Sean had always shown before, he was a complete gentleman the entire time.

He made good on his word by taking her shopping daily for bikinis for the beach, and outfits for the nightlife, which would explain the Gucci sneakers and warmup she wore on the trip home, and the Louis Vuitton duffle full of new clothes in the overhead compartment.

She was pleasantly surprised by how well-behaved he was and even considered dating him if he was interested as well-; and only if he asked, of course. She wasn't about to be sweating him like that. Sasha was kidding herself because deep down inside she knew she was falling for Sean but would never reveal her true feelings unless it was mutual.

"You can stay with me tonight, if you want to," Sean leaned over and whispered in Sasha's ear.

"Really? So you haven't had enough of me?"

"I don't think I could ever get enough of you."

"That's good to hear, because I'm not done with you yet."

'Did I just say that out loud? This man has got me all out of character,' Sasha thought, giving herself a mental kick in the butt because she couldn't believe she'd allowed her thoughts to be heard aloud.

At least now she knew he was feeling her a little bit, as well. 'But, why wouldn't he? Everything about the trip was good-; even the love making. Were we making love or just fucking? This can't be love. It's too soon. Girl, you're gonna drive yourself crazy overthinking things,' she admonished herself. 'Just relax and live in the moment. Don't rush things. If it's meant to be, it will.'

Sasha shifted in her seat as she tried to stop her mind from going one hundred miles a minute. 'I'm still going to this nigga's house tonight.' She laughed to herself as she gently squeezed his hand tighter and nestled her head on Sean's shoulder. Her thoughts were interrupted when the captain announced, "Prepare for landing."

On the ground, Agents Bradley and Belgrave were notified that the flight was about to land and in turn put their team on alert. As Agent Bradley checked his watch again he noticed four Port Authority officers approach the gate, one with a K-9 by his side. Something was off about everything he saw and it made his antennas go up. Belgrave noticed her partner's body language and approached him on his left side.

"What do you make of all this?"

"I don't know, but whatever it is better not interfere with our case."

Bradley decided to approach the K-9 officer and after showing his credentials, asked what was going on.

"I can't disclose that information, sir."

"Who's in charge?"

"I can get him on the radio if you need me to."

"Please. Use the phone if you could."

The K-9 officer instructed one of his colleagues to call their supervisor from the ticket agent's podium and hand the phone to Agent Bradley.

"Hello?"

"Yes, Captain Murray here."

"Yeah, this is Agent Bradley with the Bureau. I have a sensitive matter arriving on this six o' clock flight. These K-9s are raising eyebrows."

"We do also. It's a narcotics situation, hence the K-9 presence."

"I understand, but the U.S. government takes precedent, sir, and how come I wasn't notified of this when I called earlier?"

"This is a highly sensitive federal matter as well, Agent..., Bradley you said it was, right?"

"Yes, Bradley."

"It's a joint effort with the D.E.A, and info about this case is only released on a need-to-know basis. There are several agents all around you as we speak."

"Okay, so we have two targets that need to be taken on the plane."

"And we have a major drug trafficker on board as well as a couple of suspected mules."

"Well, all I need to know is who's going in first. I don't want the dogs to go in and alert my target."

"Normally, K-9 presence only makes *smugglers* uncomfortable. Is your target a narcotics suspect?"

"No."

"Then, he only has to worry about the Bureau, not the D.E.A. But, it doesn't matter. Your people can come in right after us."

"That sounds good to me, sir. Thank you for your time."

"No problem."

Agent Bradley placed the phone back on the receiver and ran the plan down to Belgrave and his agents. By this time, flight 712 had landed and was pulling up to the gate. With law enforcement from three different agencies about to board the plane, the targets didn't stand a chance of getting away.

The Port Authority notified the captain to instruct the passengers to remain seated for security reasons. Some of them had already unbuckled their seatbelts and were removing bags from the overhead compartments when the flight attendants asked them to return to their seats.

The main cabin was opened and two D.E.A. agents plus the K-9 officer went on board. They moved down the aisle past first class through the curtain to the rear of the plane. As the last agent passed through, Sasha turned around to look; but wasn't able to catch anything because the curtain closed so quickly.

"It's about to go down back there," she whispered excitedly in Sean's ear.

"You are so nosey."

"So what. Shut up."

As she turned to face forward, she noticed a familiar face. It was a white woman's face that had just boarded the plane and moved into the

252

aisle. Sasha couldn't quite put her finger on where she had seen her before, but it all came back to her when she noticed the tall black man that bent the corner and followed the white woman.

Sasha elbowed Sean in his ribs and pulled him closer so she could whisper, "That's the couple with the camera from when we left!"

Sean looked over the seat in front of him and his memory was jogged instantly.

'Oh shit! That *is* them,' he thought. Sasha had been right about them the entire time. He scooted down in his seat, hoping the couple would pass them by. That didn't happen. Agent Belgrave stopped in the row behind Sasha and Bradley stood by the row in front of her. The agents pulled out their credentials almost simultaneously and displayed them for the couple to view.

"Sean Prescott, this is Agent Belgrave and I'm Agent Bradley. I need you and Ms. Raymond to come with us."

"Go with you for what?!? I ain't do shit! What I need to go with you for?!?"

"Let's not make a scene, Mr. Prescott," Agent Belgrave said, leaning over Sasha's head so as not to alarm everyone in the vicinity.

"Man, I'm not going no where until you tell me what's up."

Bradley was visibly beginning to lose his patience with Sean and warned him, "I'm not going to repeat myself again. Stand up and exit this plane on your own before you have to be removed, and I don't think you're going to like that."

Sean looked at Sasha realizing this was a fight he wasn't prepared to have and began to stand up. When he was in the aisle, Agent Bradley cuffed him and draped his Akademics warmup jacket over his shoulders.

"Stand up please, Ms. Raymond," Belgrave said to Sasha.

"And what exactly am I being arrested for, may I ask?"

"It will all be explained later. Right now we need to get you off this plane."

Sasha was equally embarrassed and pissed off but didn't want the focus to be on her any more than it already was. So, she stood up and allowed Agent Belgrave to place the federal jewelry on her wrists. After Sasha was in cuffs they started to exit the plane.

By this time, the K-9 officer had returned to the first-class section through the curtain from coach and was making his way up the aisle when a passenger who had a little too much to drink grew impatient and yelled,

"What the hell is going on here?!?"

This startled the dog and it responded with a loud bark. Agent Belgrave, who was secretly terrified of dogs, lunged forward, causing Sasha to lose her balance and stumble to the floor. The commotion made Bradley turn around, releasing Sean's arm to reach for his firearm.

In the split second that Sean felt the pressure of Agent Bradley's grip soften from his arm he bolted for the plane door. Two frightened flight attendants moved out of Sean's way as he ran as fast as he could with the cuffs still tightly clamped around his wrists. A rookie agent waiting in the tunnel with his weapon drawn, heard the melee and rushed toward the noise, running head-on into Sean who blew past him, knocking him against the wall.

Sean stumbled, but managed to maintain his balance and made it to the entrance of the gate when he heard a deafening, Blaow! He whinced as he felt the sharp pain in his right trapezoid muscle from the bullet that had grazed it. Not one second ticked off the clock before another gunshot echoed through the tunnel, this time hitting Sean in the back, cracking his fifth rib and piercing his lung.

The force from the .9mm slug spun him around. He sprawled and landed on his back, grimacing in agony. Onlookers gasped in shock as Sean's eyes rolled into his head. The rookie rushed over to Sean and stood over him with both hands gripped around the gun handle, and his finger still on the trigger. He was shocked by the look on Sean's face as he was lying on the floor gasping for air, fighting to stay alive.

Inside the plane was complete mayhem as the flight attendants and officers tried to calm the terrified passengers.

When Agent Bradley saw that Belgrave was okay, he ran out of the door and into the tunnel.

The waiting area was filled with all three divisions of the law, hovering over Sean while he lay bleeding on the floor. Tears were already forming in Sasha's eyes as she was being escorted through the tunnel, but when she saw the bottom of Sean's sneakers through the police's legs, she lost it completely.

"Noooo!" she screamed. "What the hell did you shoot him for?!? Why?!?"

Agent Belgrave tried to restrain her as she became irate in the narrow walkway. Another agent assisted Belgrave as they had to practically drag Sasha past Sean's lifeless body. Amongst all of the chaos, not one officer or agent bothered to call a paramedic to try and save Sean's life.

Agent Bradley was too busy reprimanding the rookie who might have just put the entire investigation in jeopardy. He pulled the rookie to the side and asked, "What the hell happened?"

"I... I don't know. He caught me off guard when he came running through the door and knocked me into the wall. I didn't know what to think. I just didn't want him to get away."

"Are you serious? How about chasing him? Did that ever occur to you?"

"I don't know, sir. I panicked. I'm sorry."

Through clenched teeth, he got within two inches of the rookie's face and said, "That sorry shit won't cut it out here, motherfucker. I don't know where you come from, but you can't apologize your way out of shit like this. You just shot a man in the back that was unarmed *and* in fuckin' handcuffs.

Not to mention the fact that you could've hit a civilian. You better hope that motherfucker lives, because if he doesn't, your ass is going to jail. Either way, Ryan is gonna have your badge or your ass."

Frustrated with the whole situation, Bradley backed away from the rookie with his hands in the air and went to check on his prisoner. Someone had finally called 911. When they arrived they began working on Sean who was unconscious at this point. The paramedics asked for the cuffs to be removed so they could place him onto the gurney and transport him to the hospital.

Sasha was in the back seat of the government SUV crying her eyes out when Sean was brought out of the airport and placed into the ambulance. Never in a million years did she think her vacation would end this way, after spending the last seven days in paradise with the man she had now fallen for. For him to get shot and be fighting for his life was way too much for anyone to bear.

When the ambulance door was closed, Sasha leaned over until her face was on the seat and sobbed quietly while Agents Bradley and Belgrave got in the front and pulled away from the terminal. Sean was taken to Jamaica Hospital ER where the staff fought to get the bleeding under control and tried to relieve the pressure from his heart and lungs so they wouldn't fill up with air.

While Sean was being worked on, Sasha was taken to AUSA Ryan's office to be interrogated. They had no real evidence to pin on her, so they tried to see if they could extract some information, hoping to capitalize on the fragile state she was in. Although she was glad Sean was in custody, Ryan was furious when Agent Bradley briefed her about what happened with the rookie at JFK. She didn't want to concentrate on questioning Sasha, so she let Agent Belgrave handle it.

This only lasted for a few hours because nothing came from the inquisition. Sasha didn't know anything so she had nothing to reveal. Belgrave quickly realized that their theory about her was correct all along. Sasha was just a friend of Celina's who was lucky enough to get an all-expense paid vacation funded by a criminal.

AUSA Ryan decided not to release her until the morning so she could be monitored. Sasha was placed in a cell where she sat up nearly the entire night thinking about Sean and his condition. The last image of him on the stretcher was burned into her brain and all she wanted to do was get to him.

Monday December 9th

Before Sasha was released she was allowed to use the phone, so she called Celina and asked if she would be able to pick her up from downtown. She wanted to get to Sean as soon as she could so she called the only person who would understand, not knowing Celina had bad news to deliver as well. When Celina answered the phone, she had just dropped Barry off at school and was headed back home to wait for Lay's call.

Tears welled up in the corners of her eyes as Sasha briefly described the events that lead up to Sean being shot by the agent. Celina collected herself and headed to the city to get her best friend from federal lockup. After ending the call, Celina's mind wandered as she drove. Amidst all the chaos, everyone had forgotten about Sean and Sasha. She was immensely worried about how Lay was going to take the news when he found out.

She also felt a sense of guilt for hooking Sasha up with Sean because they wouldn't have gone through any of this if it wasn't for her playing matchmaker. Celina began to doubt her decision to have Lay's baby, and even getting involved with him in the first place. Even when it wasn't his fault he still found a way to hurt her. She couldn't keep doing this to herself over and over. There had to be a better way.

Sasha was standing in the lobby of 500 Pearl Street when Celina pulled up in front. Sasha grabbed her bag, walked out to the car and hugged her best friend as they both broke down in tears.

"I'm so sorry this happened to you, Sash. I feel like this was all my fault."

"I could never blame this on you, girl. I knew what I was doing when I got involved with Sean. I know what type of man he is. This is part of the game."

The women got in the car and Sasha called the hospital to get directions so she could check on Sean. On the way there Celina filled her in on all that happened in her absence. Sasha tried to keep it together but the tears just wouldn't stop falling.

When they reached the hospital, Sasha got the room number from the information desk and took the elevator up to the sixth floor. Sean's room wasn't hard to find because it had two federal agents standing guard on both sides of the door.

Sasha tried to enter, and was told he couldn't have any visitors, but she was allowed to step in for a second and see him. She stood there looking at Sean lying so still and peaceful, the same way she remembered him sleeping in the Bahamas. The only difference was, she was beside him in that bed and he was cuffed to this one. Every sound in the hospital was drowned out by the ventilator machine that helped Sean breathe as he lay there unconscious.

Celina comforted her friend as best she could, considering she needed comforting of her own. Sasha explained to the agent that she was with Sean at the airport when he was shot. She asked the taller agent if she could just kiss him before she left.

He felt some compassion and told her to make it quick. When they tried to approach the bed, he stopped Celina and said, "Sorry, just her."

"Okay, no problem," Celina replied.

Under the watchful eye of both guards, Sasha went inside, leaned over Sean's lifeless body and whispered, "You better make it, because I'm not done with you yet, Baby."

She kissed him on the cheek, touched his face and walked out of the room, past Celina and the agents to the elevator. From nowhere it seemed like the walls were closing in on her and she had to get out of the building. Celina walked as fast she could, but missed the elevator Sasha was on by two seconds.

On the ride home Celina offered her house to Sasha because she didn't want her to be alone; nor did *she* want to.

"I don't want to inconvenience you Celina. Besides, I don't want to be stuck in New Jersey where I can't get back and forth to see Sean."

259

"Sasha, you can stay in my house as long as you want. You can use my car and I'll take Lay's." After thinking for a second Celina said, "Girl, they won't even let you in the room, so how are you going to visit him?"

"I don't care. I'm going back every day and will stand at that door until he wakes up. I don't care."

"I have never seen you act like this over a man before, not even your ex. What happened over there on that island?"

"I don't know what it is either, but he was just so different than his usual irky self. He made me feel so special, girl. He really did."

"I was hoping the two of you had a good time but I definitely didn't expect all of this."

"Everything about the trip was so dope. You know what I mean? Even down to the sex. He was so-..."

"Girl, I do not want to hear about that man's sex game. Please spare me the details."

"Okay, you're right. He's off limits, anyway."

"How is he off limits, Sasha? Sean is not your man."

"He will be when he wakes up. I'm not leaving him in that hospital by himself."

"Girl, you are crazy."

"I might be, but I don't care. It's not the first time, and it won't be the last."

Celina shook her head at Sasha as they rode to her house to pick up some clothes for the week. It was almost time for Barry to get out of school so they tried to make it to New Jersey before traffic got too heavy.

Later that evening the ladies picked up some takeout from Outback and went to the house to wait for Lay's call. When he did, Celina let Sasha give the account of everything that happened to her and Sean. He held the phone, listening in disbelief.

"Damn, those motherfuckas shot my brother," he said regretfully.

After the call, Lay went back to his cell and stayed in for the rest of the night. He had to be the bearer of the bad news to the rest of the team at the library the next day. Bobby took it the hardest because besides Lay, he was the closest to Sean. Even though he was fucked up, he still had to keep it together whenever he was around the team.

On his next visit with Niecy she told Bobby that there was $285,000 in the kitty for the team's legal fees. He instructed her to take $35,000 out to pay Stacey's lawyer and divide what was left by five and give it to the ladies. Niecy's response was,

"Okay Babe, but do you really trust Sasha with Sean's money? That's Celina's friend; we don't know her like that. To be honest, we don't even know Celina like that. Besides, we don't even know if he's going to-..."

Niecy caught herself before she uttered some words she wouldn't be able to take back. Bobby looked at her with contempt. He knew she had a point about Sasha, but that last comment almost got her in hot water.

"Im sorry, Babe. I didn't mean that. He's going to pull through. I just don't want some random chick having access to his money if she's not going to do right by him. That's all I was saying."

"I know, Babe. All of this shit has us going a little crazy. It's alright. I know you didn't mean it, but from what I hear she's been at that hospital everyday checking on him, and she's not getting a *dime* for that. It seems like she really cares for him."

"I feel you, Babe."

"But, I get what you were saying, so here's what we'll do. Give her $5,000 for traveling and any other expenses she might have, and put the rest to the side for him, because he's going to need it."

"Ok Babe. I will."

At the next meeting, Bobby explained how the kitty got divided so everyone's minds could be at ease about paying their attorneys. He also advised them about going to trial against the feds and their high conviction rate. That didn't matter to Lay because he already had it in mind to counter their first offer and take it if they accepted. He knew he still had to handle his situation in Syracuse and didn't want to piss them off by prolonging the process.

After leaving the meeting they all returned to their units to find large manila envelopes had been slipped under their cell doors. Inside Lay found a copy of the complaint that the U.S. government had filed against him and his brothers.

Reading through his paperwork, Bobby was able to confirm that Maureen was the confidential informant. She got arrested with him, but her name was nowhere in the complaint.

After a visit from his attorney a couple of weeks later, Bobby looked through his discovery and found out his phone had been tapped, and a bug had been planted under the table in the booth at Jimbo's. There were also a series of very short conversations with Maureen that had no real incriminating statements on them. However, with her cooperation along with the physical evidence from Stew, it had been enough to bring the case to fruition.

The U.S. v. "The Charles Syndicate"

The courtroom was filled almost to capacity as Bobby, Tony, Malcolm, Stacey, and Lay were all seated in their respective seats at the defendant's table. Behind them stood six attorneys; including one who represented Sean. AUSA Ryan stood and stated her name to the court loudly and clearly to be sure the stenographer heard every word. After that, The Honorable Judge John Sterling turned his attention to the other side of the room and each lawyer stated his or her names and which defendant they represented.

It had been agreed prior to the hearing that Bobby's lawyer, Mr. Andrew Masino, would speak for the entire team unless there were some specific requests that needed to be addressed individually. Each attorney had assembled a bail packet before this hearing and AUSA Ryan was ready to challenge them at every angle.

The ladies had been in constant contact with the lawyers over the past couple of weeks, retrieving signatures from family members and securing properties, in hopes of getting their men released on bail.

When the applications were filed, AUSA Ryan quickly requested to have them all denied on the basis that the defendants had knowledge of the identities of the cooperating witnesses, and to release any of them-, especially Bobby- would put their lives in danger.

Masino recognized her strategy immediately and petitioned to address the court.

"Your honor, the prosecution revealed those identities to my client with the sole purpose of having his bail denied at this hearing, making the ridiculous assumption that he would cause harm to these informants if released. It is highly unorthodox for a prosecutor to reveal the identity of a confidential informant, your honor. That's usually why the title *'confidential'* is assigned to people like that."

"But the U.S. attorney had an agenda, your honor. Neither my client nor any of his co-defendants have a history of violence in any capacity. So, to deny bail based on that fact is unwarranted. They recognize the severity of these allegations and are not inclined to further worsen the situation by committing a violent retaliatory act against a C.I. I would also like to add the fact that each defendant has strong ties to the community, with children and families that love and care for them, so taking flight is not an option. All have agreed to surrender their passports in hopes of a favorable decision today."

As Masino spoke, he turned to the audience and motioned for everyone in the gallery who was there for the defendants to rise. The entire room stood on its feet.

Judge Sterling was surprised by the amount of people who were in attendance in support of Bobby and the defendeants.

AUSA Ryan interjected,

"Your honor, I ask that the court not be persuaded by the turnout of support in the audience. These defendants collectively defrauded corporations out of millions of dollars, showered their familes with expensive gifts and provided them with an extremely lavish lifestyle. One would *expect* them to show up in court. If my husband bought minks and diamonds for me, just because it was Wednesday, I would be in court, too. But the fact that they have families should have no bearing on their release. Not to be facetious your honor, but Ted Bundy was a serial killer, and he had a wife and a child as well."

Seeming to be unmoved by either side, Judge Sterling sat stoically on the bench for a few seconds and then said,

"After taking both sides into consideration, bail requests for all of the defendants are denied."

The judge's ruling seemed to let all the air out of the audience as they sucked their teeth and some even scoffed at the decision.

"This case will be adjourned until..." The judge paused and looked to the clerk for a date. "Tuesday, January Seventh."

As Judge Sterling lifted his gavel to end the proceedings, Alan Shapiro, Sean's attorney stood and asked if he could approach the bench.

After being granted permission, Shapiro walked forward, followed closely by Ryan and stood before Judge Sterling and said,

"Your honor, I'm here on behalf of Sean Prescott."

"I'm aware of that."

"Yes your honor, but for my client to have his bail denied while he lies unconscious, and chained to a hospital bed is extreme, especially considering the circumstances in which he ended up there."

AUSA Ryan chimed in,

"Your honor, Mr. Prescott has proven to be the most brazen of all of the defendants by resisting arrest in a crowded airport, showing no regard for and endangering the lives and safety of travelers. The man tried to flee while in handcuffs, sir."

"Yes, as we all know a man in handcuffs is a menace to society and one of your agents politely shot him in the back for that fact. Not once, but twice."

"My agent did his job, counselor."

"I would tread lightly around those waters if I were you," Judge Sterling warned Ryan.

"Bail for your client is denied as well, counselor."

Mr. Shapiro looked at the judge in disbelief as AUSA Ryan walked away from the bench satisfied that everything had gone her way in the proceedings. She gathered up her paperwork and made her way out of the courtroom.

When Celina and Sasha stood up and turned around they noticed Monique waiting in the aisle behind the crowd of people who were exiting the courtroom. She had been released a day after her arrest for lack of evidence, and the fact that she refused to snitch on Lay. The government had no reason to hold her any longer.

"What the fuck is that bitch doing here?" Sasha snapped.

"I don't know. She's probably here checking on her old thang."

"That shit doesn't bother you?"

"Girl, I don't have the energy to be mad at her right now." My main concern is this baby, Barry, and my man. Screw her and her agenda, whatever it may be. Besides, she can't get to him anyway. And I already told Lay if I see another chick's name on that visitor list, he won't see me again. *Ever.*"

"I hear you. But I just can't stand a disrespectful bitch."

"She's not worth the aggrevation Sash, trust me. Anyway, the ladies and I are about to get something to eat. Are you coming?"

"No, girl, you know I have to get to the hospital."

"How is he?"

"Still the same."

"Damn, girl. Give him my love."

"I will."

The holidays had passed and the time for family and festivities was instead filled with loneliness and despondence because all of the ladies were forced to spend them without their mates. Although they had more than enough money to buy gifts for the kids, the absence of the men in their lives during that time of year left them feeling a deep void. Now, forced with being the backbone of the family unit, each woman pressed on and continued to hold everything together.

The next couple of weeks proved to be equally challenging because another court date was rapidly approaching. Prison sentences were inevitable, as they all were well aware, but the mystery surrounding what terms the government would request is what had everyone on edge.

As if things weren't bad enough, even more stress was added to Celina's plate during one of her weekly visits to see Lay. She was now four months along and the baby girl inside of her was wreaking havoc on her hormones. Sometimes Celina was an emotional wreck. Other times, she was stone-faced and stoic.

On this particular day, she was waiting for the visitor form outside in the cold January air when she noticed a vaguely familiar woman standing three people in front of her. The woman wore a full length mahogany mink and had her hair pulled back in a ponytail that came down to the middle of her back. Every movement and gesture the woman made was taking Celina to a place where she dreaded more than going to the dentist. 'I know her from somewhere,' she thought.

When the woman turned her head to receive her visitor form from the CO, Celina caught a glimpse of her profile and was instantly sick to her stomach. The woman caught sight of Celina and, upon recognizing her, turned all the way around to make sure she saw who she thought it was. At that moment Celina and Josie locked eyes for the first time in about five years. The two women despised one another because of the love triangle Lay had entangled them in so many years ago. Although the encounter was brief, it seemed to last for an eternity.

'What the hell is this bitch doing here?' Celina thought. Josie rolled her eyes and turned to face forward, ignoring the fact that Celina was behind her. She bounced up and down as if she was trying to rock a baby to sleep.

Peering closer, Celina now noticed the brown straps of a baby carrier peeking through the fur on Josie's coat. She closed her eyes and silently asked God for this not to be what it most certainly looked like. She knew she was getting ahead of herself. She may not even be here to see Lavian. She prayed that that baby was not his, for his sake.

As the line moved inside the building, Josie returned her visitor form. When Josie got to the desk, Celina overheard the CO tell her that she wouldn't be allowed inside because she wasn't on the inmate's correspondence list. Frustrated, Josie turned away from the CO's desk, crumpled the piece of paper, threw it in the trash, and walked past Celina with the cutest little cocoa-complexioned baby girl strapped across her abdomen. When Celina laid eyes on the little girl, everything seemed to move in slow-motion. Every time the heel of Josie's Giuseppe boot hit the floor, it sounded like the bass drum of a marching band.

Sucking on a Nuk pacifier, the baby rested her head comfortably on Josie's bosom. Her hair was donned with red, black, and white barrettes on the ends of her ponytails. She pulled the hood of the baby's tiny mahogany mink jacket over her head before exiting the building. Celina couldn't believe her eyes as the door slammed behind Josie, making a loud commotion. When it was her turn at the desk, the CO looked at Celina's form and said, "Two visits for Taylor in one day? Somebody's got it going on up in here."

Celina remained silent, but rolled her eyes at his corny ass comment. 'CO's were so wack sometimes.' But she had bigger issues to focus on, like the fact that Josie *was* here to see Lay. Inquiring minds wanted to know why. She couldn't wait to get inside so she could confront him about whatever shenanigans Josie was up to. Placing her belongings inside the locker, Celina's rage began to rise from her gut, up to her head. She slammed the locker, locked it and waited to be led into the visitor room.

Once inside, Celina grabbed a chair and sat with her arms folded, impatiently waiting for Lay to come out. When the door opened, Lay was the third inmate to step inside. With a gentle smile on his face he approached Celina sitting in her chair, who was bubbling inside, like a pot of hot grits on the stove. He extended his arms for a hug and Celina remained seated, as tears began to form in the caverns of her eyes.

"Oh-Kay, I don't get a hug today?"

Noticing her tears, he grabbed Celina's hands, pulled her out of the chair and asked,

"What's wrong, Babe?"

When Lay wrapped his arms around her, she refused to reciprocate. Her hands dangled limply by her sides. He tried to kiss her and Celina abruptly turned her head to the side, wiping the tear that had rolled down her cheek into Lay's beige jumpsuit. The CO motioned for Lay to sit down, because at this point they were the only ones still on their feet, drawing attention to themselves.

"What's wrong, baby? Why are you crying?"

Celina looked Lay directly in the eye and said, "I just saw Josie downstairs."

"Josie?!? Okay, and?"

"Yes, Josie! And, she came here to see *you*."

"Me?!? I don't know what for! I haven't been anywhere near her since we got back together."

"Are you sure about that, Lavian?"

"Am I sure? What kind of question is that? I'm more than sure. I'm positive, Babe. I put that on everything I love."

"Oh, really? Because she was carrying a baby that looked just like you."

That was an exaggeration, although the little girl's complexion was definitely close to Lay's.

"Looks like *me*?!? Are you serious? What are you trying to say, Babe? Man, I don't care what that baby looks like. It's not mine!"

Celina's tears had stopped falling. She sat across from Lay with a look of complete exhaustion on her face.

"Lavian, I'm tired. I'm so, so tired of you and everything that comes with you."

"Babe, don't say th..."

"No, I have to say it. It's been on my mind for a while now, and after what I just saw today I'm at my wit's end. You and your whole world have drained me, completely. I'm trying to be the good girl, and stand by my man but every time I turn around something else is right there to knock me on my ass. How much is a woman supposed to endure before she reaches her breaking point?"

"Babe, I know shit has been crazy lately, and most of it is my fault. I'll own one hundred percent of it. But this bullshit with Josie is exactly that. Bullshit. I promise you."

Lay's words had no effect on Celina. She sat there looking into Lay's eyes, wondering why loving him had to hurt so badly. He understood, because although he spoke with conviction he had very little confidence in his own statements.

"I love you, Lavian. I love you with everything in me. But I will not play second, ever again."

"Babe, you will never have to. There's no one to play second to."

"What about the baby, Lavian? That could be your baby. Then, I'll have to be second to her *and* her mama. You chose her over me before. Who's to say you won't do it again?"

"*I'm* saying it, Babe. You are my world. My everything. Nothing and no one else matters. You have to believe me."

Looking into Lay's eyes as he spoke, Celina did believe him, but the events that occurred over the past couple of months had taken its toll on her. She stood up, as Lay reached out to hold her hand.

Snatching it away, Celina said, "If that baby is yours, I'm leaving you, Lavian."

She knew those words would cut him like a razor, but she had to remain firm in order to preserve some of her dignity. Lay's world had managed to suck the life out of her, and Celina was ready to throw in the towel.

Lay remained seated as he watched Celina walk through the door without looking back. He was fuming inside about the chaos Josie had caused, but was more concerned with Celina and her well-being. He was determined to get to the bottom of this baby situation, but had no idea where to start. He was honest with Celina when he told her he hadn't seen Josie, but he *had* spoken to her on occasion; just to give her money for the boys and miscellaneous matters. He definitely didn't do anything to cause a problem with him and Celina.

Celina walked out of the door never looking back, as Lay remained seated for a moment, thinking about how much he had once again hurt the woman he loved. He motioned to the CO to let him know his visit was over so he could go back to his unit. He had homework to do, and he wanted to get started on it right away. When he reached his cell, Lay sat on the bed and wondered if he had actually lost Celina for good this time. This baby fiasco had Lay totally fucked up in the head, as he tried to calculate the last time he was with Josie to try to make sense of it all.

He figured out that Josie might have gotten pregnant around July because they were only intimate a couple of times after he bought the X5. If they had sex in July and she got pregnant then, the baby would've been born around April. It's January now, so that would make her about nine months old. Celina didn't say how big the baby was. She just said it looked like him. Lay lamented, 'if my calculations are correct, that *could be* my fuckin' baby,'

"Damn!" he shouted aloud.

He put his feet on the edge of the bed, rested his elbows on his knees and covered his face with both hands. His life was unraveling right before his eyes and there was nothing he could do about it. As much as he hated to admit it, he believed Celina this time when she said she would leave him. She had never looked so hurt and defeated before.

Lay resisted calling her for a couple of days just to give her a chance to cool off. The person he desparately needed to speak to however, was Josie. The best thing for him to do was to take a chance and put her name on his visitor list just in case she decided to show up again, and hope that she didn't bump heads with Celina. That would be a disaster of massive proportions; and would definitely solidify Celina's departure from their relationship.

He left the cell and got the form from the CO's desk to add Josie's name to his list. After inserting it in the envelope he dropped it in the outgoing mailbox and went back to his cell. There was nothing left for him to do now, but wait.

Sentencing

Weeks passed by and Lay hadn't seen or heard a word from Celina. She wouldn't answer any of his calls and had not been back to visit him since the Josie sighting. As far as Josie was concerned, Lay knew she had received the visitor form because she mailed it back. She didn't show up to visit him again. This led him to believe that the whole baby situation was just another ruse to get under Celina's skin. The sad part of it is that it worked. Whether the baby was Lay's or not, Celina had disappeared, leaving Lay to wonder if there was anything left of their relationship.

Although he still met with the team regularly, he spent most of his time sitting in his cell, stressed about Celina, reading books to pass the time and take his mind away from his current predicament. Celina was that addiction he just couldn't shake. She and the baby were on his mind constantly, almost to the point of obsession. His every waking thought was of Celina and how he missed her. Nevertheless, there was a small voice in the back of his mind that said she was better off without him.

Lay woke up on Valentine's Day feeling more down than usual because this was the day he had planned to propose to Celina, and had even hoped for a June wedding date. He could only imagine what the expression on her face would've looked like when he got down on one knee and asked her to be his queen for all eternity. But now all of those plans had to be put on hold because he had bigger issues to tackle.

The team had a court date on February 28th, and they all intended to take their pleas. They were all brought into the courtroom and seated at the defendant's table where their attorneys stood behind them. Before sitting down Lay turned around and noticed all of the women were in the gallery except for Celina. Even Sasha was there to show her support for Sean, although he wasn't present in court, himself. A true sense of hopelessness came over Lay that day. It didn't matter how much time they gave him. If he didn't have Celina to come home to, he might as well stay locked up forever.

AUSA Ryan sat at the table for the government as the judge made his way to the bench and called the court to order. The proceedings began with Ryan explaining that all of the defendants had accepted their offers and the government was ready to set a date for sentencing. Judge Sterling looked to the defense attorneys and asked if this was true. They all responded in the affirmative and the judge asked that it be noted in the record. The team was asked to stand as their charges were read to them, and they were each asked individually if they indeed wanted to plead guilty to said charges. The team responded yes, and the judge proceeded to hand down the sentences.

"After reviewing the pre-sentence reports, the following shall be noted to the record. Mr. Anthony Brown, Mr. Malcolm Jones, Mr. Lavian Taylor, and Ms. Stacey Mack all fall under the sentencing guidelines of forty-two months. Mr. Prescott's matter will be handled at a later date, when his health is not an issue."

Sean's lawyer nodded his head in agreement.

Judge Sterling continued. "As for Mr. Robert Charles, because he assumed the leadership role in this organization, his guidelines have been calculated to put him at sixty months. We will reconvene on March 28th, exactly one month from today. Is that date suitable for all parties involved?"

After everyone checked their schedules and agreed, Judge Sterling ended the proceedings by banging his gavel and asking for the next case to be called.

As the team was being led to the back of the courtroom Lay looked to see if Sasha was still in the audience. When he saw her, they made eye contact and Lay quickly mouthed the words,

"Tell Celina I love her."

Sasha nodded and silently mouthed, "Okay."

Lay disappeared in the back, through the door behind the judge's bench. She felt a little betrayal inside for even acknowledging Lay, when Celina was clearly done with him. She still felt some compassion at the same time because he was the only one up there with no one in the audience for support. That had to be a fucked-up feeling. Even though she would always be "Team Celina", Sasha actually felt sorry for Lay.

The next twenty-eight days seemed to drag as the team waited in federal lockup to be sentenced. Everyone was anxious to know where the feds were going to send them to do their time, but Lay had to worry about that, plus the open case in Syracuse.

On March 28th, the team was present in court again; this time for sentencing. When they were brought out to the defendant's table, Lay looked to see if Celina was sitting in the gallery along with the other ladies; only to be disappointed once again.

'She must really hate me if she didn't even show up for my sentencing.'

He heard the voices, but wasn't listening as the proceedings took place right before him. He snapped out of his trance-like state when Judge Sterling called his name, asked him to stand and whether he had anything to say to the court before sentencing was pronounced. Lay stood up, but declined to speak and immediately returned to his seat.

The rest of the team followed suit, and the court session was basically over. After the judge sentenced the team, they all stood up so the bailiffs could escort them to the back. They tried to say their goodbyes as quickly as possible without being reprimanded for facing the audience. Bobby blew a kiss to Niecy, and Tony lifted his shackled hands as high as they would go and waved to Yvette. Malcolm winked at Tiecy and raised his chin, signaling her to keep hers up because everything was going to be alright. Stacey looked at Missy, ran her tongue across her top lip and blew a kiss at her as well.

People had started to leave the courtroom when Lay stood up to walk away from the defendant's table. Although he felt it was uselees, he looked in the gallery one more time to see if Celina had a change of heart. In the very last row, he spotted Sasha sitting close to the aisle with her arm wrapped around someone who was out of Lay's view because there was a man standing in front of them. When the man moved, Lay caught a glimpse of Celina's beautiful face covered with tears, while Sasha comforted her.

He wasn't able to blow a kiss, wink an eye, or mouth that he loved her because the bailiff had his hand in his back, pushing him through the door. But the fact that she actually showed up gave Lay a ray of hope that he hadn't felt in weeks. 'Maybe she doesn't hate me, after all. Or worse; maybe she just wanted to see me one last time, and this was her way of saying "goodbye" forever.'

The latter thought chased away all of the optimism he had just felt, with the quickness. In despair, he hung his head low and walked the long corridor that led back to his holding cell.

Later that evening, when Lay was back on his unit he called Celina to try to salvage what was left of the relationship he hoped he still had with her. When she didn't pick up, he was deflated all over again. Lay tried two more times to no avail. Hanging up the phone, he walked back to his cell, sat on the bed with his elbows on his knees and zoned out until a single tear rolled down his face.

The Federal Bureau of Prisons

Another four weeks passed by while the team sat in M.C.C. awaiting transfers to their designated prisons. During the fifth week Malcolm, Tony, and Stacey were placed on the draft to be transferred. Everyone had requested to be placed within five-hundred miles of home in order to make it easier to maintain close family ties. The F.B.O.P. didn't care about that, and sent them wherever they wanted.

For the most part, they were lucky because Malcolm was sent to the federal correctional institution in Danbury, Connecticut. Tony went to the F.C.I. in Fort Dix, New Jersey, which were both pretty close to home. Stacey was transferred to Alderson, the federal prison camp in West Virginia, which wasn't as close as the others but it wasn't too far out of the way, either. They all had made the same request, except Lay, who didn't care what facility he went to because Celina wasn't going to visit anyway. He and Bobby were the only two left at M.C.C. until Bobby was shipped out to Elkton, the F.C.I. in Ohio two weeks later.

With the rest of the team gone, Lay had no familiar faces to look forward to seeing everyday. He had found solace in those times spent in the library with the team because it kept him from losing it altogether. Bobby had been his go-to guy when he needed to vent all of his personal issues, and that had been taken away from him now.

As the days slowly crept by, Lay's sense of reality began to slip. Depression was leaning on him like an elephant stepping on a pea. He spent most of the time in his cell, staring at the four walls as they now seemed like they had closed in on him.

There weren't any suicidal thoughts, but feelings of being a failure and unworthiness defintintely crept through his mind. One morning, after brushing his teeth, Lay splashed water on his face, and wiped it with the now semi-white washcloth. He looked at his reflection in the metal plate on the wall that was a makeshift mirror. This ritual took place every morning, but today Lay noticed how different his face looked from before. His eyes were sunken with dark lines underneath from lack of sleep. He had stopped going to the barbershop once he realized Celina was never going to visit again, so his beard and mustache had grown into a wiry unkempt mess.

Losing Celina had hit him like a ton of bricks, but seeing his reflection at that moment made Lay decide to stand up, dust himself off, and step away from the pile of rubble under which he was buried for so long. 'You gotta snap outta this shit, Lay,' he said to himself. 'This ain't you.' He immediately walked out of the cell and went to the CO's desk to sign up for the barbershop.

The officer told Lay, "It doesn't make sense for you to get a cut, Taylor. You're out of here tomorrow anyway."

"Where am I going? Do you know?"

"You know I'm not supposed to say, but I'll look it up and get back to you before the end of my shift."

"Thanks, CO."

Lay went back to his cell and shaved the hair off of his chin and neck as best as he could with the razor he was issued. He decided to worry about a cut when he got where he was going.

That evening the CO informed Lay that he was going to Otisville, the F.C.I. in upstate New York. He sat in his cell all night thinking about the new jail and who he might run into when he got there. The time had come for Lay to get into his bid and start knocking the years down.

Anxiety was to be expected when going to a new spot, but Lay was up for whatever the future held. One thing he knew for sure was that his time wouldn't be spent sulking over Celina anymore, especially since he felt he hadn't done anything wrong.

Despite her recent behavior, Lay still loved Celina very much, and would never disrespect her by letting other women visit, but her feelings were no longer his concern. His main objective for the remainder of this incarceration period was his safety and his sanity. The outside world would have to be put on hold until he was a free man, once again. Yes, Celina was having his baby, and he wished he could be there to help raise his first child.

However, the circumstances he found himself in didn't allow it at this time, so he had to make do. That was a war he would have to wage whenever he touched down. Until then it was all about how he was going to get through this time alone. The next morning Lay was transferred to Otisville, where he got settled in and started his three-and-half-year sentence.

The Justice Center

It was August, and Lay was now eight months into his bid. He had made the adjustment from M.C.C. to life in Otisville, and was getting along pretty well. Although she didn't bother communicating with Lay, Celina didn't leave him completely messed up. After having to spend over $30,000 on legal fees, Lay was left with a little under twenty from the kitty money. She wrote a check out for the remainder of the $50,000 and sent it to him so there would be no need to ask anyone for help while he was down. She used the rest of the money he had in the safe to maintain everyday life in his absence.

Lay was upset about what had become of his relationship with Celina, but was very appreciative of her for at least doing that much for him. He wasn't worried about the rest of his money, because Lay knew she wasn't the type of woman to spend it frivously. She would take care of Barry and the baby before doing anything for herself.

Lay was fortunate enough to land a job in the library where he had unlimited access to reading material that he used as a mental escape from his prison life. It was a quiet job that he enjoyed, and he avoided a lot of the bullshit that went on in the jail by staying out of the way. If he wasn't at the library, Lay was working out, something he never did on the street. He knew not to get involved with any gangs, and he didn't gamble or use drugs. Those were three ways that one can definitely get into some shit in the penitentiary.

Lay was into his morning ritual when a CO told him to pack his things because he was going on a court trip. The time had come to face the music in Syracuse. While he hated to break his daily regimen, Lay was ready to deal with the situation and put it behind him.

While on the bus being transported to Syracuse, he looked out of the window and noticed a beautiful woman driving a black 3 Series BMW, just like the one he had bought for Celina that had an empty car seat in the back. Lay's thoughts immediately went to his baby, who by his calculations was probably two months old by now.

He hadn't spoken to Celina since January and had no idea how she or the baby was doing. She thought for sure that they were having a girl, but Lay had no idea what the sex of his baby was. He didn't know anything, and the thought made him sick. As much as he tried to block it out of his mind, it bothered him a great deal. Lay faced forward and avoided looking out of the window for the rest of the trip. He didn't want any more reminders of Celina and the baby, nor the freedom that was beyond his reach.

When he arrived at the Justice Center, Lay spent the entire day being processed into the system. By the time he was moved upstairs to a housing unit, it was after lights-out so he made his bed and tried to get some sleep. For some reason being transferred from jail to jail took a lot out of him, so it wasn't long before he was out for the count.

The next morning Lay was awakened by the sound of his cell unlocking, signaling it was time for breakfast to be served. He quickly brushed his teeth, washed his face, and went downstairs to see what was on the menu. Prison food was sub-standard but he had to eat something in order to survive. Lay dealt with what was presented to him.

While pouring milk over his crispy rice cereal he noticed two Hispanic guys taking a tray of food and coffee upstairs to the corner cell that was located two cells from his. 'Whoever that is must be sick or something, in order to have room service in this motherfucka,' Lay thought. He couldn't see the man's face from where he was sitting but he noticed that he too was Hispanic. After a brief minute, the two men brought the food tray back downstairs along with a laundry bag which he assumed belonged to the man in the corner cell, and ate their own breakfast.

When Lay was done eating, he stacked his tray on top of the others and approached the deputy to ask when he was scheduled to go to court. He was relieved to find out that it was on for the next day, so he wouldn't have to spend that much time in Syracuse after all. He went back to his cell to put his cup away and decided to watch some daytime TV, something else he rarely got a chance to do while on the street. There were two rows of chairs set up in front of a nineteen-inch TV that was suspended from the bottom of the top tier. Lay sat in the second row in the last seat on the right because from there he could see the TV and most of what was going on in the pod.

After sitting for a few minutes he noticed the diversity of the pod. It was made up of approximately eighty-five percent Black, ten percent White, and five percent Hispanic. It made him wonder what the population in Syracuse was, and why no matter what jail he was in, there were always so many more black faces than others.

His thoughts were interrupted by a conversation two black guys in front of him were having. Lay overheard one tell the other that his friend was in another pod for shooting someone on the city bus in broad daylight. He told him he was in for violating his house arrest because he kept going on his porch to talk to his friends.

Over the next hour or so he heard numerous jail conversations and was confused by the fact that no one was locked up for trying to make money.

As the day progressed, Lay also noticed how every now and then, the deputy had to tell inmates not to hang out on the top tier. No one was allowed to enter a cell that wasn't theirs, so all conversations had to be conducted on the first level.

But that rule didn't seem to apply to everyone. Although the deputy repeatedly told people to stay off the top tier, the mystery man in the corner cell always had two or three Hispanic guys hanging around outside his door without a word of resistance from anyone, not even when the sergeant came to the unit.

This gave Lay the indication that the mystery man wasn't sick at all. Whoever he was, his name had some clout attached to it. This piqued his interest even more, and made him wonder who in the world could have that much juice in the joint.

A few minutes later, one of the guys standing by the mystery man's cell went downstairs, tapped on the shoulder of someone who was using the first phone on the far left, and asked him to hurry up. The man quickly ended his call while the guy waited. As soon as he hung up, the Hispanic inmate placed the receiver on the small ledge under the phone. This alerted other inmates not to touch the phone because it was about to be occupied.

Just then, the deputy yelled, "Count time, gentlemen. On the count!"

The inmates went to their cells and shut the door behind them as the deputy made his way around the pod securing the entire unit. When the count cleared inmates were released from their cells to carry on with the rest of their day.

After washing his hands, Lay dried them and stepped outside of his cell, closing the door behind him. Before going back downstairs to watch TV, he paused to look over the rail and observe the entire pod. From where he stood he could see all of the phones were in use except for the one that was left off the hook by the Hispanic inmate. The deputy was writing something in the log book and a few guys were playing basketball in the gym.

Lay was about to go downstairs when out of the corner of his eye the door to the corner cell opened, and the mystery man finally emerged. He stood in the doorway of his cell for a brief second, looking over the entire pod. His jet-black hair was neatly cut and faded while his face sported a perfectly groomed close-shaved beard that looked as if he had just stood up from a barber's chair.

There was a thin gold chain hanging around his neck with a two-inch cross dangling from the bottom of it. On his ring finger was a gold wedding band worn on the perfectly manicured hand that he used to grip the banister. On his feet was a pair of brand new Salvatore Ferragamo loafers worn with no socks. The mystery man was sipping on a beverage from the cup he held in his right hand, when one of his minions walked behind Lay to greet him and relieve him of the cup. It was only then that the mystery man and his sidekick began walking toward Lay to get to the stairs.

As he moved closer, Lay felt a sense of familiarity about the man who looked more like an expensive attorney than an inmate. When he got close to Lay, he nodded and kept walking past him to the staircase. That's when it hit him! Lay couldn't believe it. It was the facial hair that threw him off, but behind the beard was the face of none other than, Mr. Alfredo Lopez.

Lay watched from the banister as Alfredo walked down the stairs to the phone that was purposely left off the hook for him and him only. Alfredo picked up the phone and began dialing as the sidekick placed his cup on the ledge and stood directly behind him like a security guard on duty.

Lay observed all of what was happening and had to admit that he was thoroughly impressed. He went downstairs and took his same seat in front of the TV, keeping his eye on Alfredo at the same time. Lay watched the TV and time tick away on the clock as Alfredo used the phone over and over without once turning around to face world behind him.

By then it was time for lunch. Several inmates began setting up for everyone to eat. An old-timer who was sitting two seats from Lay leaned over and said, "Hey Youngblood. You ain't from 'round here, are you?"

"Nah."

"Yeah. I could tell. You don't act like these other fools running around here. Muhfuckas make me sick."

Lay had to chuckle a little bit.

"Say, if you ain't from 'round here, where you from, New York? You look like one 'nem city boys."

"I'm not from New York. I'm from Harlem."

"Well, where the fuck is Harlem at if it ain't in New York, Youngblood?"

"It *is* in New York, but there's a difference. Trust me." "Where are you from?" Lay asked.

"Born and raised in Durham, North Cackalacky, but my wife from up these parts, so I been here fo' 'bout twenty some odd years now."

"That's a long time. How long you been down?"

"Oh, I been in here fo' 'bout two months now. Goin' home soon, though."

"What about you?"

"I just got here yesterday. I gotta go to court tomorrow. I caught a bullshit charge last year. Just gotta clear it up, that's all."

The old-timer was speaking, but Lay's focus was on Alfredo. He hung up the phone and walked to the deputy's desk with his security carrying the cup behind him. He said a few words to the deputy and walked away from the desk toward the stairs. Another Hispanic inmate went to the desk and the deputy handed him a large brown paper bag. He grabbed it and walked briskly up the steps so he could catch up to Alfredo before he reached his cell. The two men went inside of the cell while Alfredo stood outside, leaning on the rail. After a few seconds they came out, he went inside, and they stood outside of the door on guard.

"What's up with the dude up there in the corner cell?" Lay asked the old man.

"Oh, him? He's whatchu call one 'nem uh, uh, kingpins or somethin'. You know, like dat uh, whatchucallum, uh Pabo, Pabo Escoban."

"You mean Pablo Escobar."

"Well ain't dat what I said, Harlem?"

"Yeah, you did. My bad."

As the old man continued to talk, Lay tuned him out. 'Damn. Fredo wasn't lying. But what the hell was he doing all the way up here from Miami? He did say his coke was everywhere in the U.S. I guess that meant up here too.' He wondered if Fredo would remember him if he spoke to him. 'I better not,' he thought. 'In here it might be even weirder than when he had me trapped in that damn bathroom.'

"I wonder why he's locked up all the way in The 'Cuse," Lay wondered aloud to the old-timer, who was still talking when he interrupted in mid-sentence.

"His shit is on the news all the time, Harlem. You ain't seen it yet? It'll be on there this e'enin' prolly. Watch. He got some kinda' beef wit' his brother. The news say his brother gon' flip on him to get less time. But I feel sorry fo' him if he do. Dat man got too much power fa' somebody to be snitchin' on him. But we gon' see."

Fredo was in the same boat he was in. Well, kind of, except Lay wasn't facing kingpin time. That's for sure.

"You ever spoke to him before?"

"Yeah, a couple o' times. He don't come out dat cell much fa' nothin' else but to use da' phone. Don't watch TV or nothin'. I think he got one up in dat damn cell, if you ask me." The old man chuckled.

"What about food? He has to eat."

"Dat muhfucka' don't eat what we eat. You see dat bag da other Spanish boy took up there? I think dat's his food."

"Man, I've been down twice. Been in prisons all over New York state, and I never seen no shit like that in my life."

"Yeah, he a different type of muhfucka', Harlem."

Lay laughed. "My name is Lay. You don't have to keep calling me Harlem because I'm *from* there."

"Lay?!? You mean, like lay down?"

Lay laughed again. "It's short for Lavian."

"Lavian! Damn! Dat's a black ass name fo' yo' ass! You ain't gon' catch no white muhfucka' wit a name like dat. I bet my life on dat shit!" "Lay is aww-right I guess, but I like Harlem better. It fits you."

"Okay, Harlem it is."

"Grab a chair Youngblood. Let's see what these hacks gon' feed us fa' lunch tuh-day."

The two men got their trays and sat down to eat what was supposed to be lunch.

"You never told me your name, sir."

285

"Oh, please excuse my manners, Harlem. I'm James Bridgeforth, but er'body call me Jimmy Lee."

"Okay, Mr. Jimmy Lee. I got you."

Lay sat at the table facing Alfredo's cell so he could monitor his activity. The two Hispanic inmates who usually stood by his door, ate lunch with everyone else, and returned to their post immediately after. When lunch was over, the inmates had an hour or so to kill before the afternoon count. Jimmy Lee filled Lay in on all of the who's who and what's what of the pod. He wasn't really interested, but listened anyway just because he quickly found out how much Jimmy loved to talk.

The deputy called for the count and everyone began moving to their respective cells. Jimmy's cell was upstairs as well, but at the other end of the tier. As they walked up the steps, Jimmy said, "I'll see you when we come back out. I got some cards. You play Casino?"

"Yeah, I play."

"Good. I can cut yo' ass in some Casino, den. It make da' time go by faster. Ya' know, Harlem?"

"Yeah, I got you, Jimmy. See you in a minute."

"Okay, Youngblood."

The two had reached the top of the stairs, walked in opposite directions to their cells and closed the doors behind them.

After the count cleared, and the shift changed all of the inmates were released from their cells. Lay had fallen asleep during the one-and-a-half hour count period, so he was still brushing his teeth when Jimmy yelled, "Yo Harlem!" up to his cell from the first floor.

Lay spit in the sink, rinsed his mouth, wiped it, and then stepped out from behind the heavy steel door. He acknowledged Jimmy downstairs with a head nod, noticing Fredo and his security standing to his right, from his peripheral view. This time he got a nod *and* a smile from Alfredo. Lay returned the nod and walked toward the staircase to meet Jimmy who was waiting for him at the bottom.

The two men sat down and spent the next two hours playing cards as Lay listened to Jimmy sharing his life story. He learned that Jimmy was a truck driver who was about to retire in a couple of years, and that he had been arrested on a small possession charge. Jimmy said most truckers messed with that "Booger Sugar" so they could stay awake while driving.

"I didn't know that," Lay said.

"Yeah man. We gotta do somethin'. Ain't nobody tryin' to die out 'dere on 'nem roads."

"You're right. I hear you, Jimmy."

The whole time Jimmy spoke, Lay's attention was back and forth between Jimmy's mouth, the Casino game, and Fredo. Jimmy talked so much he could never tell if someone was listening to him anyway. As Lay picked up a set of threes he noticed one of Fredo's guards had left his post to go speak to the deputy for a few minutes before returning to whisper directly into Fredo's ear. He was sitting quite a distance from Fredo, but Lay was able to see a smile form on his face as the guard continued to speak.

The smile turned into a full laugh as he tapped the same guard, mouthed a few words, and pointed in the direction of Lay and Jimmy's table. The Hispanic inmate immediately started walking down the steps toward Lay as he watched all of this unfold before his very eyes. Jimmy was oblivious to what was going on. He was in mid-sentence when the Hispanic inmate approached the table and asked, "What's up? Is your name Lavian?"

"Why? What's up?" Lay responded.

"Someone wants to speak to you. Up there," the Hispanic inmate said. He pointed toward Fredo and the other guard.

"Okay. Let me finish this game and I'll be right there."

"I think you should come now." Jimmy looked on in astonishment. For the first time since Lay met him, Jimmy was completely silent.

"Okay. I'm coming now."

"Thank you."

"No problem."

Lay rose from the table and placed his cards face down. Jimmy grabbed his wrist and said, "Aww shit, Harlem. What you done did? That muhfucka' ain't talk to nobody but dem Spanish boys since he been here. What da hell he want witchu?"

Lay wiggled his wrist from Jimmy's grip and responded, "Chill out, Jimmy. I got this."

Jimmy released him. "Okay, Big Harlem. I'm here if you need me."

The Hispanic inmate looked down at Jimmy wondering, 'What the hell are you gonna do?' Jimmy shot a look right back at him in defiance.

Lay walked to the stairs, paused and yelled to Jimmy, "Don't look at my cards either, old man."

Jimmy waved his hand at Lay. "Go 'head, boy. Ain't nobody tryna' cheat you."

Jimmy turned his chair all the way around so he could watch Lay walk up the steps to meet Fredo at the end of the tier. When Lay was in arms reach of the mystery man, the two men extended their hands to be shaken and hugged with the others.

"Lavian Taylor. It is good to see you again. The circumstances are not so good, but it's still nice to see an old acquaintance."

"I thought I had recognized you earlier, but the beard kinda threw me off, and I didn't want to approach you because, you know, I didn't think you remembered me."

"Well, I didn't at first. But when I heard the old man call you Harlem, I knew you weren't from this area. So, I watched you for a while and I noticed you weren't running around with the rest of these young guys. You were quiet and reserved. I could hear the old man's voice from all the way

288

up here, but not yours. That intrigued me so I sent my associate to find out what your name was and what you were charged with. When he returned and told me that you were in for cashing checks, it all came back to me."

"I'm not in here for cashing checks. I'm only charged with possession of a forged instrument. How did you know it was a check? It couldv'e been anything; like a fake credit card."

"Lavian, I can find out who everyone in this jail is, and what they're in here for if I want to, including the deputies. Also, the fact that you have a court date tomorrow was in the newspaper yesterday. That is how I put two and two together and figured out it was you."

"Are you serious?"

"Absolutely, my friend."

Lavian looked at Fredo skeptically.

"I see you have some doubt."

"No, I don't," Lay lied.

"It's okay, Lavian. In time you will get to know me and the influence I have on the people around me."

"So, you know why I'm here, but what are you doing so far away from Miami?" "And how are your wife and those two beautiful daughters?"

"Ah, you remembered. I like that."

"Well, you left a lasting impression, Fredo."

"Unfortunately, my situation is a very complicated one, Lavian. Maybe I will explain it some time."

"The old-timer was telling me something about a beef with your brother. Is that true?"

"I hate the media. That is what the government wants people to believe. I don't think my brother is going to turn on me. It's their tactic to pit us against one another. I'm not budging, and I don't think he will, either."

"How much time are you facing?"

"I'm looking at the death penalty, Lavian. The best case scenario is for them to offer a number that will let me see freedom one day, but the reality is, I'm probably going to die in prison."

"Damn. Are you serious?"

"Sadly, I am."

"Why would the death penalty be on the table for a drug case, especially if there wasn't any violence?"

"Who said there wasn't?"

"Oh, damn. But with all the millions you have, can't you pay your way out of this?"

Fredo laughed at Lay's last question. "What's so funny?"

"I'm laughing because you said millions. Lavian, I don't have millions. I am a billionaire. You really have no idea who I am, do you? Don't you pay attention to the news?"

"Apparently not! Shit, if you're a billionaire, shake my hand again. Maybe some of that will rub off on me."

Fredo chuckled for a second, then continued, "It's a funny thing my friend, but if I only had millions I probably *would* be able to buy my way out of this mess. But when you climb to the echelon that I've been fortunate enough to reach, it becomes a gift and a curse. My occupation influenced economies on a global scale, which allows leaders of countries all over the world to weigh in on my case, especially my own. Now do you see what I mean?"

The more Fredo spoke, the more he wished someone else would've gone into that bathroom in Miami.

"So, what are you and your brother going to do?"

"There's nothing we *can* do but bargain for our lives, and hope to at least get the death penalty removed from the equation."

"Damn, Fredo. You seem like such a good guy. If there was something I could do to help, I would."

"There may be a way you can, my friend."

"How? What could I possibly do for a billionaire?"

"You keep saying billionaire like it's a bad thing."

"It's not bad, but it damn sure is scary. I never thought that having too much money could be a problem."

"Don't be afraid, my friend. Money doesn't have to be scary."

"That sounds funny coming from a bill... You know what I mean."

After a brief pause, Lay got up enough courage to ask, "How much money *do* you have, anyway?"

"I don't know. I stopped keeping track after I touched my first billion. That was six years ago. When you think about it, after that it really didn't make sense to count it." "But that's not important. Let's get back to how you can help me."

"I'm listening."

"The government has brought my entire operation to a screeching halt. I have no way of moving my product to generate income."

"But why do you need to make more money if you already have so much of it?"

"You know how the government does. They seize everything they can get their hands on. I need to get my network up and running again because my wife is being detained, Lavian. They arrested her in Florida, forcing us to send my babies to Colombia to live with her parents. I need to raise some money under the government's radar in order to secure her release."

"But, how can money secure *her* release and not your own?"

"They were never after her. My brother and I were the targets. She was just used as a casualty to make this whole thing personal. They wanted to hurt me, and they did."

"So, what do you need me to do?"

"How much time do you think you're going to receive for this case?"

"I don't know. I'm hoping its three years or less so they will run my state time concurrent with the three-and-a-half-year sentence I'm doing with the feds. I have eight months in already, so I guess you can say another three years."

"That just might work. Do you think your team will be able to generate 100 million in two years?"

"Wait... what?!? Two years?!? I don't know if we'll ever see that kind of money in a lifetime."

"You will, if you have my network at your fingertips."

"But you just told me the feds shut your whole operation down."

"They did, but only the people in my organization got taken down. The people I supplied are still out there, starving for my product. There's a panic right now, and there has been one since my brother and I have been inside."

"Even if I decide to do this for you, Mrs. Lopez will still have to sit for five years."

"You *will* do this for me. I have faith in you. But, as far as Eva goes, it's better for her to do five years and go be with my babies, than for her to do life in prison, which is what they're trying to give her."

"Damn. This is a lot to think about, Fredo. I want to help, but I also don't want to let you down if I fail. How are you going to look at me if I don't meet the deadline?"

"You worry too much, Lavian. You will have my backing. That is all the help you will need. You're a smart man. I believe if given access to the supply, you would find a way to meet that deadline."

"This is some heavy shit, Fredo. But I think you're a good man, and I hate to see you go through this. I feel especially bad for your wife and kids. I understand what it feels like to be separated from the ones you love."

Lay shared everything that happened with Josie and the mystery baby, and how Celina found out about it. He told Fredo how he hadn't seen or heard from Celina since January, and didn't even know if he was a father or not, because of that fact. Fredo saw how defeated Lay looked as he spoke of the turmoil that had plagued him for the past few months, and wanted to help in any way he could.

The two men talked all the way up until the last count for the evening, while Jimmy sat at the table watching them like a hawk. After the count Lay and Fredo resumed their conversation and exchanged information so they could keep in touch during the bid. Fredo gave Lay an address in Miami that they would both use, so the letters would be forwarded.

"I've taken up enough of your time, Lavian. Please, go back to your card game. Tell Mr. Jimmy I apologize for keeping him waiting. It was great to see you again, Lavian. We'll talk tomorrow when you come from court."

The two men shook hands and embraced simultaneously, then Lay proceeded to put the information Fredo gave him inside of his cell so it wouldn't get lost. After closing his cell door behind him he returned to the table where Jimmy sat looking like a parent who was about to scold their child.

As Lay pulled up his chair to sit down Jimmy asked, "Now what the hell was that all about, Youngblood?"

"Nothing to worry about, Jimmy. We just realized that we knew each other from another time and place, that's all. I'm good."

"You sure? 'Cuz I ain't got time to be fightin' up in here. I'm on my way out da do'. You feel me?"

Lay chuckled at Jimmy's attempt at machismo.

"Don't worry Jimmy. I'm more Martin than Malcolm on any given day. Trust me, violence is not my forte. Besides, I'm not trying to explain to your wife how I got you up in here breaking people's legs."

"Okay now. Just so you know, I done had my share of ruckus in my day."

"I believe you, Jimmy."

"Come on now. Let me finish cuttin' you up in 'dis here game."

"So, tell me more about your truck driving career."

For the rest of the evening Lay listened to Jimmy go on about his life as a truck driver. The other half of his brain's wheels were turning in the direction of how to meet Fredo's deadline once he was back on the street, and how Jimmy could play a major part of it.

That night, Lay didn't get much sleep, thinking about all that was now piled onto his plate. He had a court appearance in the morning, a federal sentence to complete, Celina and the baby to think about, Josie and the possible daughter with her. And to top it off, a two year-one hundred million dollar deadline to meet for Fredo. 'This is too fuckin' much," he thought as he turned over on his side to try and get some sleep.

Lay was called for court bright and early the next morning. When he was brought into the courtroom in shackles, Kev was sitting at the defendant's table with his and Lay's attorney, Milton Chase. He hadn't seen Kev since last year when they initially got arrested. Lay was happy to see Kev, and was glad that he looked like he was doing okay.

The judge sat on the bench and was ready to start the proceedings. Lay's attorney, Mr. Chase and the state had discussions prior to this date and a three-year offer agreement was reached. Mr. Chase relayed the message to Lay, and he accepted the offer.

After pleading guilty, Chase pushed for sentencing to take place immediately so as not to waste the court's time and money on another date. Everyone agreed. Lay was sentenced to three years in state prison to run concurrent with his federal term. Lay nodded to Kev as he was escorted to the back of the courtroom and through the door to the tunnel that led back to The Justice Center.

When he returned, the deputy informed him that he would be leaving first thing in the morning. Lay spent the remainder of the day finalizing things with Fredo and talking to Jimmy-; or listening, to be more accurate. Before locking in for the night Lay exchanged information with Jimmy and promised to keep in touch.

The next morning Lay was awakened at four o' clock to be processed out of The Justice Center and placed on the bus back to Otisville. There was so much for him to think about on the three-hour drive to the place he would call home for the next three years. It was a long trip but Lay was too amped up to go to sleep. Instead he looked out of the window and let his mind carry him three years ahead to the plan he was determined to execute and the freedom he could now taste.

An exerpt from

Part 2

By Lou Black

Miguelito Lopez

On September 9, 2003 Miguelito Lopez was being transported from a federal safehouse in the suburbs of Binghamton, New York to the James M. Hanley building, which is the federal courthouse for the Northern District of New York. It appeared that he had struck deal with the Assisstant U.S. Attorney to testify against his brother Alfredo, in order to avoid the death penalty.

Escorted by three federal marshals with his hands in cuffs and, his legs in shackles, the five-foot-ten Miguelito ducked his head as he stepped out of the van in the rear of 100 South Clinton Street. Miguelito had been locked away in the safehouse for so long he had become void of color. On this beautiful sunny day he looked up at the sky, closed his eyes for a second to bask in the rays, and soaked in the vitamin D he had been so deprived of.

In that split second, his head was thrusted backward as the .308 bullet from a Ruger American sniper rifle cracked his skull, piercing his brain, killing him instantly. The unexpected weight of the dead body brought the two marshalls holding each of his arms to the ground as they failed to support the now deceased Miguelito. All three marshalls drew their weapons and looked around trying to figure out what happened as blood began to seep out of the hole directly between Miguelito's lifeless eyes.

Almost Home

In May of 2006 Lavian Taylor sat in his two-man room at the halfway house on a cell phone that had been smuggled in by one of the CO's. An old-timer nick-named, Getaway stood on lookout for any guards that might happen to be passing by.

Lavian was on the phone with Alfredo Lopez, who sat at the helm of one of, if not *the* largest cocaine cartels to come out of Colombia. His empire's distribution had tentacles that stretched throughout the United States and across the globe.

The two men met a few years back in Miami, when Alfredo was at the height of his career as an importer of some of the purest cocaine to ever touch American soil.

Lavian had been in town attending a dinner to celebrate his brother Tony's last days of being a bachelor when Alfredo approached him in the restroom and introduced himself. To say it was a strange encounter would be putting it mildly, but the two parted ways that night in amicable fashion.

It was by chance that they were reunited while incarcerated at the Justice Center in Syracuse. Lavian had been arrested a few months earlier for possession of forged checks, and Alfredo was facing drug trafficking charges, amongst other things. There, the two men got reacquainted and promised to stay in touch.

Lavian had made a commitment to Alfredo to help raise $100,000,000 to secure his wife's freedom within two years of his release, a promise he had no idea how he was going to keep, but for the sake of his newfound friend, was going to give it his best shot.

"So, my friend, you will be going home soon," Alfredo said.

"Yes, I only have a few more months to go."

"That is perfect. Everything is going as planned, my friend. Are you ready?"

"As ready as I'll ever be. What's going on with your case?"

"You know how complicated my situation was. Well, it got worse for me after my brother was killed."

"I know. I saw it on the news. I'm sorry about Miguelito."

"It's okay. I'm delaying my trial as long as possible in order to make things happen the way I need them to. Some unforeseen developments have occurred and I have to make some adjustments. There are always setbacks in life, but we must push through them, regardless."

"You know I'm going to do all I can to help you, Fredo."

"I know, my friend. I've set everything in motion for when you get released. You won't have a problem at all getting set up."

"That's good. I like the way that sounds."

"There's one more thing I need you to do, Lavian."

"Anything, Fredo. What is it?"

"I need you to kill my wife..."

Connect with Lou Black

Respectthepen.com

Respectthepen139@gmail.com

Instagram: Respectthepen_139